I AM WITH YOU

I AM WITH YOU

Tell of My Kingdom's Glory
Book Three

Sonya Contreras

 Bull Head Press

Published by Bull Head Press
Squaw Valley, California
Paperback ISBN: 978-0-9990009-0-8
eBook ISBN: 978-0-9990009-1-5

Library of Congress Control Number: 2017907097

Cover Design by Kirk DouPonce of DogEared Design
Copy edited by Titania Porter
Formatting by Joseph Contreras, Jr.
Typeface: Felix Titling, Bell MT, and Constantia

Printed in the United States of America.

"I will insist the Hebrews have [contributed] more to civilize men than any other nation. If I was an atheist and believed in blind eternal fate, I should still believe that fate had ordained the Jews to be the most essential instrument for civilizing the nations. If I were an atheist of the other sect, who believe, or pretend to believe that all is ordered by chance, I should believe that chance had ordered the Jews to preserve and propagate to all mankind the doctrine of a supreme, intelligent, wise, almighty sovereign of the universe, which I believe to be the great essential principle of all morality, and consequently of all civilization....

They are the most glorious nation that ever inhabited this earth. The Romans and their empire were but a bubble in comparison to the Jews. They have given religion to three-quarters of the globe and have influenced the affairs of mankind more and more happily than any other nation, ancient or modern."

John Adams, Second President of the United States

(From a letter to F. A. Van der Kemp [Feb. 16, 1808] Pennsylvania Historical Society)

TELL OF MY KINGDOM'S GLORY

This love story between God and His people continues in the series Tell of My Kingdom's Glory. In Book One *Until My Name Is Known,* God brings His people to see Him as He frees them from the bonds of Egypt. In Book Two *I Have Called You by Name,* God draws them to know Him more personally, providing safety in the demands of His Law and dependence upon Him to reach their Land. Now, in Book Three *I Am with You,* God reassures them that as He has been with Moses, so shall He be with them. He brings them into the Land promised them, giving rest from their journey.

Dear Reader,

The Book of Joshua is a book about battles. Joshua leads the Israelites into the Land promised by God, but they must destroy those who reside there. Joshua learns to wait God's timing for each battle as God assures him that He is with him. Through their battles, they see God's holiness, His hatred for evil, His desire for justice.

In the midst of the battles, the book also tells of God's redemption and mercy with Rahab. Evil preys strong in her mind as she struggles to believe God's love for her, in spite of her own evil.

Evil hasn't disappeared, nor does it compromise nor negotiate; it consumes those it takes. It must be eliminated or it grows.

The Book of Joshua inspires us for our battles against evil. Like Joshua, I, too, must depend upon God for each victory. I grow weary.

God comes beside me, and reminds me He is with me in the battle and afterward when I want the credit and forget His glory. Or when I doubt my own worth, like Rahab, and wonder how our great God could chose to use me.

I Am with You is a testimony to the faithfulness of our righteous God Who helps us to the end.

Sonya Contreras

"Oh that they had such a heart in them, that they would
fear Me and keep all My commandments
always, that it may be well with them and with their sons
forever.
Deuteronomy 5:29

"...You have said, I have known you by name, and you have also
found favor in My sight...My presence shall go with you,
and I will give you rest."
Exodus 33:12-17

Tell of My Kingdom's Glory.
"So that all men may know of My Mighty Acts."
Psalm 145:11-12

CHAPTER 1

Someone grabbed Michael's shoulder and jerked him around. Michael's foot slipped in the loose gravel of the mountaintop of Mount Nebo. The dust coated his legs and shining garment. He scowled at the being standing behind him. What did he want now? Michael tightened his grip on his shovel, preparing to use it to fight, if he must.

"I want the body."

Michael stood his ground. "It's not mine to give, nor yours to take. The Lord wants it buried."

Satan smiled. "I'll bury it for you."

Michael also smiled. He knew Satan's motive. It would never be to please God. "You'd save me from burying him, would you?"

"He'll be rewarded for his service here on earth."

Satan's smug response irritated Michael. Why must he always try to defeat the Lord's plans using God's chosen creation?

God had sent Michael to perform this simple task. God had warned him he'd have problems. Michael shook his head. "He will not be worshipped."

Satan's grip on Michael's shoulder tightened. His smile disappeared. He hissed through clenched teeth. "Give me the body."

Michael stood straighter and stepped back. Everything must be a fight over who received the glory. Michael would make sure God received it. "The Lord needs the body."

Satan's dark eyes glowed with intensity as he tried to persuade Michael. "He could create another. Give it to me."

Satan wouldn't deter him. Michael was finished squabbling. The Lord wanted it buried and he would finish burying it. Still holding the shovel, Michael, the archangel, faced him directly and pulled his sword. "The Lord rebuke you!"

Satan left, snarling his hatred.

Michael watched him leave, before resuming his digging.

Moses had interceded for God's people before Pharaoh in Egypt and had taught them to look to God as they journeyed through the desert these past forty years. Now his work was finished. God would lead His people into their promised land by another.

Michael buried Moses's body well, so this people would not worship his body. No one deserved worship meant only for God.

Michael surveyed the mound, covered with boulders. It would not be found. He nodded, satisfied. He left the way he came.

Joshua stood partway up Mount Nebo with the sun overhead. Sweat tickled his back as it dripped down the inside of his tunic. He wiped his face with his cloak sleeve. He had begun the walk with Moses before the sun had risen. How much longer should he wait?

Joshua thought back over when Moses led the people away from Pharaoh's power. Joshua had stood in his shadow to learn how to lead. As Moses judged the people, Joshua learned God's Law. When Moses walked up Mount Sinai, Joshua watched from the rope where God allowed the people to stand as the mount smoked and poured out flames. Whenever Moses returned from seeing God, his face glowing with God's presence. Joshua yearned for that same intimacy. Yet he feared to get too close. What would being close to God do to him?

Moses had given him charge over the army training. Joshua had led the men to victory over the countries around the land promised them. They had conquered Sihon and Og, allowing the Reubenites, Gadites, and half the tribe of Manassites to settle there.

Now, when Moses walked up the mountain for the last time, Joshua had come with him to hear his last words.

Joshua felt a heaviness. Following God in the shadow of Moses was not the same as following God without Moses.

He glanced again at the top of the mount, out of habit, waiting for Moses to return. The sun glared in his eyes as if to tell him he had no business up there. He shook his head. He didn't. Moses had told Joshua to lead the people, and God would be by his side. He breathed deeply. He hoped so. Not that he doubted God. But how would he know what to do?

He glanced at the campsite of six million people, the Lord's people. Their campsite stretched as far as he could see. Their tents rippled like the waves of an ocean, but they were far from any ocean as they waited on the east side of the Jordan River for God's permission to cross. Banners rose above their tents, marking where each of the twelve tribes camped.

Even at this height on the mountain, Joshua heard the rumble of the people, preparing their mid-day meal. His stomach grumbled, and he licked his lips in anticipation of the flatbread from the morning's manna.

Must he return to the noise of the people? He had known peace, following Moses, as he had looked to God for answers.

He sighed, then smiled. He sounded like Moses when the people wearied him. How much of Moses's mannerisms did he mimic after having shadowed him these forty years? His smile faded. There was more to leading this people than sighing over their actions. What if he couldn't hear God's voice? Moses was the only prophet who talked with God face to face. How would Joshua know what the Lord wanted?

Joshua looked to the land promised by God, the land flowing with milk and honey.

When he had spied out the land with Caleb and the other ten spies, he had been excited about the land. The ten spies had reported the giants, but he and Caleb had told of the rich resources God was giving ... a land ready to harvest God's bounty.

When the people had doubted God, believing the ten spies, God demanded judgment. They spent the next forty years in the desert, weary of sand, heat, barrenness. During that time, all men twenty years and over had died, except the Levites. God, in His mercy, hadn't killed them all in a sudden plague that would have devastated every family in the camp at once. Instead, He had allowed natural incidents and battles to take them.

Joshua had been spared, along with Caleb, for their faithful report.

Joshua missed his father's support and counsel. His father, family, even close friends were gone. Now Moses was gone too. Joshua's tears streaked the dust on his face. He didn't bother to wipe them with his cloak sleeve.

Death was so permanent. Joshua was now one of the oldest men alive, besides Eleazar. He felt alone.

He breathed deeply, watching the Jordan River threading its way over the land. Its water overflowing its banks. How would they cross Jordan and enter the land God promised?

He turned around, startled by a man standing beside him. How had he approached without Joshua hearing him? Who was he? The ledge didn't allow much room. Joshua fingered his dagger hilt in its sheath.

The man's cloak was pure white. It almost shone. How could he keep it so white with all the dust? The man spoke. "Whom do you seek? Moses is dead."

How did He know Moses was gone? Even the people didn't know yet. They'd be vulnerable without Moses, until they accepted Joshua as their new leader. Joshua breathed faster. He looked to the top of the mountain where Moses had gone to die. Was this a friend or foe?

The man repeated. "Moses, My servant, is dead."

Joshua stepped back at the distinction. His servant? Who was this man?

"Cross Jordan. I give you this land. Every place your foot touches will be yours. No one will be able to resist you. As I was with Moses, so I will be with you. I will not fail nor forsake you."

Joshua fell on his face. How could he do anything but worship? Now he knew why he had lingered on the mountain. He needed to be assured that God was still with him, even if Moses was not.

"Be strong and courageous. Obey the law of Moses. Don't turn from it to the right or left. Meditate on it day and night, so you may obey and prosper. The Lord your God is with you wherever you go."

Joshua was not alone. God was with him. God would help him do his task. His breathing returned to normal. He had nothing to fear.

He hadn't come to the mount to see Moses. He had come to see the Lord. And he had.

The sun was setting when he returned from the mountain. He returned with confidence that his God would lead him, just as He had done with Moses.

The people remained camped at Mount Nebo as they mourned the loss of Moses. His absence seemed more acute to Joshua, as he would look for Moses's direction, only to remember that he was gone. His loss left not only a hole in his insides, but brought a weight as he thought of the leadership that now fell on him.

Zipporah, Moses's wife, had also died. The people had mourned, but most had treated her like a foreigner. The Lord had spared her Moses's death.

Joshua woke in the pre-dawn light. He felt beside him for Dorona.

She lay asleep.

He could dimly see her chest rising and falling with each breath. Her presence gave him completeness. He covered her with the sheepskin against the desert's cold morning air.

He laced his sandals and tied them securely, then rose and grabbed his cloak before stepping outside his tent. He looked to the east for the cloud of fire.

It was too early to see God's guiding cloud for the day, but the nighttime fire cloud was gone too. Moses had looked to the cloud for every step their people had taken through the wilderness. Where was it now? He scanned the horizon for any glimpse of it. The sky seemed empty without it, like a hole had been left in the sky.

His heart raced. He stood unmoving, though his thoughts raced. If God's presence had left His people, how could he lead?

The tent flap stirred behind him. Joshua continued to stare to the east. As if he could make the cloud appear.

He felt a hand tuck into the bend of his elbow and squeeze.

Dorona's voice was barely above a whisper. "The fire cloud is gone."

In hearing the words spoken, Joshua felt the finality of what it meant. Had God left them? In that one statement, all their people's needs fell onto his back.

The silence stretched between them as the ramifications of the cloud's absence settled over him.

He felt her gaze on him. He couldn't meet her eye; she would see his fear. What could he say? He continued to study the horizon as if the cloud would appear if he stared long enough. Fear, uncertainty, and the responsibility of leading this people without the presence of God made him tremble.

Dorona rested her head on his shoulder.

He put his arm around her shoulders and squeezed. She depended upon him to get them to their land. The entire people depended upon him.

Her voice broke into his thoughts. "We've reached the border of our land. God has already given His direction. All we have to do is the next thing."

Her words brought calmness.

The cloud had only shown them the way through the wilderness. Moses hadn't had it in Egypt when he obeyed God's words.

Joshua knew what he must do. God had already told him. The land was for their taking. The cloud was no longer needed. He knew how to take the people to victory. A new confidence seeped through him. Not in his leadership skills, but in God's faithfulness to tell him each step. He squeezed Dorona's shoulder once more. He felt complete, not only with Dorona by his side, but with God leading him, even without the cloud and fire.

The women searched the sand at sunrise, a habit formed after forty years of gathering food spread on the desert floor.

There was nothing.

God had stopped the manna.

This was the first the people had noticed God's distance. But had He left? Or was His presence still with them, but not visible? They didn't consider what it meant, for they only saw with their eyes and not with their heart. They gathered around the mountain and waited for Joshua to return to the campsite. "What should we eat?" For some, their fear consumed them. They demanded, not only of Joshua but of God, "Where's our manna? Who are you to take that away?"

Joshua could see the whites of their eyes and felt their fear.

But what made them think they could demand an answer from God? Didn't they sense God's greatness?

Joshua looked to the east where the cloud had been, but it wasn't there. He would like to ask for the cloud and fire to return, too. If Joshua hadn't felt God's presence earlier in the dark, he would have panicked. God's reassurance hovered him, like the cloak he wore. He tightened the belt of his cloak as if reminding himself God was still with him. He had nothing to fear. He swallowed and sighed. When he turned to face the crowd, he raised his arms, waiting for them to quiet. "God has given us the fruit of the land. Eat from the land on this side of Jordan. The orchards are loaded with fruit, fields are heavy with barley, flocks flowing with milk, waiting for cheese."

The panic melted from their faces. Excitement grew in their eyes. Several licked their lips.

Cheese would be good. Joshua smiled and nodded. "Prepare provisions. In three days, we'll cross the Jordan. The Lord is faithful." He nodded and knew it in his heart. *He is indeed.*

The Tent of Meeting was where the people were judged when any disagreement arose among them. As Joshua entered it, he considered what he must do to bring the people into the land. He needed leaders from each tribe to help counsel for the land's conquest. How should they be chosen?

Leaders from the Reubenites, Gadites, and Manassites approached him.

Hezron, a spokesman of Manasseh's tribe, nodded. "Shalom, Joshua."

Joshua nodded. "Shalom." He motioned to an empty area in the Tent of Meeting.

Joshua had first met Hezron after watching him use his rod with his flocks. Hezron had redirected a wandering lamb back to his flock by nipping it with the thrown rod. Joshua thought Hezron's accuracy was luck. How could anyone throw a stick with such precision? But then Joshua saw him kill a lion with a single throw. "Let me see your rod."

Hezron handed it to Joshua with visible reluctance.

Joshua noticed his hesitation. "You don't want me to touch it?"

Hezron shrugged. "I feel naked without it. It's my right arm. I use it to check my sheep's fleece for wounds and insect bites."

Joshua checked its balance in his hand. "It does more than check their skin." He motioned to the lion carcass, already drawing flies. "Could you teach our army how to do that?"

Hezron shrugged, as if Joshua had witnessed nothing unusual for a shepherd to do. "My youngest son knows the skill; any man could learn it. It takes a balanced rod, a flexible wrist, and practice."

Joshua shook his head. "A lot of practice."

Hezron's humility made him a good teacher and leader. "Begin at once to train the men."

Hezron's men didn't just improve their skill, they mastered it. He also had suggested adding slings and bows to their list of battle skills.

Joshua smiled. He had entered the Tent of Meeting wondering how to find leaders for his war council. He already had them.

Hezron cleared his throat and leaned on his staff. He motioned to the two other men with him, "We spoke to Moses about claiming this side of Jordan, where the land is good for our flocks."

Joshua's smile faded. He hoped they wouldn't ask to stay behind as the rest of the people moved into the land. Once people built homes and fences, they wouldn't want to cross the Jordan to help their brothers in the new land. Settling brought comfort. He nodded, his eyebrows lifted. "With conditions."

Hezron met Joshua's gaze. "We are ready to cross the Jordan, armed for battle until the Lord gives our brothers rest."

Joshua let out a breath and nodded. He didn't have to confront these men about their responsibility.

Hezron nodded. "We will do as we promised."

Madron, Hezron's brother, added, "Anyone who doesn't obey your command will be put to death. Be strong and courageous."

The other leaders nodded their assent.

Joshua smiled. The Lord had told him the same thing. Did he look as fearful as he felt?

"Help!" Salmon lifted his head above the raging water of the Jordan one last time before he was sucked into the swirls of the current. Icy waters felt like liquid snow, numbing his limbs and stealing his breath. He bounced against a boulder, hitting his head, as if he was nothing more than a leaf tossed by the waves. Pain exploded inside his head. How could he see stars under a blanket of water? Then blackness covered him. He sank deeper, as if falling into a black hole. Who would care if he never surfaced again?

When he woke, he felt warmth, wonderful warmth. He shivered in spite of the fire's heat. He stretched and moaned. His hands and feet tingled like hundreds of needles stabbing him. His head pounded.

"You're awake. Take a drink." The familiar voice was distant, spoken as if through a long cave.

Salmon lifted his head and groaned again. He felt water dribbling onto his lips. He licked them and swallowed, opening his eyes. "Ethan."

Ethan held his head so he could drink. "Stop jabbering and drink this."

After several swallows, Salmon leaned back and closed his eyes again.

A trumpet blast split the early morning air.

With great effort, Salmon opened his eyes and looked across the Jordan River at their people's campsite. He breathed deeply. "We missed the morning sacrifices."

Ethan broke a twig, adding it to the flames of the small fire close to Salmon. He nodded toward the Jordan River, then studied Salmon's face. "Jordan almost took you for good."

Salmon felt his scrutiny. "I feel great." He tried to sit but a wave of dizziness made him hesitate.

Ethan laughed. "Denial won't make you feel better. Rest until your clothes dry. Unless you want to meet Jericho's people naked."

Salmon noticed for the first time that he was covered by Ethan's cloak. His clothes and cloak were spread over the sand and nearby bushes. "Why weren't your clothes wet?"

Ethan grunted. "Remember how we tied them to our heads so they'd be dry enough to wear after we'd crossed? Mine were. You decided to drench not only your clothes but yourself."

Salmon shrugged, but then winced as his head pounded.

Ethan nodded to Jericho. "There's no hurry. Joshua didn't expect us to return for a while."

Salmon closed his eyes and rested again. He could hear Ethan adding more wood to the fire. His fingers and toes began to gain feeling. He must have rested again, for when he opened his eyes, the sun was warming the sand. Sitting slowly, he ran his hands through his dried hair. He felt the bump on his head gingerly. "What do you think we'll find?"

Ethan shrugged. "Are those walls as strong as they look?"

Salmon nodded, then winced at the pain that it brought. "The height alone makes me feel small. What do you think the people will be like?"

Ethan raised his eyebrow.

"What?"

Ethan gathered the dried clothes scattered around the sand and tossed them at him. "If you can wonder about a people whom God told us to destroy, then you're ready to walk to their city."

Salmon took his tunic from the sand, wincing as he put it over his head. His entire body ached with every movement, but he wouldn't tell Ethan.

Ethan lent his hand to help Salmon stand.

Salmon felt Ethan studying him. He smiled to reassure him.

Ethan grunted. "That wobbly, attempted smile tells me more than the lie you wish me to believe that you are fine."

Salmon shrugged.

Ethan gestured toward Jericho. "We'll move slowly until your head catches up with your body. That was quite a bump you got."

Salmon would have laughed if his head hadn't hurt so much. He fingered his head. "We should make the hill country around Jericho by evening sacrifices."

Ethan tied his tunic between his legs, so he could walk unencumbered. He kicked dirt over the fire he had made to dry their clothes. "We'll wait 'til morning to enter the city."

Salmon braced against a tree that hung over the water and stooped to fill his waterskin. His head swirled like the current. He paused, trying to focus, before slipping his waterskin into the water to fill it. That bump must have been a good one. He felt himself swirling like the waves and falling, again.

Ethan grabbed his shoulder and yanked him back from the water. He took his waterskin from him. "Let me do that! I saved you once. You'd think you'd spare me the problem of saving you again." He squatted beside him and filled his waterskin.

Salmon laughed, but stayed where he was, letting his head stop circling. "I wouldn't want you to get wet again on my account."

Ethan put the stopper on Salmon's waterskin and handed it back to him. "See that you don't."

Salmon tied the waterskin to his belt and nodded.

Ethan helped him to his feet again. He seemed more concerned than he wanted Salmon to think.

Salmon looked across the horizon to where Jericho lay.

What would they find in Jericho?

CHAPTER 2

The king of Jericho stood on his palace roof, looking toward the Jordan River. If he squinted, he could see beyond the river to the campsite of this people who waited on the other side. "The desert people are great, as many as the sand." His voice broke as he swallowed.

His adviser nodded. "The Jordan River stops them. We have time."

No one could cross for several weeks with the Jordan flooding.

The king sighed. Reports had come to him of this people fleeing Egypt after leaving it desolate. Nothing had come from Egypt's borders in forty years. Nor had the Reed Sea stopped their progress. Their God had dried it so they could cross, yet had drowned the Pharaoh and his army. This news hadn't brought him comfort. Now, the only thing between this God's people and his own was the Jordan River at flood stage. What is that to a God Who had already created a dry path through a lot of water?

"What hope do we have to fight a people whose God destroys everything in His path?" He didn't expect his advisor to answer.

He didn't.

The king's palace was located in the center of the city, beside the temple. His army could surround his palace, leaving his people to their own death, but he doubted even that would stop this God from finding him.

He looked at the wall surrounding their city. It was actually two walls, layered on a mound to give the appearance of a huge fortress.

The city was an old one, having lived through many battles. It had won by the strength of its walls. But through its battles, both walls had been rammed, weakening its structure and mortar. Shifting underground had brought greater internal cracks no casual observer would notice.

His sentries were scattered around the wall. But even as he watched, several stopped their patrol and turned around, not passing some areas. "Why don't our sentries walk the entire wall?"

His advisor looked at him, then looked away. "Remember when the mason worker reported the walls were crumbling?"

The man had discovered cracks, not in just a few places, but all around the city. He had walked the entire wall and marked them on a map.

The king chewed his lip as he studied his adviser, who had grown more outspoken with the presence of this people across the river. Did the presence of death allow him to see more clearly? Or was he just willing to risk more, because he would die soon anyway?

He shook his head. "What about him?"

The advisor hesitated.

That mason had thought he would be rewarded for his information and given the job of its repair.

The king shrugged. He had been annoyed by the warning of danger. Where did danger fit into his life of comfort and pleasure? The king had sacrificed him to the gods. He had forgotten the danger as soon as the man was gone.

Now it was too late to consider repairs. Regret, but not repentance, brought the king to say, "Our walls are nothing but a deception."

The adviser looked at the king. "Did walls keep this God out of Egypt?" He was becoming bolder with the danger.

The king met his glance. Would he lose the people's respect if he didn't do something? He must show his authority and power. "Lock the gates early this afternoon. Question those who enter or exit." The king studied the hillside around their city. A stream ran within their walls, and with the recent harvest, the people had plenty of food on hand as well. He shrugged. "We have no reason to tempt the gods."

Pounding woke Rahab and she covered herself with her cloak before unbolting the door. The sun's low rays through her window showed it was only late afternoon, not time for her normal visitors.

As she opened the door, the general barged passed her into her one room.

His armor clanked loudly in the quiet room.

She bolted the door behind him. She clutched her cloak around her, tying the belt at her waist. Perhaps he wouldn't stay long. He wasn't one of her favorite visitors. She pushed her shoulders back and swallowed a sigh.

He adjusted his sword and sat on the bench by her table, his large frame filling the bench.

This was different. What did he want?

She lit a candle in front of him. His shadow covered the entire wall behind him. She dipped a vessel from the jug on the table and pushed it toward him, then sat across from him. Men didn't come to talk. Especially not this one. She waited, knowing he must fill the silence with his words.

He drank until the water was gone, fidgeting with the vessel. "Rahab."

She tensed. Men rarely called her by name. Most didn't even know it. She was an object for their pleasure. If they knew her name, they might use it at a wrong time. Like the general, who threatened or bribed with it.

She licked her lips and waited, leaning away from him to give distance, protection.

He swallowed. "The king demands more sacrifices."

She cringed. Whenever the king demanded sacrifices, she must work in the temples. Not that her work was different in her own home, but here she earned payment enough to live. At the temple, she must give freely for the gods' pleasure. The gods required more than any man.

The general leaned forward and stroked her face. His calloused hand felt rough against her skin.

She braced herself, trying not to shrink from his touch. Sometimes when he had been drinking, he hit her. His breath didn't smell of drink now. But still he wanted something. He licked his lips. "The army has been told to watch for strangers."

Soldiers filled the streets.

She had heard their marching throughout the day.

"The king closed the gates early, as if we're under siege." He stroked her cheek with his thumb.

She struggled not to flinch. She forced herself not to look away as he touched her. Wouldn't a siege be better than sacrifices?

"You are more beautiful than those of high stations, Rahab."

She shrugged. Again, he had used her name. As if she could be special. It was hard to feel beautiful when no man wanted her for long. Her beauty kept her alive.

"The king demands more sacrifices."

He had already said this. What did he really want? She was startled when she looked into his eyes.

They held tears. His voice broke, "My son must be sacrificed."

Rahab shuddered.

How much did this god want? Wine did nothing to block the screams from the children offered to Baal. She numbly nodded. She understood that grief. She still woke, sweating, heart pounding from nightmares after her own son's agony. She shook her head, unable to remove the memories. No drink was strong enough to keep those screams from piercing her heart.

She could drown the hurt of men using her by drinking, but she could never fill the emptiness of her son's loss.

He held her face, cupped in both hands.

She leaned closer to him, stroking his hand. She could pity him tonight. "You must be there?"

He nodded. "The king expects me to honor my gift."

Now Baal wanted more. How did any man know when sacrifice was enough for the gods?

The general interrupted her thoughts. "You'll be there?"

She closed her eyes, unwilling to look at him. He would soften his hard features and make her consent.

"Rabab."

He had used her name again. She looked at him, against her better judgment.

His expression pled with her.

Her shoulders fell. She would agree, and she hated herself for it. "You may not get me."

He spoke with confidence, "I'll stand in line for you."

He would have to. If she went to the temple's prostitution, all the men stood in line for her. She was cursed with beauty. She closed her eyes and nodded.

"Good." He pushed the bench back from the table. He placed a gold piece on the table as he left.

Why did she trust him? He had already taken her only baby, his child, and given him to Baal. He denied the child was his, but she knew. Now he would feel the pain she had. She should feel satisfied that his pain would match hers, but she couldn't. No one should know the pain of their baby's sacrifice.

She listened as his footsteps echoed down the stone street. When she could no longer hear them, she threw the gold piece across the room. It bounced off the wall, rolled under her bed, and rattled to a final stop. No amount of gold was worth what she would do tonight.

All their people must sacrifice, worship, and beg the gods for protection against this God from the desert.

She would be there. She depended upon the general's gifts to survive. She must appease him, even if no god could be pleased.

The sun's rays were casting long shadows from the walls of Jericho as Salmon and Ethan strode through the fields of barley already gathered into bundles, tied for threshing. They reached a house nestled in the foothills. Salmon looked around the yard as they waited for a response from their knock on the door. Chickens pecked the ground in a small fenced area. One tried to reach a barley stalk dropped just beyond its reach outside the fence.

After no response to his knock, Salmon pushed the door open, warily stepping into the one room. Glancing around its interior, he noticed signs of its occupants leaving in a hurry. Water filled the vessels by the door. Embers still smoked in the cook fire. A flatbread hardened on the stone nearby. The bed had been stripped of its blankets, leaving only the mattress stuffed with wheat shocks. Salmon turned back to drink from the dipper at the door. "They left in a hurry."

Ethan pushed his hood away from his face as he stepped into the house. He still watched the city's gates and the straight road that led there. He searched the surrounding hills. "The city gates look closed already, like they're under siege. Where's the enemy?"

Salmon returned to the doorway. After watching for movement, he sank to the bench by the table in the middle of the one room. He rested his head in his hands. "We'll wait until morning."

Ethan settled on the other bench across from him and chewed on a fig. "Head still throbbing?"

Salmon lifted his head. "Like a pounding drum."

"Maybe a cold poultice would help the swelling." Ethan took a cloth hanging by the water vessel at the door and dipped it in the water.

Salmon took the cloth and held it to his head. "Thanks."

"What do you think we'll find?"

Salmon closed his eyes and sighed. "The city is big. Look at the walls. They rise to the clouds."

"The distance deceives. It appears as one wall, but look," Ethan pointed out the door to where they could see the city's silhouette as the sun set. "One lies on an embankment above the other."

Salmon opened his eye and lifted his eyebrow. "From this distance, they appear as one rising to the heavens."

Ethan chewed slowly. "Wasn't it strange that all the houses we passed were empty and no one worked the harvested wheat?"

Salmon sighed. "Your chewing reminds me of my hunger."

Ethan reached into a bag for another fig. "Want some?"

Salmon grabbed a few. "Where'd you find these?"

Ethan motioned toward the plains. "In the last house." They had stopped at other houses on the plains. No one had been home.

Salmon chewed, thinking. "The people left in a hurry. Their vessels were filled with their recent wheat and barley harvest. Even their water vessels are full and cold. What frightened them?"

Ethan gulped a drink from his waterskin. "I think the people ran to Jericho for safety."

"And left everything behind?"

Ethan ate a date, considering. "We've lived with God's presence our entire lives. We lose the awe of His greatness."

Salmon paused in his chewing. "They fear our God?"

Ethan nodded.

"My father spoke of God as the Friend of Abraham. I'm not afraid when I think of God."

Ethan shrugged. "Look what we did to the Amorites." They were a neighboring country who hadn't allowed Israel to pass through their borders. Instead, they had attacked Israel.

Salmon drank from a dipper and wiped his mouth with the back of his hand. "The Lord gave us victory."

"And no one remained. That is cause for Jericho to fear, don't you think?"

Salmon woke with a foot on his chest.

"Do you plan to sleep the day?"

Salmon threw Ethan's foot off. "I'm awake." He stretched and sat, surveying the space within the dry-mortared walls of the one-roomed house. "Any manna close by?"

Ethan laughed. "No, but I did make flatbread."

Salmon's eyebrow rose. "You? Without Kamon's help?"

Ethan gestured toward the cook fire. "Hungry people become desperate."

Salmon reached for a warmed flatbread and took a big bite. After crunching one bite, he stopped chewing.

Ethan had watched him. His attempt at hiding a grin failed. "What's wrong?"

Salmon spit the bite into the embers of the small cook fire. "Did you grind the wheat kernels into flour first?"

"That wastes too much time, so I just mixed the flour with the kernels for a ... a crunchy, chewy taste."

Salmon nodded, massaging his jaw. "Crunchy, chewy taste ... You achieved that to perfection. I'll have to thank Kamon for wasting her time grinding the wheat next time I eat at your tent."

Ethan laughed. "I will too." He gestured to the flatbread. "These were awful. I about cracked my tooth on my first bite."

"But you saw no reason to warn me with mine?" Salmon reached for his sandals and laced them on his feet.

"Motivation for you to find someone who will care for you."

Salmon humphed. "I can grind my own flour just fine. No pun intended." He stood and stretched. "These people are tall. I don't even have to hunch to stretch."

"The other spies did say that."

Salmon nodded. Their news of giants had caused a revolt. Their entire nation had been condemned to wandering forty years in the wilderness until a new generation had risen. Salmon didn't want to re-do that mistake. He took several handfuls of wheat kernels from the vessels against the wall and dropped them in his pocket. The last handful he put in his mouth. He spoke around his mouthful. "Most of the time, I didn't grind the manna into fine flour." He smiled as Ethan had stopped putting out the fire.

"Do you have holes in your teeth?"

Salmon laughed. "I soak them until they're soft. Then they don't break my teeth."

Ethan grabbed a couple handfuls of kernels and tried a few.

Salmon shrugged. "Fills me up until I go to your tent for Kamon's fine-ground flour flatbread."

Ethan spoke through a handful of kernels. "You need to find someone."

Salmon shrugged. "God will bring me the right wife." He stepped outside into the early morning sunshine. He didn't want to talk about it. How could he explain to Ethan that the girls Ethan and Kamon had introduced him to seemed more interested in his riches and not in him? Except one. He shook his head.

Ethan's eyes twinkled. "Since you run from any woman who even gets close to you, would you know the right one if she came along?"

Salmon ignored him. He was finished with this conversation. He needed to focus on the city and what news they must find out about it to help their people. He studied the road leading toward the gates.

Some merchants were making their way to the city gates. "We could flee in fear of Israel's God."

"You might have something there. I'd thought of stealing from a merchant, but your idea is better."

Salmon rubbed his belly. "Your stealing fits better with my empty insides."

Ethan poked him as Salmon stretched again. "What about your soaked wheat kernels?"

"Takes too long when I'm hungry."

"You need someone who will care."

Salmon rolled his eyes. Ethan had brought the subject up again. He grabbed the last fig from the basket. "You don't care?"

Ethan shook his head. "Not enough."

Salmon shook the dirt from his cloak and threw it around his shoulders. Ethan meant well with his advice, but food wasn't all that he needed in a wife.

Being around Ethan and Kamon showed Salmon what he was missing. Kamon fitted Ethan's needs, made him complete. Salmon was old enough to marry, but he knew of no woman who wanted to know God. His people saw God but did not search for Him. The deeper things of life, where his heart ached, motivated him to wait. Did such a woman exist?

Ethan surveyed Salmon. "Perhaps, if you looked less like you were taking a stroll, and more like you were fleeing, you might convince someone."

"Like I slept in the dirt and hadn't eaten a meal in a day?" Salmon tied his tunic between his legs so he could walk faster. He looked at Ethan when he finished. "Better?"

Ethan shrugged.

They moved toward the city at a good pace. They conversation had only awakened in Salmon's loneliness again. He turned his thoughts from what had been, and focused on what the city would bring.

As they approached the city, they noticed soldiers at the city gate were questioning all those who entered.

Salmon's insides began to churn.

They increased their pace, hoping to slide into the crowd without being noticed.

The guard towered over them. "Stop! Where do you come from?"

"The mountains from the west." Salmon spoke quickly as Ethan answered, "From the east."

The guard looked from Salmon's to Ethan's faces. "Which is it, the west or east?"

Salmon looked at Ethan and shook his head. "We came for protection. Allow your servants to enter and be safe."

The guard turned to Ethan. "Why the east?"

"We came from the west to visit my Amorite relatives in the east. None remain. But we saw those people camped on the other side of the River. We feared for our lives and thought to reside here until these people pass by."

The guard lowered his sword. "Go on."

As they hurried inside, Salmon heard the soldier mutter to himself, "These people don't just pass by. They conquer and destroy; then they pass by."

Salmon and Ethan didn't look back. After walking several streets, Salmon whispered, "Allow me to do the talking. 'Coming from the east,' indeed."

"Isn't that where we came from?"

Salmon sighed in disgust. "Are you going to tell them that you're a spy too?"

A voice behind them whispered. "Come this way, for you are followed."

A figure pushed between them, weaving through the streets, looking back once to see if they followed. His hood covered his head. He kept his face down.

Should they trust him?

Salmon looked at Ethan. If they were wandering the desert, Salmon would have felt at home. He studied the wildlife, tracks, the terrain; but here, the tracks these people left all blended into a mess on the street in front of him. He noticed Ethan's eyes reflected that same lost look.

Salmon could never find his way back to the gate on his own. The twists and turns of these narrow streets reminded him of an ant trail hunting a flake of manna. They were at the mercy of this person wherever he led them.

They followed.

The streets narrowed. The crowd thickened as they moved through a marketplace. Merchants' wares were spread on blankets, arranged in baskets, and hung at eye level to catch the attention of possible customers. Garments of fine silk shimmered even in the shadows where the sun could not reach, their colors telling of the riches required for purchase.

Blankets overflowed with baskets of dried grapes, dates, figs and other fruits that Salmon didn't even know. Other merchant stalls had stacked chickens in cages, squawking their ability to lay eggs.

Salmon slowed as smells of roasted meat tempted his nose. His mouth watered as he tried not to think about the food he had missed for his morning meal or the day before. He licked his lips. This land would make his people rich.

He glanced ahead. Where was Ethan and the one they followed? He'd only looked away for a moment. How could they have disappeared?

His heart raced. He backed toward a doorway on the side of the street. Rather than wander aimlessly, he could take note of his surroundings. How could he have lost them so quickly?

Someone grabbed him and tugged him into an alcove of a doorway.

He raised his arm to defend himself, but found himself facing the one they had followed.

His head stayed down, his hood covering his face.

Salmon slowly lowered his arm. He looked around for Ethan. Where was he?

Soldiers pushed through the crowded street.

Crowds parted, making a path for the soldiers.

An officer directed, "They came this way. I saw them with the harlot."

Salmon hunched farther into the doorway.

The hand that still held Salmon's arm trembled.

The soldiers were looking for them.

He had just missed being seen. He glanced down at the small figure beside him. His eyes grew accustomed to the darkness. They had followed this one. The soldier had called her a harlot. They had followed a woman?

He glanced back the way they had come, then bumped into Ethan, squatting behind him, the dark corner hiding him.

Had they walked into a trap?

The woman stepped from the doorway, and motioned for them to follow.

What choice did they have?

They continued to follow. The crowds thinned and the streets were emptier, but still they stayed to the sides of the streets.

They passed a beggar, lying in a doorway away from traffic. His deformed limb not hidden by the meager clothes he wore. "Show mercy." His voice was as weak as his wasted body.

The woman hurried by, ignoring his plea for help.

Salmon fingered a silver piece from his cloak's pocket. He stooped to look into the beggar's face. His face was wrinkled with more than just age. His eyes reflected a blank, hollow, hopeless look. Salmon took the beggar's gnarled hand in his own. It felt like bones with only a thin, dirty protection of skin. Salmon dropped the silver piece in the man's hands, closing the gnarled fingers over it.

The man grabbed his arm with surprising speed. His eyes met Salmon's with almost a hint of hope. "May the gods reward you."

Salmon squeezed his hand gently. No god but his God would reward him. How could he share the plenty of His God with one who knew such poverty?

Salmon stood and met the woman's gaze, although most of her face stayed hidden in the cloak's hood.

She shook her head. "That'll ruin him."

Salmon hurried to walk beside her. Didn't they help their own? God's people had poor who didn't have much, but all had eaten from God's manna. How could people with some, watch others with nothing and not give? Was this woman heartless?

She whispered even as she hurried. "He'll be beaten."

Salmon lengthened his stride to keep up with her. She almost ran. What would make people so cruel? "Why?"

"No one will believe he got it honestly."

Salmon didn't understand the ways of this people, but felt rebuked. His kind act would lead to further abuse.

Ethan stepped beside him. "Try not to wear your heart on your sleeve. We must destroy these people, remember."

Salmon nodded, but felt torn. Destroying in the heat of battle out of obedience to God was one thing, but seeing those destitute made him want to show them his God as Friend. Salmon shook his head. Ethan was right. He shouldn't care too much. And he mustn't cause attention. They must return to their own people alive.

They left the noise of the merchants' stalls. The crowds thinned. The streets narrowed to a pathway where he could almost stretch out his arms and reach the houses lining both sides of the street. Salmon shivered. In their camp, they had space and sun. Here he felt trapped, their houses towered over him like dungeons without light.

The smells changed from the tantalizing cooking meat and baked breads sold to people in the marketplace to the smoke of burning straw, unwashed bodies and waste. Down the center of the street, a ditch ran where refuse lay, swarming with flies. His insides churned in spite of their emptiness. He tried not to breathe in the smell.

When a door opened, Salmon paused in the shadows.

A person stepped from the doorway, paused long enough to toss something in the street, then returned behind the closed door.

Looking at what had been thrown, Salmon saw human waste. Didn't these people know sanitary laws? God had told them to cover their waste outside of camp. That kept their people clean and healthy. He caught Ethan's glance and shook his head.

Salmon hurried to catch up. What more would they learn of this people?

The woman stopped before a door. She looked up and down the street before opening the door, entering and bolting it behind them.

Salmon remembered the soldier's words, "Harlot..." His eyes adjusted to the greater interior darkness. What had they walked into? With all Ethan's teasing of his need for a wife, Salmon stayed away from women. They distracted him from knowing God. Their culture didn't allow them to be alone with a woman, nor speak to one without her father or older brother present.

This protected the woman. Salmon swallowed and shook his head. And the man.

Not only were they alone with a woman, but the woman was a harlot. Would she offer her services? His face flushed with the thought. What would she expect from them?

She removed her hood and shook her hair from its confines. It flowed down her back, shining like a raven's, even in the dim light.

Salmon could only stare. He wanted to step forward and touch it. Did it feel as silky and soft as it looked?

She didn't face them, but pointed to a bench. "I only have flat-bread."

Salmon shook his head. She was offering to feed them. Surely that couldn't hurt. He removed his cloak, placing it on the small bench beside the table. He washed his head and arms at a bowl on a bench by the door, wiping back his hair. He drank from the dipper in another vessel. He squared his shoulders and sat at the bench, resigning himself to the fate God had given.

Ethan sat opposite him and mouthed, "What have we done?"

Salmon shook his head.

As he watched the woman grind wheat into flour and form flat-bread, he realized how hungry he was. Last night he had fallen asleep without eating. That morning they had only eaten dates and wheat kernels. Flatbread would be a feast.

She interrupted his thoughts, "It'll not be long before he comes."

Salmon studied the woman. She kept her face down and hidden. Could they trust her? "Who?"

She stirred the embers to life, adding dried leaves from nearby wheat stalks to encourage the flames. She placed the flatbread on a stone warming near it. "The general." She kept her face hidden. "I didn't know where else to take you."

Salmon took several steps toward her. He worked to keep his voice level. "You brought us here to give us to the army?"

She started to raise her face to look directly at him, but seemed to think better of it. She betrayed control and confidence. "I brought you here, because that was the only safe place for you to be."

Salmon glanced at Ethan. How safe were they? What would she do when the general arrived?

She didn't speak again until she placed the flatbread before them on the table.

Salmon spoke a blessing on the meal, even as he listened for any noise outside the door.

She sat across from Ethan and watched them eat. "Your blessing honors your God?"

Salmon shrugged. He couldn't think of not thanking God for the meal, especially when every meal of manna had been a direct gift from God. "His presence is with us. We speak to Him throughout the day."

She considered this. "And He hears?"

Salmon nodded as he took another bite.

Ethan chewed his flatbread. "What do your people think of us?"

She shook her head at the change of subject. "The gates shut early. Soldiers march the streets." She huffed. "As if that could protect us."

Ethan paused in his chewing. "You don't feel safe?"

Her house was part of the city wall. She pointed to a pile of crumbled rocks by her sleeping pallet. "Look at the walls. They won't withstand any battering. Our walls give a false impression of our strength."

Salmon savored the wheat texture. It was fresh. "Why do you tell us?"

"Your God already knows. If He can take mighty Egypt and make her like the sand of the desert and move the waters of the Reed Sea so your people can walk through, then what is a mere wall for Him to climb? Especially a wall that is falling down."

Salmon exchanged glances with Ethan. "You have more faith than our own people who have seen these wonders." He looked around her room, as if seeing it for the first time. How could someone who did not know their God have such faith?

"What does this God want from us?" She kept her face down.

Salmon studied her. He couldn't see her entire face, but she was beautiful. He lowered his eyes, surprised he had even noticed. He normally didn't notice women. To cover his embarrassment, he offered her a piece of his flatbread. "We're grateful for your kindness."

Her eyes widened at the gesture. Women ate after the men finished and only with family, not with a stranger. She shook her head.

Hearing heavy feet and clanking armor in the streets, Salmon straightened.

She rose and motioned them to be silent and follow her up a ladder to her roof.

As Salmon moved from the darkness of the room to the brightness of the roof, he breathed deeply, savoring the openness and light that the rooftop offered. These confines of the city made him long for the sky and the mountains.

They were on the north side of the city. He could see the sun falling over the mountains in the west.

The woman shoved aside sheaves of drying barley and wheat. "Lie here."

Pounding at her door began. "Hurry."

Salmon and Ethan lay down.

She piled the sheaves over them.

All this confinement heightened Salmon's senses. He smelled the fresh cut wheat stalks as their drying leaves scratched him. He slowed his breathing, trying to ignore their weight.

The sun filtered through the leaves and shone in his eyes as it moved closer to the horizon.

He squinted through the sheaves and saw her glance once at their covering before climbing down the ladder. He didn't like the feeling of helplessness or vulnerability.

Could they trust her? Salmon closed his eyes and strained to hear.

The pounding at the door stopped.

A man's voice demanded, "Where are they?"

Would she betray them? Salmon's insides tightened. He didn't realize that he held his breath until he heard her response.

Her voice was controlled. "Would anyone visit me, after last night?"

The man's voice softened, "Your beauty was sacrificed to the gods. We secure our safety."

"What safety is there from a God Who controls it all?"

The man responded, "Baal will save us."

Salmon felt a growing desire to know this woman. Even in her limited knowledge of God, she showed a deepness in understanding Him.

She spoke again, "Did you sacrifice your son?"

Salmon choked back a gasp. They sacrificed children? His body tensed. What kind of favor could that bring to any god? He almost missed the general's next words.

"There was no need. I gave your beauty."

What did that mean? Salmon didn't understand their sacrifices.

"What is this?" The man's accusing tone raised Salmon's hair on the back of his neck. "Where are they?"

With a sudden realization, Salmon remembered his cloak. He had left it on the bench. His flatbread turned as he realized he wouldn't need her betrayal. He had given evidence of their presence.

The woman didn't waver. "They were here. But left."

There was a smack.

Then a gasp.

Something clattered to the floor.

What was happening? Salmon clenched his fists. He couldn't lie still and allow her to be hurt. He started to rise and caught Ethan's eye between the stalks of wheat.

Ethan shook his head.

Salmon slumped back against the roof. How could he just listen to her get hurt? He closed his eyes and concentrated to hear her next words.

"I trusted you."

The man's voice took a pleading tone. "It's for our people's safety. We all must sacrifice."

"What about your son who was supposed to be sacrificed?"

The man softened his voice. "I love my son."

She spat. "You once told *me* of your love too. Do your words mean nothing?"

"You still have life. My son would not."

"I would rather not live."

The man's tone changed, demanding. "You will live long enough to tell me where those men are."

"How could I have thought you cared for me?"

The man laughed. "I've found another."

"You destroy me before you move on."

His voice softened, "It's for the pleasure of the gods."

"The men that you seek—" She paused as if waiting for his complete attention.

Salmon held his breath for her next words. Would she tell?

"I led them to the gate before it closed. If you hurry, you'll catch them."

Salmon released a breath he had held. He heard another loud smack before he heard the door slam shut. He listened as the clank of armor moved down the street. Then he heard nothing. He stood and nudged Ethan with his foot. He lowered himself through the roof's opening, not even using the ladder, but dropping to the floor. He paused, adjusting to the dark interior.

The woman huddled on the floor by the door, her face in her hands, weeping.

Salmon touched her shoulder. "You have saved our lives."

She raised her face to look at him. "Does your God demand such a sacrifice?"

He flinched as he looked at her face. Even in the darkness, he could see the fresh burn on half her face. He tried not to lower his eyes. What kind of god demanded their people to burn their faces? He remembered the beggar and Ethan's warning, but he must tell this woman of their God. "Our God desires a broken and contrite heart."

She laughed without feeling. "That's all I have." She squared her shoulders and sat up straighter. "Does your God demand your babies to be sacrificed?"

Salmon swallowed the lump in his throat. He saw such pain in her eyes. Pain and longing to believe what he said. What horrors had she known to please these gods?

He still held her shoulders. "Our God sent food every day for forty years so that not one of His own perished."

She wiped her face, gingerly, around her burn. "Would your God save me?"

Salmon looked at Ethan. At his nod, he nodded.

She swallowed. Her eyes showed hope, then resolution. "What do you want to know about the city? I know many secrets from men who come to my arms at night."

Ethan moved to the door, listening.

Salmon sat beside her on the dirt floor. He wanted to protect this woman who knew such pain. "What do they think of us?"

"We heard what you did to the two Amorite kings, Sihon and Og. Our hearts melt. No courage remains. Your God ... He is God in heaven above and on earth beneath." She paused. "But you say, He won't demand any child sacrifices?"

Salmon leaned forward. What else did these people do to please their gods? "Could you love a God Who demanded such horror?"

She paled at his response. "You love this God?"

Salmon smiled. "God saw our fathers suffering in Egypt and came to our aid. We owe our lives to God."

"You are His slaves?"

Salmon nodded. "He demands our obedience to His laws."

Her voice returned to the panic of earlier. "His laws? What does He demand of you?"

"He tells us how to treat our animals, our slaves, even foreigners who come. He gives us rules for sacrifice."

She shook her head in alarm. "You do sacrifice! You told me He didn't demand your children."

Salmon took her hand to calm her.

She shivered at his touch.

He lowered his voice, "Only animal sacrifices are acceptable. By them, we show we love Him."

She lowered her head. "I know little of love."

Ethan paced. "We must go before they close the gates."

She rose and dusted her tunic from where she sat. She shook her head. "They watch for you. I know a better way." She searched her room.

Salmon watched her. What was she looking for? She had nothing but a bench, table and her pallet for sleeping.

Her eyes rested on her pallet lined with fine sheets.

His insides dropped. He held his breath. They were in the house of a harlot. Would she expect to give her services before they could leave? Salmon threw his shoulders back and opened his mouth to speak. He caught Ethan's eye.

Ethan shook his head.

Did Ethan always read his mind?

She tugged off her sheets and ripped them into strips, tying them together to form a cord. She moved with greater purpose, even hope. "I have saved your life. When your people take the city, save me ... and my family."

Ethan looked at Salmon and nodded. "Our lives for yours, if we do not save your life."

Salmon added. "When we come, we will deal kindly and faithfully with you."

Tears welled in her eyes. She pushed back her hair. "Kindly ... I don't know what that is."

Salmon couldn't imagine a life without kindness. He remembered her rebuke about the beggar. How could a people survive without love?

They followed her as she returned to the roof. The sun had set. Darkness crept over the city.

Ethan tightened the knots in the sheets. "We won't be held responsible for anyone who isn't in your house when we come for you."

She nodded. "Take some wheat." She pulled heads of wheat from the sheaves and handed them some.

Salmon put a few kernels in his mouth to chew, then took several handfuls for his pocket. He stopped when he remembered not seeing any vessels filled with harvest in her room. "Will you have enough?"

She paused as she tied the rope securely to a pillar on the wall and faced them. Her surprise that he would care was evident.

Had no one ever cared for her?

She eyed them before handing the rope to Ethan. "I'll make do."

Remembering her conversation with the general, Salmon wondered, could she trust anyone? He took her by her shoulders.

She shrank from his touch.

He waited until she looked at him. "Leave the rope on the wall. We'll use it to find you again. If anyone leaves your home, they won't be spared."

Ethan added. "If you tell anyone our business, we will be released of our oath."

She nodded. "According to your words, so be it."

Ethan tested the rope before climbing over the ledge. He slid down the sheet and was swallowed by the darkness.

When Salmon felt the tension of the rope lessen, he swung his leg over the edge of the roof.

She grabbed his arm. "Don't take the road. Go to the hills west of us. Stay there three days. The men who look for you will return; then you'll be safe to return to your people."

Salmon looked into her face. Even in the darkness, one side was so beautiful, the other marred by a brand. "You can trust our God to take care of you until we return."

She gasped, as if she could not believe such a thing.

He lowered himself down the rope. The image of a beautiful face marred by a brand lingered long in his mind.

What would it be like not to know God? Without God, would life have any goodness?

After waiting three days in the western hills, Ethan and Salmon retraced their steps across the plains to cross the river. Ethan gestured to Salmon's dry cloak on his head. "You made it this time."

Salmon rubbed his head where the swelling had gone down. "Glad for your help the first time."

Ethan looked into Salmon's face. The glance relayed more concern than his words. "Don't let it happen again."

Salmon nodded. "Eat and meet me at Joshua's."

Ethan nodded. Salmon would allow him privacy with his wife. Ethan retraced his steps to his own tent and paused before the entrance.

He thrived with the danger that spying brought, but now he must adjust back to acting civilized. Though gone only a few weeks, time away seemed long. He had missed Kamon. What he had seen of the city's inhabitants made him want to protect Kamon from its evil. He swallowed the lump in his throat.

Ethan glanced through the tent opening as Kamon bent over the fire. He took the few steps that separated them and hugged her from behind.

She squealed and struggled, until he laughed.

"You frightened me." She turned in his arms to face him.

He tightened his embrace and raised his eyebrows. "Do other men grab you?"

She laughed. "I wasn't expecting you."

He had missed her laughter. In the city, he had heard no laughter. He hadn't realized the loss until now. Laughter represented peace. He felt the stress of the danger, even the evil, melt as he held her. He was home.

She pushed away from him and looked into his face.

"What?"

She hesitated. "Your eyes show such intensity."

He studied her face. Her eyes glowed with life. The contrast from the city's inhabitants with no life in their faces moved him. His voice was thick with emotion, "I've missed you."

She lowered her eyes. "What did you find?"

He bowed his head and shifted his thinking. "The people are afraid."

She squirmed out of his arms to retrieve the smoking flatbread from the embers. "Hungry?"

"Always. But I want to see your face first." He bent down and cupped her face in his.

Kamon shook her head and pulled from him. "Why do you gaze so long?"

Ethan didn't understand why she still grew embarrassed by his gaze, but he loved her more for it. He dropped his hand. "The people are afraid. The houses around the city are empty. Their people seek refuge in the city, leaving everything behind."

She searched his eyes. "So why the sadness in your eyes? Isn't that good?"

"A woman," he swallowed and hesitated. He must tell all. He kept no secrets from Kamon. He had done nothing wrong, yet in their culture they would think so. Would she believe him? "A harlot," he corrected. "A harlot led us to her home."

Kamon gasped and looked down.

Ethan raised her face to his. His heart quickened. Could he make her understand? "The army was searching for us. The harlot saved us from capture. We owe our lives to her. We promised her deliverance." He sighed.

Her eyes relayed trust. She believed him.

Ethan's love for her deepened.

"Why the sigh?"

Ethan shrugged. "I feel that by delivering her, we will bring problems to our people and to Salmon."

"Why to Salmon?"

"Salmon has fallen for the harlot."

Kamon repeated, "The harlot?"

"He doesn't know it yet, but if I know Salmon, he has fallen hard."

"Why?"

Ethan shook his head. "She has a faith in our God that surpasses even our own people's faith."

"How can that be?"

Ethan laughed. "She already believes our God has conquered her city. And she wants Him to."

Kamon pressed. "But you will honor your word to save her?"

Ethan nodded. "She doesn't understand our God."

"Do we?"

Ethan laughed, then shrugged. How could he explain the harlot's thirst for God, yet her lack of knowledge? How did someone bring a person to trust? "It's not just understanding; it's trusting."

Kamon brushed his hair from his forehead. "She'll trust when she finds God is trustworthy."

CHAPTER 3

Rahab looked around her one-roomed house. She hadn't eaten all day. Her meager supply of food was gone. Word had spread that she was marred. Her visitors had stopped coming. She wouldn't be paid for any more services.

Would the spies come soon?

The spies intrigued her. They were strong, though short. She laughed. They were taller than she was, but smaller than her people.

When she had pulled the one spy through the doorway to hide him from the soldiers, his arm had held strength. When he had turned with his arm raised, she expected him to strike her, but he had reacted quickly, not harming her when he saw who had grabbed him.

Yet with his strength, and even the power of their God, they showed ... was it humbleness? Or tenderness? He had given to the beggar. Almost like he cared for him. Why did he care? She had hated telling him the beggar would be abused for his kindness. It made her feel like she was evil for not caring.

Even when he was leaving, he seemed to realize the wheat she offered was all she had. He had stopped taking some for his trip and asked if she would have enough. Had anyone ever shown such kindness to her?

His eyes had blazed with passion when he spoke of his God. Like his God cared. Did his God teach him to care?

Was she deceived by this man or could she hope he would be trustworthy? She sighed. She wanted to believe they would return.

Her thoughts were interrupted by pounding on her door.

The general always pounded. He always demanded. He always tried to control her.

She hated giving in to his desires. She had supplied his needs, for her own survival. If she hadn't, she wouldn't have eaten. But now, with the promise of the spies' return, Rahab felt a power over the general. She didn't have to bow to his needs. She wouldn't have to please him. In that knowledge, she felt hope, almost a freedom. Rahab answered the door with a new resolve. She blocked the doorway, hindering the general from entering.

He barged past her. "Where are they?"

Rahab blinked in the light from the doorway. She leaned against the doorframe. "Couldn't you find them?"

"You know I couldn't. We've been looking for two days. What did you do with them?"

She pushed her hair from her face. "They left before the gate shut. That was the last I saw them."

He slapped her. His slap opened her scabs that had started to heal.

She gasped as pain shot through her face. She felt blood drip down her cheek.

He had caused this brand on her face.

She would not forget. Nor would she allow him to know how much pain he had caused her. She swallowed her pain and glared at him.

He wasn't finished. "The people have crossed the river."

In flood stage? How? She would have liked to see how this God protected His people as they crossed. But she knew better than to ask. She waited.

The general would tell her what he knew. He always did.

He swallowed, studying her. "We thought we had more time."

She had once been at his mercy to do whatever he said. But now, if she could believe the spies, she would be taken away from him and his threats and control. With this realization, she found strength to stand against him. "More time for what? To prepare for a God Who controls the wind?"

He raised his hand to smack her again, but held it in the air over her face.

She did not flinch, but continued to taunt. She wasn't dependent upon his money for her meals anymore. She would be taken away from this city and its gods. She would be able to know this God Who cared for His people. "Go ahead. Prove to me your love."

He stepped forward and touched the unmarred side of her face with unusual gentleness. "You are still beautiful. I have loved you."

Rahab was not deceived. Her eyes did not falter from his. Her voice grew hard. Why had she ever believed him? "Your love is fickle, just like the gods you serve." She could see his eyes flicker, and she braced for his slap.

This time he did smack her. He hissed his next words, "Do not speak ill of Baal. We depend upon him to save us."

She glared at him. "You don't worship Baal. You use Baal to sanction your own pleasure."

"We sacrifice tonight." His eyes held a look of something besides lust. Was it fear?

Rahab pressed. "Will you meet with man or woman?"

His eyebrows raised as he smirked. "Whatever the gods desire."

She mocked him. "And everything is sanctioned, because it's for the gods."

He shrugged. "If the gods are pleased, then I am pleased."

"Demand your sergeant's attention. You may find pleasure in what he can give."

He smiled. "I know. I already have."

"Then I'm not needed."

He shook his head. "He only fills my need as I wait for you."

"There will be no men in line for me anymore. You took care of that last time. So why are you really here?"

His voice took a pleading tone. "What did the spies tell you? What are their plans?"

"Do you think they would tell me?"

He stroked her arms lightly. "All men tell secrets to a woman in their arms."

Rahab shivered, rubbing her arms as she stepped away from him. "They were too good to use me. They spoke of a God Who does not demand evil for His pleasure."

"We offer our best to Baal. Our children hold the hope of our nation."

Rahab challenged. "So you can continue to find pleasure where you will?"

"Baal promises fertility. We offer what we have."

Rahab turned from him. "What you offer will never be enough for Baal."

"It gives me pleasure." His voice changed as if he were commanding his army. "It must be enough."

Rahab turned to face him. "And if it's not?"

His voice fell almost to a whisper, "Then we perish."

After the general left, Rahab grabbed her cloak and hurried to her father's house. They lived in a better area of the city, not between the two walls. She must convince her family of their chance for deliverance. Recalling the general's reaction, she slowed her steps as she came closer she came to their house. Her insides knotted. The general had feared this God, but not enough to serve Him. Would her father be like the general, or would he want deliverance?

When she entered their house, her mother hugged her. Rahab kept her face down and avoided eye contact.

Her mother seemed distracted. She watched the door nervously, as if she expected someone. "When did you eat last?" She rubbed her hands down her tunic before turning to make flat bread.

Rahab smiled. Her mother's solution to anything was eating. Rahab didn't want her father to find her eating his food, but flatbread would settle her insides. She knelt by the embers and stirred them into flames. "I have news."

"Tell me after you eat." Her mother glanced at the door again.

They were alone. Did her mother expect someone? Rahab looked around the one room. Their harvest was arranged in jars on shelves on the wall. "Do you have enough to spare?"

"The harvest was good."

Rahab smiled. She remembered her brother Galon's appetite when she had lived here. He could eat all the time. "Does Galon have enough?"

Her mother wiped her hair from her face with a floured hand and laughed. "Even Galon is full."

When her mother handed her the flatbread, she noticed Rahab's cheek for the first time. "You were marred at the temple, Rahab?"

Rahab nodded.

Her mother sighed. She bent beside Rahab. "Let me see."

Rahab raised her face for her mother to see.

"How did you displease Baal so, child?"

"Mother, it's impossible to please Baal. My baby's gone. My face is marred. And still Baal wants more. When is enough, enough?"

A shadow fell across the doorway and her father bellowed, "We don't question the gods. We appease them."

Rahab's mother jumped and stepped away from Rahab.

Rahab stood as her father strode across the room. He threw his cloak on the bench beside the table and continued to where she stood. He lifted her chin to examine her face. "How did you displease Baal?"

"Papa," She used the term of endearment that had soothed his anger when she was small. "I sacrificed to please him."

"You never do enough. I sold you for good money. You were provided for life."

"I tried, Papa. The man was cruel. He wearied of me."

He pointed to the flatbread burning in the ashes. "I weary of you. And now, you steal food from me again."

"Papa, I've come to tell you, we are saved." Rahab bowed, moving the burnt flatbread out of the ashes with her foot, but keeping alert to what he did with his hands. Sometimes she could avoid being hit if she moved fast enough. "The people who camp on this side of the Jordan—"

"What do you know of this people?" His voice broke. He paced like a caged lion. "They hinder me from working my flocks. The gates stay shut, and I can't leave."

She sensed his hesitation. Did he fear these people enough to want deliverance? "Two men from their camp promised me deliverance before they destroy our city."

"What did you promise them? Did you offer my flocks?"

"No, Papa, those are yours." How could she convince her father? "The men told of a God Who doesn't allow babies and children to be sacrificed to Him."

Her father's voice rose, "What kind of God would not sanction the pleasure of His people?"

Pleasure? Did her father enjoy the sacrifices? Did he find what the men did under the cover of darkness pleasing? She felt sickened by his admission. She had feared her father but never despised him. She had considered his selling her as what had to be done. Now, she saw her father differently as she compared his actions and words to what the spies had told her. His words reminded her of the general's. Did he seek his own pleasure no matter whom he hurt?

He stalked to the shelves on the wall lined with jars. He grabbed a handful of kernels from one of the jars and sifted them through his fingers. "We have plenty because Baal is pleased."

Rahab stepped toward her father. How could he always praise Baal? She was tired of pleasing this god. She was weary of their people seeking their own pleasure as if the gods cared. "We have plenty because the sun shines and the rain falls at the right time. Baal only takes; he does not give."

Her father took two long strides and struck her.

Her father respected strength. She would show it to him. Rahab gulped air. She would not show pain. She would not cower. More of her scabs ripped open. Her cheek dripped blood. Blood tickled her skin where she still had feeling. She wouldn't wipe it in his presence.

He hissed the next words in her face. "No daughter of mine will discredit the joy Baal brings to me. Get out."

Rahab stood still. She didn't want to leave without their consent for deliverance. She clenched her fists. How could she convince him their lives were held by this God outside their city? She softened her tone. "Papa, when the people from the desert destroy our city, they will save those in my house. If you come, I would welcome you."

She glanced at her mother from the corner of her eye.

Her mother had wilted in the corner during their argument. She would never come without his permission.

Her father feared destruction. She could see it by the way his hands trembled, even as he clenched them at his sides to keep them still. But was that fear enough to bring him to deliverance?

"Get out!"

She walked to the doorway. Before leaving, she turned back, and looked at her mother, then at her father. "This God can deliver us."

CHAPTER 4

Joshua stood before the Jordan River. Its waves piled high, spilling over the banks. Trees on both sides of the bank were submerged, showing their upper branches above the rolling waves. As he watched, a branch from a tree farther north bumped its way from boulder to tree as it was swept downstream. In the early sun's rays, he couldn't see the bottom of the river. The black waters looked like a grave. He stepped away unconsciously.

He no longer heard the noise of the people behind him in camp. They had moved their camp here three days ago, from Shittim to Jordan's banks, by the Lord's command. But he only heard the crashing waves and the roaring rapids. Was this how Moses felt when God brought them to the Reed Sea?

He sighed. What should he do?

Last night, Ethan and Salmon had reported to him. The city of Jericho was in their hands. Now would be the time to take the city. They weren't expected to cross the river until it went down.

Joshua had told the people last night during evening sacrifices to be strong. He had even consecrated the people to God. But now in the morning's early light, he looked at the waters and felt helpless. Why could he not simply trust God?

As he watched the waters gush before him, it was as if the icy waves stopped their hammering. The deafening waves stilled. Quietness surrounded him. He looked at the river. Had it stopped flowing?

The waves were as large as they had been.

But Joshua couldn't hear them.

He fell to the ground on his face as he waited in the stillness.

Out of the quietness, the Lord spoke, "Today, I will show the people that you will lead them to My Land. As I have been with Moses, so I will be with you."

Joshua waited for more instructions.

None came.

He must lead the people to the Lord's Land.

And God would show him.

It was enough.

The quietness stopped and the waves resounded as they beat against the sides of the bank and roared down the narrow passageway, but as Joshua rose to his feet, he felt the Lord's presence. Not like before, when he had followed in Moses's footsteps, waiting to be told by Moses what to do. Now, he must spend time listening carefully to the Lord's Words, so he could lead the people.

He would take the first step of obedience, like Moses always told him, "Obey first; then ask how."

They would cross the Jordan River today.

The river spilled over its banks and ran toward the south. The morning sacrifices included instructions to the tribe of Levi. They were responsible for worship and carried all the tools and furniture of the Tabernacle. Most of the curtains, poles, and hangings could be placed in carts and pulled by oxen. But not the Ark of the Covenant.

The Ark of the Covenant must be carried by poles on the shoulders of four men. They could not rest it on the ground for any reason. The presence of the Lord rested in it. The people could see and know He was with them by the cloud that rose above it.

Korah's clan was assigned the task of carrying the Ark of the Covenant.

Ebiasaph, Korah's son, and his three sons held the four poles.

Although the sun shone brightly, the morning air was still cool. The water looked even colder and blacker.

Ebiasaph held his pole, waiting for Joshua's directions. He tried not to look at the raging waves before him, nor think about how cold it would feel to be buried in that water. He would obey. He had learned that much in the desert. "Today God will deliver His people from this river."

His son Rafa snorted. "While our shoulders grow weary of holding this Ark."

Ebiasaph's own shoulders ached already under the weight. The Ark was plated in gold. No one needed to remind him of how heavy gold was nor how quickly it could make him sink in the sandy riverbed. He shook his head of such thoughts. He must obey, and he must have his sons obey if they were to live. "Do you seek God's displeasure? Your grandfather sought to change the plan of God. He was swallowed by the very ground where he stood. And he didn't go alone. He took his wife and young children."

His words silenced his sons. They had heard the story of *Korah's rebellion* before. When Korah had sought to overthrow Moses's authority, God had shown the people that no man would usurp that authority. Korah and those of his family who still resided in his tent had been swallowed by the ground.

Korah's actions had caused Ebiasaph to serve God whole-heartedly. Now, Ebiasaph renewed his desire to serve God, even as he watched the waves. The swirling madness at his feet made it easy to fear and doubt. They all could be submerged by the waves. Easier than being swallowed by the ground. He shook his head and tried not to think such thoughts. He caught Joshua's eye.

At Joshua's nod, Ebiasaph signaled his sons to walk into the icy waters.

Ebiasaph swallowed his gasp. The water numbed his legs and feet. He couldn't feel his toes grabbing the sand through his sandals. The waves swirled around his feet, tugging at him, threatening to topple him. He concentrated on standing firm and watched the distant shore. The weight of the Ark was enough to make all four men sink to the bottom like rocks. Would he let go, if it started to sink? What was it like not to breathe, swallowing water with every gulp? Would his body even be found on the beach afterward?

He shook his head to stop his thoughts. He must trust in God Whose presence kept them safe.

He stepped forward. He could hear nothing but water.

When they held the entire Ark over the waves, he stood still.

Did the waters tug less?

Air cooled his legs where water had just been. He could feel goosebumps rise on his skin.

He looked to the north where the waters started.

No water came. Only a river bed filled with rocks and buried branches.

He turned to the south.

The waters continued away from his feet, as if fleeing before the presence of the Ark.

He stood on sand.

No water swirled around his feet. The waves, so loud a moment before, were gone.

In their place was quiet.

In the stillness, he heard the cry of an eagle, soaring overhead. He raised his head and watched it circle. Even God's creatures cried out His praise.

Ebiasaph smiled and breathed deeply. He would not die in the waters this day.

What power of God that even the waves of an overflowing river would be stopped to allow God to pass!

Ebiasaph adjusted his grip on the pole. He followed the pole through the rings of the Ark of the Covenant, then studied the Ark. God had given specific instructions for its construction, for it would house His presence in their camp. Their Creator God choose to reside in a thing made by His creature's hands.

He shrugged. Not that they could ever contain God in a box. He was, after all, God, Creator of everything, but He allowed Himself for the sake of the man that He created to rest where they could worship and know Him. That in itself was incomprehensible.

Two cherubims of gold faced each other, their wings spread upward, covering the mercy seat which was lined with gold.

Ebiasaph looked at Rafa across from him. "Ready?"

His son's expression showed worship. He nodded.

They set out as one. As they walked, Ebiasaph felt with his toes. Even the sand beneath him was dry.

No cart or wagon would bog in its bottom.

The people had nothing to fear.

And neither did he. He would not be found on the beach of the river today. He would be spared to live for God another day. He breathed deeply and walked.

When they reached the center of the river bed, they waited for all Israel to cross.

The people had been instructed to leave two thousand *cubits* around the Ark for the holiness of their God. After seeing the power that the Ark contained, it should be easy for them to remember.

Ebiasaph firmly held the pole and watched the people cross.

Even though the families hurried, carrying all they owned, Ebiasaph heard his sons sigh and shift as they held the Ark. He could no longer feel his own arms as the weight of the gold-plated box grew heavy. He relaxed his grip to adjust his hold, flexing his fingers to allow the blood to circulate again. He then grabbed it firmly, reminding his sons, "Keep the Ark on your shoulders, men. Don't grow weary."

As the last herd of sheep and goats crossed the river bed, he heard his sons sigh. Nothing remained of their campsite on the east bank. Ebiasaph encouraged, "We're almost finished."

But almost was not finished. They must wait for twelve men representing the twelve sons of Jacob to choose a stone from beneath the Ark to represent each tribe.

Ebiasaph and his sons remained in the center of the river bed while the men carried their stones to the bank of the river. They made a memorial.

Joshua instructed, "When your children ask, 'What do these stones mean?' Tell them of God's mighty works and His care for His people, not only to save them here, but to deliver them from Egypt. Teach your children to remember. Fear the Lord your God forever."

Joshua chose twelve more men from each tribe to collect a stone from the bank of the river and pile them under the Ark.

Once finished, Ebiasaph and his sons walked from the river. When all four men were standing safely beyond the river's reach, the water burst forth, rising above its banks as it had before.

The quietness, even of the people, as they walked across the river, was replaced by the roar of the waves and the power of the water crashing against the rocks. The waves covered the twelve stones in the center of the river.

Ebiasaph swallowed. He shifted under the Ark's weight. The Lord's protection and mercies in the midst of such power was hard to comprehend. But he was grateful for it.

The people had crossed the river yesterday, making camp far above the flowing waters. Today, after morning sacrifices and further instructions from Joshua, Amos searched the river bank for the right kind of rock.

He had been young enough, under the twenty years, when the spies returned forty years ago. He still sewed and repaired canvases and tents. He and Pelia had raised their family to look to the cloud and obey the Law.

He watched as his grandson Nadir searched the banks of the Jordan for a flint stone.

"Why, Grandfather, are we circumcised?"

Amos paused in his search. "Circumcision sets us apart as the Lord's people."

"No other nations do it?"

"None."

"Will all our men be circumcised?"

Amos explained again the words of Joshua. "All men from the oldest who left Egypt, who were not counted as warriors, to those who are newly born in the desert sand."

"Even babies?"

"They are part of our nation, aren't they?"

Nadir nodded.

"God wants us all to be set apart."

"Why does He set us apart?"

"So we may know Him." Amos studied his grandson to make sure he was listening. "Didn't you listen to Joshua when he told us? These questions were answered then."

Nadir bowed his head, and then raised it with a smile. "When Joshua instructs, he speaks to fathers and grandfathers like you. But when you tell me, the words sink into my heart and become mine."

Amos tussled Nadir's hair. "Then I'm glad to repeat them for you." He pointed to a rock. "Let me see that one." When Nadir handed the stone to him, he shifted it in his hand and nodded. "This is what you want." He limped on his wooden leg to a tree where he could lean against it. "The stone must be one and a half handbreadths for the three-finger blade."

Nadir knelt beside Amos and watched. "How do you know how to make a flint knife?"

Amos laughed. "I once apprenticed as a stone carver like your Great-Grandfather Hakeen."

Nadir brought his knife from its sheath. He began chipping with another stone. "Why can't we use the knives from Egypt? They seem sharper than any stone knife that we could make."

Amos settled against the trunk of a tree. "You'll see." He struck the rock at an angle with his knife, so that the blows were close to the edge of the rock. As he chipped, he inspected his grandson's work. "Good. Make it narrower on the edge."

Nadir flexed his fingers. "I know why Great-Grandfather was so patient, if he worked with stone his entire lifetime."

Amos took a drink from his vessel, wiping his mouth with the back of his hand. "Any skill requires patience to do well. My father's hands were strong. But he wasn't very patient when he sewed soldiers."

Nadir stretched his legs. "He sewed soldiers?"

Pelia had come from camp. She knelt beside Amos. "He didn't sew. He put pressure on the wounds. Your Grandfather was the one who stitched. That's when I found how patient your Grandfather was."

Amos squeezed her knee and smiled at her. "Your Grandmother, here, could make any soldier forget his wounds."

She laughed.

Nadir shook his head. "I thought with victory, there would be no wounded."

Amos shook his head. "No battle is without cost from both sides."

Nadir stopped chipping. "I thought living in the desert was boring."

Amos rubbed the knife on his tunic to scrape away the loose chips. He tested the sharpness against a branch. The knife sliced through it with ease.

"Let me see that." Nadir tested it on a piece of leather. "That's sharp!"

"Now we need a handle." Amos dug in his cloak pocket for the leather piece he had brought. He handed it to Nadir. "Try this piece."

Pelia looked over the valley toward Jericho. "It'll be nice when we are settled in the land."

Amos watched Nadir's work. "Tie the knot where your hand won't rest, so it won't irritate your hand when you cut."

Nadir readjusted it.

"There, that's it." Amos responded to Pelia's comment. "There'll be other worries then."

Nadir handed the knife to Amos for inspection.

Amos smiled. "Good."

Pelia sighed. "I used to wonder what the land would be like. Now I don't care. I just want to be there."

Amos nodded to Nadir, but spoke to Pelia. "Settling down will be good. But we don't want to settle down too soon."

Pelia still watched the city. "Why not?"

"The people of the land must be conquered and destroyed before we settle. If we rush to settle without obeying the Lord, the people will snare us." Amos looked up from tightening the knot. "We've waited this long for our land, we must wait until it's completely cleared before we settle."

Pelia shook her head. "Waiting is hard."

All the men of Israel were circumcised. They camped until the men healed.

Hannah smashed herbs to make a tonic for some whose wounds had become infected. Known as a healer ever since she had helped Aaron in caring for those afflicted by the Egyptian plagues, she had learned desert herbs and helped Phinehas when they married. "Why do some cuts turn hot, red, and inflamed, while others don't?"

Phinehas, trained as a physician in Egypt, turned from treating one of the men. He hesitated. "Those with problems didn't use a flint knife but an Egyptian knife."

"What difference does it make?"

Phinehas shook his head. "I don't know. But God told us to use a flint knife. God rewards those who obey."

Hannah shook her head. "We always think we know best."

They worked in silence for a while. Hannah licked her lips before speaking. All the men twenty and over had died, except the Levites. Phinehas was a Levite. "Why weren't the Levites counted with the warriors?"

Phinehas stopped mixing the herbs and smiled. "Looking to get rid of me?"

Hannah laughed. "I can't imagine life without you. I only think of how young the men seem to be warriors."

Phinehas shrugged. "Youth has its advantages. Over the last forty years, they've all been taught the Law and watched God provide. Joshua couldn't have done better training them."

Hannah sighed. "I'm ready to be settled in the land, but not ready for the battles that must come before that."

"No one seeks battles. Yet God commands them. His holiness demands that the evil of the cities be removed."

Hannah shook her head. "I remember the wounded, even when we win...."

Phinehas nodded. "Your tender heart reminds me of the man behind the wound."

"And you remind me of the rightness of the battle."

Phinehas spoke with assurance. "God commands sin to be removed. The people in the land have turned their back on God. God will judge them by our hand. Which reminds me, are you ready for Passover? Those lambs raised by Amos's boys will make a great feast."

The Passover Feast reminded them of the Death Angel in Egypt who had killed the firstborn of all who didn't have blood painted on the door mantle and sides. Those who obeyed were spared. Their people remembered it every year. They would soon prepare the feast again.

Hannah nodded. "We even have grain and cakes from the land. It was hard not to gather manna. When it didn't come, I panicked thinking what will we do?" Hannah laughed. "Then I remembered the Lord has given us the Land. He will provide."

Idle times in the lives of six million people do not bring good. The men had been circumcised. They had healed. The people had celebrated the Passover. Now they were restless to conquer the Land.

Joshua walked through camp. He was ready to conquer Jericho. He reached the outskirts of the campsite and looked back over the settlement. On the outskirts of camp, he saw a group of boys acting out a battle with sticks. They had watched their fathers practice in the desert, preparing for real battle. They now brandished their "swords" as if trained like their fathers.

Joshua laughed. He took his flint knife from its sheath and peeled a fig picked from a tree by the river's edge. He held each piece in his teeth before eating it, savoring its sweetness. He reached the inside, filled with tender seeds. This Land was good. The people were ready to settle down. Their wanderings were coming to an end.

But before peace came, many battles must take place. Were the people ready for that?

First was Jericho. He looked across the plains. Outside the city, harvested wheat stood in shocks, waiting for its people to thresh and winnow the wheat from the chaff. Few had left the city's safety since Israel had crossed the river.

Flocks of sheep, goats, and cows grazed unattended. They spread across the harvested fields, feasting on the bundled shocks.

Some of his people had started to herd them away from the wheat to keep the wheat for their people.

No one from the city came to claim them. It was like the city held the dead already. Could people be that afraid?

Ethan and Salmon had described its crumbling walls.

How could they use that knowledge to their advantage? Joshua had no experience fighting a walled city. How could they enter the city, even with its crumbling walls?

A twig snapped.

He jerked up his head.

A man stood with his sword drawn, pointing at him. The blade shone. This man was not one of them. His tunic was long sleeved and of shining white material. His face glowed with a radiance, like Moses when he had returned after seeing God.

Joshua choked on his fig. How could he have been caught unprepared? How foolish not to be alert on this side of the river, where enemies lay within a half day's journey.

Joshua dropped the remaining fig, wiping his hand down his tunic to bring his hand closer to the hilt of his dagger. What would a dagger do against a sword?

Joshua coughed. "Are you for us or against us?"

"No."

Joshua licked his lips. What kind of an answer was that? He glanced back at the campsite.

The boys were gone.

He was alone.

The stranger continued. "I come as Captain of the Lord of hosts."

This was God of Heaven talking to him! He dropped to his knees, bowing before Him, trembling. He would have been less afraid if it had been an enemy catching him unaware. But to stand before God? He couldn't dig a hole deep enough to hide from His presence. "What must I do?"

"Remove your sandals, for you are on holy ground."

Joshua fumbled with his straps and removed his sandals. He bowed his head, quivering that he could live in His presence.

Time stood still.

Joshua did not remember what had happened before this moment, nor did he think about what should happen next. He was just here in the moment.

Space was empty.

He felt a weightlessness. He could not feel his dagger against his leg, nor his cloak against his back. Like the pressures of this life had been lifted and he could float free if God wanted.

Sounds ceased.

All the noises of camp, the river, and life stopped.

He seemed transported to where nothing else mattered.

Light was intense.

Even while he kept his eyes on the ground and closed, he saw God's brightness, shining greater than the sun.

He felt so utterly attuned to God.

He felt communion: a completeness he had never before felt.

He felt, not one *with* Him, for he could never be God. But made *for* Him.

God wanted him.

His entire focus was on God. And he worshipped.

He didn't know how long he stayed on the ground.

When the Lord left, Joshua stumbled to his feet. All his senses that had stood motionless while he worshiped flooded back now. He sensed the time and light. The sun was slanting over the western hills, making long shadows by the walls of the city and mountains. The coolness of the evening was sweeping with the shadows, bringing darkness. The campsite's noises as people finished their evening meal, the smells of flatbread, and the cook fires made his stomach growl. Why must he come back to the world of time, with its burdens, its noise, and its darkness?

He yearned for God in a way he never had before.

He didn't need to know what he should *do* for God.

He wanted only to *be* with God.

CHAPTER 5

The day began with the trumpet announcing the morning sacrifices. The people, out of habit, looked to the desert sand for the manna that once was gathered. They found contentment in their tents, where they stored what they had found in fields ready to harvest by people they had conquered on the other side of the Jordan. Their jars were full. Their bellies were satisfied, and God had told them to move today.

The Levites stood ready to obey.

Ebiasaph, with his sons, prepared to move the Ark of the Covenant.

Rafa shifted the Ark on his shoulder as they made their way in the line-up. "Shouldn't we carry swords?"

Ebiasaph shook his head. "There'll be no need for swords today. We'll walk around the city and return to camp."

Rafa asked, "That's all?"

At his father's nod, they started walking.

The city was big.

The walk was long.

The sun beat on their uncovered heads.

The priests held the trumpets but did not blow them.

All walked with a march that stepped in tune to their God Who gave the commands.

After returning to his tent, Rafa lay on his pallet in the shade of his tent.

His wife knelt beside him. "What does walking around the city do?"

He closed his eyes. He was weary of the heat. He repeated his father's words, although he didn't see it as his father did. "We obey the Lord."

She nodded. "I'm tired of moving from place to place. When will we have a house?"

"When the Lord wills." He closed his eyes and breathed deeply. She sighed. "Does this God control even the air we breathe?"

Rahab heard marching outside the city wall but didn't hear a war cry. A piece of the wall crumbled and fell at her feet. Alarmed that the men had not come for her, she climbed to her rooftop and shook the cord resting against the wall. Had they forgotten her? Or had they lied? Had she trusted them, only to have them fail her?

She watched the soldiers march by her wall, followed by seven men with trumpets. Four men carried a gold-covered box on their shoulders. A rear guard followed, protecting the box that shimmered in the sun.

The wall crumbled as they marched passed her. She watched their retreating forms disappear around the corner of the wall.

Would the spies come for her? She tugged the scarlet cording again. She had believed this God would care enough for her to deliver her. Was this just a false hope she had foolishly believed?

She lived on the north side of the city and could not see their campsite. She hurried to the gate on the east side, facing Jordan. It remained locked.

Others had gathered. One called to a guard watching on the wall. "What are they doing?"

"Returning to their campsite."

"You mean, they just walk around our city and return to their campsite?"

The guard shrugged. "That's what they did."

The crowd mumbled their thoughts and drifted away.

After hearing the report, Rahab ran to her family's house. Bursting through the door, she stopped as her entire family sat around the table. "What's wrong?"

No one spoke. Their solemn expressions reflected fear. Were they ready to seek deliverance?

She looked at her mother, but she kept her head bowed, avoiding eye contact.

Rahab glanced at Galon.

Her younger brother nodded to her but didn't speak.

She swallowed. "Come to my house. Wait there until they come for me."

Her mother looked at her father as if pleading. Would he allow them?

Her father cleared his throat, but didn't look at her. "Why do you trust these men?"

She looked around the room. She fixed her eyes on Galon, hoping for confidence. He tried to mask his fear by the hardness of his expression, but Rahab could see through it. They had heard of the Israelite's victory over Egypt and the Reed Sea. Those weren't lies. "They gave their word."

Galon snorted.

Rahab defended them, for she wanted to believe them. "Isn't that better than believing in Baal who gives no promises?"

Her father didn't even raise his head to look at her. "Do not speak of Baal again."

"Your fear makes you do anything, except trust these men."

Her father stood, and strode toward her. "They are our enemies!" He lifted his hand to strike her.

Rahab didn't flinch. "Maybe their God doesn't like what we do. Maybe we need to change." Even as she spoke, she realized the truth of her words. This God had a better way. She watched her father's face. She softened her tone, appealing to him. "Their God brings destruction on our city. But He also shows love to His people. I don't understand. But I trust Him."

Rahab looked at each member of her family. "For those who want to know this God, my house stands open. It's the only chance at life that you'll be given."

Rahab woke rested but famished, not like the weeks after her son had been sacrificed. Her body then couldn't even acknowledge her need for food. When she had eaten, it stirred and stayed unsettled. Nor had she slept, but had wrestled all night with nightmares of her son. But since the spies' visit, not only did she sleep, but she felt rested and hungry.

The general no longer came. In fact, she'd had no visitors for days. In a way, she was relieved. She hated what she had to do to buy food. Now she couldn't even please the men for her food. Maybe she would starve to death. Wouldn't that be better than serving at the temple? She brushed her hair from her face. Her scabs were healing, but would scar.

Beauty was a curse.

Now, ugly was also.

Was she just cursed?

Her father thought her so. He had traded her for gold as soon as she was of age. And made sure she didn't return home.

She shook her head. She wished her family would come to her house for deliverance.

The city gates had remained shut for days.

No one sold their produce.

No one walked the streets.

No one left their houses.

The streets' silence was as if death had already come.

As if by hiding, they would be protected from this God.

Rahab filled her vessel at the city's well inside the walls. She scooped a handful to her lips and drank. At least the city had water.

Others came for water only to scurry back to their houses, like some nighttime insect running from the danger of the light. Most showed some new burn or disfigurement.

Their blank stares reminded Rahab of when her grandmother had died. When Rahab had entered her room, she smelled death before she actually saw her grandmother's motionless body.

Her city hadn't died, but she could feel fear holding each person. She shivered. If she could taste death, this is what it would taste like.

She wiped her mouth with her sleeve and licked her lips, trying to remove the image from her mind.

Water only reminded her of her hunger. Without visitors, she would have no food. But she preferred this to having to please men.

The two spies had promised.

Their people had circled her city every day.

The days dragged by. Without night work and gleaning from the fields during the day, she had nothing to do but wait and hope.

She returned from the city's well and bolted her door. She climbed the ladder to her roof and watched the moon rise. It would be a full moon. It was cooler on the roof. She wrapped her arms around her.

The priests would be busy tonight. She could already hear the streets filling as people moved toward the temple. Their fear kept them inside during the day, but made them run to the temple at night to beg for protection from a god who could not care.

What would it be like to have a God really care for you?

The spies held a different spirit. They were confident, assured, not desperate. Was it peace?

Rahab sighed. She longed to know this God. Would this God love her, or was His love only for His people?

She turned at a noise from the streets. Someone was at her door. The knocking grew urgent. She didn't want to please anyone to-night, even if she starved. Sighing, she climbed down the ladder and unbolted the door.

Her mother and brother stood there.

They had come! Her family would be saved. She felt relief. She stepped aside for them to enter.

They shuffled in, uncertain. Mother set a few baskets down.

Galon carried bundles and bedding, but he didn't look happy.

She looked for her father. Was she relieved or disappointed that he wasn't with them? "Will father—"

Mother shook her head. "He went to the temple."

Rahab nodded. She took the bedding, arranging it on her bed. When she had finished, she motioned for her mother to take her bed. Her mother seemed frail, little. Rahab tucked a blanket around her.

Galon sat at her bench by her table. "They will come?"

She nodded. Didn't she have their word? Was she right to trust them?

But as she looked at her brother, she thought of her father. Her chest tightened. What would her father do when he sobered from his night at the temple, and found his family gone?

When her family was settled for the night, Rahab returned to the roof. After the darkness of her house, the moonlight flooded the rooftop. The light promised hope that would soon come. She wrapped herself in her cloak and lay in its light. The chanting and screams of the temple worship came clearly through the night air, piercing through her. She knew she wouldn't be able to sleep. But she would rest and wait.

A noise startled her. The moon had moved across to the western sky. She must have fallen asleep. She rubbed her eyes to help them focus. The stalks of wheat crackled under her as she shifted onto her elbow to hear better.

Something scraped by the wall.

She crawled to the wall. Just as she reached it, a hand reached over the top.

She stiffened. She grabbed the hand to throw it over the wall if it was an intruder. "Who are you?"

His voice was a low whisper. "I've come for you as we promised."

She could now see his face. It was the spy who had given her so much reassurance the first time.

He finished climbing over the wall and wiped his hands down his tunic. "You are ready?"

"My family waits in the house. I'll get them." She hurried down the ladder and returned with Galon and her mother.

The Israelite shook the rope. "Who goes first?"

Rahab led her mother toward the edge. "Just hold on."

Her mother wrapped her hands in her cloak. Her eyes filled with tears. "I can't go, not without your father."

Rahab pushed her toward the rope. "The city will be destroyed."

Galon placed a hand on Rahab's shoulder. "I'll find him."

Rahab wanted all her family to be delivered. Her heart tightened. "But you'll be left behind..."

He looked at their mother. "I'll go."

Rahab watched him leave, tears filling her eyes. She hugged her mother tightly. "Come."

Her mother shook her head.

Was this the last time she would see her? Would she lose everyone she cared for?

The spy looked at the position of the moon. "We must hurry. Light is coming soon."

Rahab grabbed the cord to lower herself over the edge of the roof.

The spy held her arm as she took hold of the rope. "Use your feet to slow you down. Walk down the wall."

She nodded. Her insides twittered as she remembered how much of a drop it was, if she let go and fell...

Her feet flung out and hung in the air for a long moment. Her elbow bumped the wall. Tears stung as pain radiated up her arm. Her feet hit the wall. She stood sideways.

The spy hung over the edge and held her arms. His face was right against hers. "All set?"

She couldn't find her voice. She could only nod.

He squeezed her arm. "Just walk."

She concentrated on his words. "Walk. Down. The. Wall."

She couldn't think about her mother, brother, or father. She concentrated on "Walk."

When she came to a knot, she panicked. She couldn't just slide her hands down, she had to let go and put them below the knot. She bit her lip in concentration. Move one hand at a time. She lifted one and grabbed the rope on the other side. That wasn't so hard. Now for the other. She did it.

For a moment, she felt excitement. She was doing this. She wasn't falling. But she wasn't moving. She looked at her feet. She could see the ground. It was far away. She looked up.

The spy at the top called down, "Keep your feet moving."

She walked again.

The next knot came sooner. How many knots had she tied? She kept walking.

Someone touched her back. "You're almost there. Don't let go." The other spy braced her as she dropped her feet to the ground.

She let go and fell back into his arms. She had made it.

He held her until her feet were stable under her, then directed her toward the wall, away from the rope. "Stand there."

She breathed deeply. Had she held her breath the entire way down? She leaned against the wall and waited. Now she had time to worry if she would see her family again.

The one at the top whispered through the darkness, "Ethan, three more come."

Rahab's heart skipped. Galon must have found their father. She listened as her mother slid down the rope. Was her mother strong enough to hold the rope? When she reached the bottom, Rahab hugged her. They both leaned against the wall. The shadows of the wall closed around them. "Galon found father?"

Her mother nodded.

If father had been at the temple, would he be able to hold the rope and walk? Rahab watched the top of the wall. She could see the outline of the edge. The moon shone at an angle from the top.

Her brother swung over the edge. He stayed there suspended at the top as the spy lifted someone else over the edge. That must be her father. A shower of pebbles and mortar fell as Galon adjusted his feet.

Rahab covered her head with her hood and leaned against the wall.

The spy at the top called down. "Ethan, hold the rope taunt, he's carrying another."

Rahab bit back a gasp. Galon would carry Father? Would the wall support them?

With each step, Rahab heard pebbles and mortar drop around her. She closed her eyes. Mentally, she followed her brother's descent down the wall. She counted his pauses.

They descended slowly, reaching the bottom.

The spy grabbed her father from Galon, putting him on the ground, so he could hold the rope for the other spy.

Galon stepped aside as the spy at the top made his way down. He shook his arms, bringing back circulation.

When the spy landed, he looked over the group. "We must hurry."

Galon heaved his father over his shoulders.

The spies grabbed some of the bundles and baskets they had sent down.

Rahab picked up several baskets and glanced around. This was all she would save from the city. It wasn't much.

One of the spies asked, "Ready?"

The other spy nodded, leading the way to their campsite.

Rahab's insides fluttered. The men had kept their word, and her family was with her. Surely now her family, even her father, would want to know this God.

She would soon meet this God. She could hardly wait.

Salmon and Ethan brought the harlot's family to the outskirts of their campsite. As foreigners, they must go through a purification process before they could assimilate with the people. By the time the sun began to shine over the eastern horizon, Salmon and Ethan had left the harlot and her family, and reported to Joshua. They were returning to their own tents.

Ethan yawned. "Can't wait to sleep before we walk around the city today."

Salmon laughed. "Up too early this morning? I was just going to sleep when you came for me."

"Why couldn't you sleep?"

Salmon shrugged. He wouldn't tell him he wondered about this harlot they would save. She had come to his mind a lot since they had spied the city. "What will the land do to our people?"

Ethan shrugged. "My wife's anxious to be settled."

Salmon nodded, "Aren't we all? How will God bring victory?"

Ethan laughed. "Sounds like you're trying to be God."

Salmon laughed too. "Just wondering how He'll do it."

Ethan nodded. "Joshua has a harder time leading the people than Moses did."

"Moses set a high standard. It's not a task I'd want." Salmon slowed his pace. "Did you feel His presence with us when we were in Jericho? Moses described it in his song ... as being in the shelter of the Almighty and under His wings."

Ethan smiled. "Even in the midst of evil."

They settled to a quick pace. Salmon looked sideways at Ethan. "I'll ask Amos for a tent for the harlot's family. They'll need something for shelter before the sun sets."

Ethan studied Salmon without responding.

"What?" Salmon could feel his face flush.

"Don't become too involved with the harlot."

Salmon challenged. "They need a tent. Shouldn't we help them?"

"It's not for you to help them."

"Then who will? They have almost nothing. They are taken from their city, their home, everything they know, and must live with a strange people."

Ethan laughed. "Strange people?"

"Look at all our laws. They don't know the sanitation laws; remember the slop that almost hit my face?"

Ethan laughed. "You also got reprimanded by the harlot for helping a beggar."

"They will need to know our ways."

Ethan shook his head. "I don't want you hurt, Salmon. Remember what she is."

"How can finding a tent hurt?"

Ethan squeezed Salmon's shoulder. "Do they want help?"

Salmon felt his anger growing. "Why wouldn't they?"

Ethan softened his tone. "Just stay away from danger."

"Danger?"

"She's a woman, Salmon. Remember what happened with the Moabite women and our men." The Moabite king had been afraid to fight the Israelites. Instead he sent women to feast with Israel's men. They led them into Baal worship. God's judgment had been worse than any battle they'd fought.

Salmon shook his head. "I'm not going to worship anyone but God. And the harlot seeks to know our God." Salmon felt Ethan's gaze. He walked faster. "Besides, haven't you been the one to tell me that I should at least give women a chance?"

Ethan increased his pace to match Salmon's. "Feelings in the wrong place will get you in trouble. Don't go to their campsite alone."

Salmon didn't like Ethan's insinuation. As if he couldn't control his emotions. He bit his lip to keep the agitation from showing. He was a leader of his tribe. "It's not like I'll be led by a mere woman." They had reached the path where they each went different ways. He turned to leave.

"There's safety in numbers when women are involved." Ethan looked away for a moment. "Sometimes." He laughed, but then grew serious. "Women can make you forget what you value."

Salmon resented Ethan's caution. He could take care of his emotions.

How could helping someone bring trouble?

The Israelites had walked around the city again. The sun was falling in the sky, leaving a pink glow around the silhouette of the mountains in the west. Rahab watched as the spy brought another to her campsite. She wiped her hands down her tunic. What would they expect of her family? What would this God expect from her?

She glanced back at her father and brother. Custom dictated that her father would welcome them to their fire and offer food.

Her father lay where he had all day. His mood was surly and unpredictable. The drink from the temple worship had left him angry.

Galon was no better. Several times during the day he had muttered under his breath about defending their city. He seemed torn between acknowledging their city's destruction and resentment for being an outsider among these people.

Rahab swallowed. What should she do?

The spy smiled. "Shalom. You have settled?" He looked over her shoulder at her family. No one else rose to meet them.

She nodded. "Be at peace. Thank you for remembering your promise."

He gestured. "This is Joshua. He leads our nation."

Rahab bowed low to the ground. "You have saved me and my family. We are grateful."

Joshua nodded, glancing at the men. "It's not I who saves, but our Lord Who is holy, yet forgiving." Joshua pointed to her family. "I must speak to the entire group."

Rahab led them to her family. Would her father cooperate? She felt caught between pleasing her father and knowing this God. What would this leader do if her family didn't cooperate?

Her father remained seated, not even acknowledging them.

Rahab felt her face flush at his rudeness. What should she say?

Joshua began as if welcomed. "Shalom. Your family will stay apart from the people until your purification is complete. All men must be circumcised."

Galon snorted.

Joshua explained, staring at Rahab's father. "Without circumcision, you cannot participate in the sacrifices or the feasts." He summarized their laws briefly and excused himself.

Rahab followed them. "I'm sorry for my family's response. All these rules are different from what we know. Perhaps in time they will want to know your God."

Joshua fingered his dagger at his side. "He will show Himself to them, and they will know Him."

They had reached the boundary of their camp. Rahab hesitated. She had waited in her city to know this God. Now that she was so close to their campsite, she didn't want to wait. She wanted to meet this God. But how should she make herself ready? She blurted, "Will it hurt to know Him?"

Rahab felt Joshua's scrutiny. She didn't lower her gaze.

Joshua nodded, as if he found what he was looking for. "God will change you." He turned to walk back to camp.

Her thoughts went to the temple, where priests marred their victims for the pleasure of the gods. Would this God demand such sacrifices? She had to know. She lifted her tunic and ran after him, touching his arm to stop him. She left her hand on his arm, afraid he would turn away. "Will it hurt?"

Joshua had stepped away.

Was he insulted that she touched him?

He studied her face. "Doesn't any change hurt?"

Rahab dropped her hand. Her face still hurt from the burn, even though some parts would never feel pain again. Would this be any better than what her people did? "How?"

"God makes what is inside pleasing to Him." Joshua walked away.

Rahab watched them go but didn't understand.

It was some minutes after they left the harlot's camp before Salmon spoke. "That woman has faith that surpasses many of God's people."

Joshua shook his head. His pace slackened and he turned to look at Salmon. "If that family is any indication of the attitude of the people of that city, it's no wonder God wants the entire city destroyed."

"Why?"

Joshua faced the path again. "Because they're a rebellious people who don't even want to know God."

"But the harlot has a different spirit."

Joshua shook his head. "She wants to please anyone who will give her what she wants."

Salmon's voice rose as he responded, "She doesn't seek God out of desire, but because she believes."

Joshua's pace slowed and studied Salmon. "She knows how to manipulate men to get what she wants. Look at the information she gave you. How do you think she got that information? Do you think she'd hesitate to tell her king about what she's seen of our camp, if she thought her city would be saved?"

Salmon shook his head. "She lied to the general to protect us."

"That's my point. She will say and do what it takes to get what she wants."

"She doesn't know our Law and therefore doesn't know what is wrong. But she searches to know God, as if the longing of her very soul must be met or she will perish."

Joshua stopped walking and stared at Salmon. "You care for this woman?"

Salmon paused, but didn't answer his question. "She is one of the few people I've met who lives to know God."

"Do not be deceived by her looks."

"But didn't you tell her that God would change her?"

Joshua shook his head, frustrated. "Salmon, God changes us all. If we do not change, then we become hardened like her family, and God cannot use us."

"But God changes us for His good. You said so yourself."

"Salmon, you forget one thing. She's a harlot."

"She *was* a harlot. We delivered her from the evil of her city."

"But she has the same heart. And the evil still resides there."

"We were delivered from Egypt."

"Salmon, that's different. We're God's people, chosen by God way back to when Abraham believed."

"Does our blood make us more pleasing to God? Or does what we choose to do with our heart?"

"Salmon, you are taken by her beauty and her spirit."

"That's my point. She has a different spirit about her."

Joshua stopped in the middle of the path and turned to face Salmon. "Remember one thing. She may be delivered from the city, but her city will be destroyed, totally, according to the word of our God. I don't know what she has done to charm you, but she is a harlot. And so, she deceives to destroy you. Do not let her." He began walking again toward camp.

Salmon didn't say anything more, but he knew in his heart that he wasn't deceived.

CHAPTER 6

For six days, the Israelites walked around the city of Jericho. The trumpets remained silent. The swords stayed sheathed. And no one spoke.

Achan returned to his tent after walking around the city. His sword hung sheathed at his waist.

Bara, his wife, offered him a drink as he settled against his cushions. "How does walking around the city do anything?"

He shrugged. "The gate stays shut. Can the city be deserted?"

Bara sat beside him. "Are we going to fight or be laughed at by the countries we want to conquer?"

Achan shook his head. "Do you know if the harlot brought any valuables from the city?"

She nodded. "She didn't bring much. Our people had to give them a tent."

Achan said, "Do you think the city has nothing?"

Bara shrugged. "What does it matter? We must give it all to God."

Something in her tone caught Achan's attention. Did she wish for more as much as he did? "What would you do with riches?"

Her entire countenance changed. "If I had riches..." She even smiled.

Achan couldn't remember when she had last smiled. Had this journey to their land been so hard for her that she had lost her joy?

She suddenly stopped smiling. "It's foolish to wish for things that can't happen." She shook her head, frowning again.

Achan was sorry to see her smile go. She had looked younger, more beautiful. How could he make her smile again? "Where would they hide their riches?"

Bara ignored his comment, changing the subject. "I went for water. These people brand their women to please their gods. Can you imagine such a thing?"

Achan snapped his fingers. "Bara, you're right!"

"About what?"

Achan rubbed his hands together. "They give their riches to their gods. That's where I'll look."

"But all must be given to God." She said it with such dejection.

Achan tilted his head and laughed. "Would God know?"

The king of Jericho shivered, even as the sun rose to warm the new day. He studied the Israelite camp from the roof of his palace. His advisor stood by his side. "They leave their campsite like other days, with the trumpets leading."

His adviser added, "That golden box must hold power, for they don't come close to it."

"It's not just the warriors today; the people are coming along."

"Are they deserting their campsite?"

The king leaned over the roof, trying to see better. A chunk from the wall fell as he touched it. The king stretched his neck over the wall, trying to see the damage. Piles of crumbled rock lay at its base.

The Israelites circled the city like before.

The king and his adviser watched in silence.

"They circle again!" The king touched his sword. "Call for my shield bearer."

When the king's adviser returned with the shield bearer, he looked over the city's walls again. "They're still marching?"

The king nodded. "They have circled five times."

"Where does the line begin?"

The king pointed to the golden box.

The people circled without speaking. Their marching in time without a drum to call the beat sounded through the early morning air, echoing off the walls of the city.

The king closed his eyes. He could feel the ground tremble beneath his feet. He opened his eyes to watch again. "They have circled seven times!"

Trumpets sounded.

The people shouted. "The Lord has given us the city!"

The king felt a great rumbling under his feet. The wall that stood for his strength and protection cracked, crumbled, and crushed inward like a rolling wave of Jordan.

Israel's warriors poured into the city over the broken wall from all directions.

The king shook himself into action. "Sound the trumpet for my army."

His advisor shook his head. "It's too late."

Achan's feet had grown hot through the burning sand, as they had walked seven times around the city. He shifted his feet as he waited for the trumpet signal. Each warrior faced the wall. He sighed, wondering, like Bara, what good walking around the city did.

Achan licked his lips, seeing again the look in Bara's eyes and her smile as she spoke of riches. He wiped his sweaty hand down his tunic. Then he wiped his forehead. Once the sun rose, the heat made standing in the open unbearable.

He pushed his way closer to Caleb. Caleb had been one of the two spies who had given a good report of the Land forty years ago. Caleb would know where the temple with its riches would be.

The trumpets sounded.

He licked his lips again, anticipating what they were to shout. He hoped their words wouldn't be spoken in laughter across the land when nothing happened.

When the last trumpet note stopped, there was a moment of silence before he shouted with all the other people, "The Lord has given us the city!"

Even before the words were finished, Achan braced his feet against the moving ground. It rolled and pitched. He brushed his hand over his eyes. The wall blurred. Was it moving? He stared, unbelieving that the wall, so strong and defensible, shook.

Then hearing a loud crack, he looked down the wall. Not just one crack but numerous fissures appeared down the wall. The noise was deafening. Even as he watched, the wall rolled as one giant wave, crashing inward on the city. The sound was like thunder without end.

When the wall fell, it bounced from the ground and landed again. Mortar and chunks of brick flew through the air. Dust rose, coating his cloak and head with its fine powder. He coughed as he breathed it.

He stood stunned, watching the dust settle.

Then there was silence.

The wall had fallen and lay destroyed.

He stood amazed.

Caleb nudged him. "Let's take the city."

Achan, startled by Caleb's bump, shook his head. He looked at the fragments of the wall. He unsheathed his sword, holding it ready as he followed Caleb through the dust cloud into the city in front of them. He picked his way over the fallen blocks, stepping over splintered benches and tables and broken vessels from the houses built on the city's wall.

They were inside the city.

Salmon flanked his right side. "May our great God be praised."

Around them, as the dust settled, other Israelites entered.

The city's people had already run from their houses heading to the center of the city.

Achan flanked Caleb through the streets. They followed the people pushing in panic to find refuge at the city's center. They pushed and shoved. Some fell. Others were trampled to death. Screams echoed off of buildings as the people rushed in front of the Israelite warriors.

Jericho's army spread through the city, shoving through the mobs, trying in vain to keep the warriors from entering. It was like closing a wine bottle after the wine had spilled.

Israelites barged into houses, the occupants already gone. They followed the crowds as they headed for the palace and the temple.

Caleb pointed to the center of the city. "Follow the crowds. They'll lead us to the king."

Achan nodded. Where the king was, Achan would find riches.

They came to a place where the people could not move. They were packed like bricks against a wall. No one moved.

Achan looked to see what was ahead.

Jericho soldiers stood, surrounding stairs that rose above the heads of the people.

A man stood on the stairs behind them. His purple cloak and his crown told who he was. His armor bearer stood before him.

The people cried and fell on their knees before their king.

Achan could hear their pleas for help.

He saw the king gesture to the man beside him; then turn his back on the people and retrace his steps up the stairs.

Achan watched as Jericho's soldiers began slaughtering their own people. Those stuck between the soldiers and those behind fell by the sword and were trampled by those who moved forward.

Achan raised his sword and followed Caleb as they cut a path through the people to the palace stairs.

The people fell before their swords like melted butter. Bodies littered the street, so numerous they walked on them.

When Achan reached the palace stairs, guards stood unmoving. Achan held his shield before him, pushing into the unmoving barrier. He swung his sword horizontally, cutting down a guard caught off balance by his shield. He finished him off with a thrust.

The guard deflected the first cut with his own sword but was off balance to counter the second thrust.

Achan followed with an overcut.

The guard, still off-balance, couldn't recover to guard the cut. The sword struck through his shoulder. He caught Achan's eye before falling to the ground.

Achan looked for others. The guards were all down. Only his own soldiers fought behind him.

Caleb motioned for the stairs. "Let's go."

They climbed the stairs leading to the massive doors of the palace. When they entered the palace, they stood in a large open chamber. Light flooded through the windows at the top of the archways. They stopped, allowing their eyes to adjust to the bright sunshine after the darkness of the high-walled streets.

They left the noise of the street with the sounds of fighting, the moans of wounded, and the cries of the people and found silence.

After a moment to catch their breath and evaluate their direction, Caleb pointed with his sword to a flight of stairs. "Let's take these." No warriors stood guard here. Their sandaled feet echoed loudly over the hollowed chamber as they climbed the stone stairs. At the top of the stairs, they entered a hallway. Caleb entered a room and paused, his sword drawn.

Achan paused to catch his breath from climbing the stairs. He stepped behind Caleb, surveying the room. Death-like stillness contrasted to the screams and groans of the streets. Their steps echoed on the marble floor. It was as if they had entered a lavishly decorated tomb, but waited for the corpse. Achan shook his head. By entering the room, had he committed to something beyond the fight of the city? His heart beat loudly.

His eyes roamed around the room. The marble floor foretold of riches. At the window, a tapestry covered the opening, fluttering in the wind. A stream of light entered through the opening of the tapestry, revealing a chair, lavishly upholstered with rich cloth. A silk cloak draped over its back. He took in the room's contents quickly.

At a movement at the door, Achan turned with his sword ready.

Salmon entered.

Achan lowered his sword.

Caleb stepped forward to touch the walls. "Where's the king? Doesn't the room look bigger from the outside of the palace than inside?"

Achan hadn't noticed. He studied the walls. "The walls aren't made of the same large bricks as the outside wall." He touched the wall's tapestries of purple and blue. Their silk was soft, fine, like baby's hair. He fingered it. He didn't want to let it go. If they found the king, they could find his gems and gold.

Salmon nodded. "The room is smaller. Do you think there's a secret refuge built into the wall?"

Caleb nodded, feeling along the opposite wall.

Achan touched the cold, stone wall. "What do you seek?"

"This." Caleb pushed a brick from the wall and shoved a lever.

The wall moved inward, revealing an opening.

Caleb stepped through it. His sword pointed forward.

Achan followed.

The room was dark, lit only from the window of the room where they had left. The room was a storehouse for the king's treasures. Piles lay stacked around its walls, overflowing into the center of the small room.

The king faced them, backed against the corner, with his sword drawn. He blinked from the brightness of the light that streamed from the other room.

Caleb stepped forward and struck him before the king could even parry.

Achan barely noticed the fight. He saw only the treasures: Gold. Silver. Gems. Even in the dim light from the doorway, everything sparkled and shined. Achan fingered the riches.

Caleb wiped his blade on the king's cloak. "We must hurry. The city is burning." He pointed to the riches. "Remove what we can for the Lord's use." He grabbed what riches he could carry and hurried down the stairs.

Salmon left with Caleb. His arms loaded.

Achan lingered. He sifted through the riches, remembering his wife's smile. Would the Lord need it all? Would He even know?

No one was watching.

Achan ransacked the piles and found a bar of gold. He'd hide it in his tunic beneath his belt. How could he hide more? He brushed against his waterskin. Grabbing out the stopper, he gulped down its contents. He fell to his knees and jammed silver into its opening.

Did he hear footsteps? He paused to listen.

Everything was quiet.

He went back to filling his waterskin. He shook it down before jamming more through the narrow opening. When he had filled the waterskin, it was bulging and heavy. He replaced the stopper.

Smoke poured, heavy and thick, into the closed room. It swirled around him. His nose stung. His throat burned. He coughed. His eyes watered till he could barely see. He wiped them with his cloak sleeve. But still he stayed, staring at the mound of treasures he could not take with him.

Smoke filled the room. Achan could not break away from all the riches. When he could barely breathe or see, he groped through the smoke and ran through the entry room; then stopped and re-traced his steps. That mantle draped over a chair was pure silk. He remembered the softness of the one on the wall. Wouldn't Bara be thrilled with such a gift? The thought of her delight made him grab it. He would bring back her smile. He wrapped it around his legs under his tunic. It restricted his movement, but the battle was over. It would stay hidden.

Now, for the Lord's spoils...he fell to his knees again, this time scooping anything within his reach. He bundled it in a cloak. The Lord could use any of this.

When the cloak was full, he rose and shifted the weight so he could carry it. He hurried through the hall and stumbled down the stairs. When he reached the streets, he bumped into Caleb. He could feel the silver jingle in his waterskin. Could Caleb hear it?

"There you are." Caleb's eyebrows lifted. "You bring the Lord a rich reward."

Achan nodded and swallowed. He kept his eyes down, not looking at Caleb.

Caleb lit a torch from one of the fires and set fire to the curtains of the lower floor of the palace. The rich tapestries caught the flames quickly and began to smoke.

Achan took his time adjusting the treasures gathered in the street for the Lord. His waterskin banged against his leg. It hung low. He adjusted it. The weight tugged downwards.

Caleb spoke over his shoulder, "Everything all right?"

Achan stopped adjusting and looked up. "Yes. Just a lot of gifts for God."

Caleb smiled. "Won't He be pleased?"

The heat of the city and the black smoke swirled around them as they brought the spoil over the crumbled walls and away from the flames. They dropped their armloads into piles outside the city.

Achan looked at the smoke rising toward the sky and coughed. So many riches lost forever.

He was startled when Salmon put his arm around his shoulder.

Salmon wiped his forehead with his sleeve. "It's hard to conquer a people, isn't it?"

Achan nodded. He hadn't thought about the people at all. All he had seen were the piles of gold he couldn't take.

Salmon nodded again. "They will no longer sacrifice to gods that cannot help them."

Caleb leaned against a boulder, wiping sweat off his forehead. He tipped his waterskin to his mouth. "Empty."

Achan shifted his waterskin behind him with his elbow so that Caleb wouldn't see it. He wasn't in time. His waterskin bulged with the silver. He hoped it wouldn't rattle as he moved.

Caleb's eyes lit up. "Your water is full. May I?"

Achan pushed it farther around his waist. "No, I mean, it's empty."

Caleb raised his brow but did not pursue it. "Thanks for watching my back in there. What a storehouse!"

Achan nodded, not trusting his voice to speak.

Caleb wiped his ash-stained hands down his tunic. "God will be pleased with our gifts."

Achan touched his tunic, reassuring himself the mantle was well hidden. "He will indeed."

As the people left to walk around Jericho that last day, Rahab's family watched from their campsite outside of Israel's camp. Even though they were part of the Israelite campsite, in a way, they still were not. They were alone, in the midst of many people.

Even when Rahab went for water, she felt isolated. No one spoke to her. They avoided her, whispering to themselves, sometimes loudly enough for her to hear them speak of her.

Her father remained sullen, lounging around the cookfire, scrutinizing her. He made her feel unworthy, somehow evil, by just watching her. She shivered and bowed her head.

Her mother was quiet, like a frightened hare trying not to be noticed. Had she always been so skittish?

Her brother, restless and pacing, climbed a nearby hillside to watch the people march.

Rahab made flour from the grain they had brought with them. She had forgotten how much her brother could eat. She had just fed him the morning meal, yet it would soon be time to make the noon meal.

The people had been gone longer than on other days.

She stood, stretching her back, as she looked toward her city. Even as she watched, she heard the trumpets and shouting. A roar like thunder rumbled, even as her feet felt the ground vibrate.

Clouds of dust and smoke surrounded her city. When it sifted enough for her to see, she gasped. The walls had fallen. The Israelites charged into her city.

She bit her lip. These were her people. People she knew.

She hurried to the hillside where Galon stood. Should she feel sadness that all she knew was being destroyed? Or hope that the oppression and weight of pleasing the gods and the priests would be gone?

Rahab heard a gasp.

Her mother had come beside her to stand.

Rahab put her arm around her. How frail her mother seemed. What would this do to her?

Galon's initial yells had stopped. He stood mute, watching the soldiers run over their city walls.

She placed her hand into his.

He glanced at her briefly, squeezed her hand, then turn back to watch.

That squeeze reassured Rahab. It reminded her of other times, while growing up. Her father would hit her, then leave in anger. Her brother would hold her. She'd feel safe. Now, with his strong hand covering hers, she again felt protected. She looked into his face.

He had grown up while she had been away. He had changed. Rahab wanted to believe he was still that caring brother who would protect her from the world's evil, but looking into his face she saw her father. Galon had followed her father and accepted the city's ways. His expression showed hard lines, telling of his determination to have his own way. Even his stance reminded her of her father, challenging anyone who opposed them. Yes, her brother had grown up, and she was not sure she liked what he had grown to be.

Galon's concentration on the city drew Rahab to look again.

She didn't want to watch. She wanted what the city represented to be gone. If the city was gone, would her hurt be gone? No more children would be killed. No more men to please. No more gods demanding what she couldn't give. Would she then have peace? Would she then feel whole?

Smoke rose above the city.

She felt a loss. She was torn. Even though she hated the gods and what they made her do, that was all she knew. What if this God didn't want her? What would she do?

The smoke rose to the clouds. The air became thick with ashes and smoke. The city would smoke for days, reminding her of its evil.

Winds brought the smoke to their camp.

She choked over the smell. Her eyes burned and watered. Ashes floated from the sky, drifting over her. They clung to her. She wiped a flake of ash from her arm and streaked the soot. It reminded her of her unworthiness.

What made her think she could forget her past and please this God? She sighed. She looked from her brother to her father. She wasn't free from the city. Instead, the city's oppression had followed her, just like the smoke had. She may have escaped the fire, but not the sin of the city. It weighed upon her.

Had she chosen a different death, not by sword, but a slower death, that sapped her strength as she lived with her own unworthiness?

Her danger didn't lie with Baal and its followers any more. Those gods were fickle and hard to please. She wouldn't have to please them anymore. Nor would she make her living pleasing men. She knew God's displeasure with that. But could she please this new God?

Rahab's thoughts were interrupted as the people returned to camp. They shouted victory as they passed, carrying the spoils of her city. They piled their spoils outside their camp.

One man, the spy began burning it. He stood over the fire, watching as it turned everything to ashes.

Nothing but ashes.

But as the ashes cooled, she saw, reflected by the sun's lowering rays, sparkling, glittering gold, silver, and gems tested by fire.

Rahab stepped closer to see. She watched the flames lick the fabrics.

That was all that was left from her city.

Hidden in the ashes, she could still see the glittering gold and silver.

She was so absorbed in watching, she was startled when the spy spoke to her.

"It's hard to watch what you thought was valuable burn."

She looked at the man in surprise. His words had been her thoughts.

Culture didn't allow a man to speak to a woman without a family member present. She looked back at her campsite. Her father hadn't protected her in many years. Nor had she needed his presence when the spy had visited her own house.

She didn't know what to say. She stared at the flames. Someone felt what she felt. For that moment, she wasn't alone.

The man leaned on the stick he used to poke the fire. "Fire reminds me of judgment. God uses fire to burn the dross." He poked a piece that wasn't burning deeper into the flames. "Yet when the fire is finished, the gold is refined. It is better. It is perfected."

Rahab watched the flames burst from the ashes that he stirred.

The man met her gaze and held it. "You were saved from God's judgment, just like the spoils that we brought back. The flames may have touched you, but they did not destroy you. They refined you. Just like the gold. They will make you better."

Rahab held her breath. Did he know how unworthy she was? How she was unloved and unprotected even within her own family? Could such redemption be possible?

The man used his stick to push a piece of gold to the edges of the ashes. The metal glowed from the heat.

She stared as it cooled.

The sun's rays were sinking behind the distant mountains, and the coolness of the night seeped into her skin. In spite of the waves of heat from the fire, Rahab shivered. She wrapped her arms tighter around her waist. She sensed wholeness in his words. Could this God judge and yet heal at the same time?

The moment was interrupted by a trumpet call.

The man nodded toward her. "It's time for evening sacrifices. We honor the Lord for our victory."

He picked up the gold piece he had separated from the fire. He tossed it a few times in his hand, then stepped toward Rahab. He handed it to her. "The spoils belong to the Lord."

Rahab was confused. Why was he giving it to her? She wouldn't accept it. She backed away from him.

The man smiled. "You are the Lord's. He has set you apart for Him."

She shook her head. "I am not worthy of your God."

He nodded. "That's what makes Him special. He takes the un-worthy, and makes it pleasing to Him." He took her hand and placed the gold piece in her palm and closed her fingers around it. Then turned and walked toward camp.

Rahab watched his retreating form and squeezed the piece of gold in her hand as if she would never let it go.

After the spy left for sacrifices, Rahab wondered about their worship. He had shown an eagerness to go. How would they cele-brate their victory?

She heard tambourines, flutes, and harps. The notes soothed her. Their voices rose in unison, worshiping their God Who cre-ated, provided for and protected them. The beat started out loud, almost warlike. Their chant called their attention to the message. Their words reflected the glory of their God Who was holy and would allow no evil before His presence.

But as one song melted into another, the mood changed to re-flect a peace that Rahab had never felt. Another song was sung by the men. Their voices reflected power, discipline, yet security. Not the anger that came from her father. The words flowed over her like a soft blanket, soothing her and allowing her to focus on this God.

She was drawn by the music to watch from the outer edges of the people.

The people were gathered outside a tent.

The golden box stood before them.

Men no longer carried it, but it rested on a stand of gold.

Joshua and another older man stood beside it. Joshua's voice carried easily to where Rahab stood. "Let's sacrifice to our God."

Rahab's heart dropped. Hadn't the spies told her they didn't sacrifice children?

She felt rather than saw someone beside her. She glanced without turning her head.

It was her father and Galon. Her father muttered, "They sacrifice without Baal? Where are the women to appease their gods?"

She didn't answer. She had hoped their worship would be different, because their God was different. So far, it had been. Would their sacrifices also be different?

Her father strained to see over the people. He shook his head. "Without women, why should they worship?"

Galon's disgust showed on his face. "Where's the wine and dancing?"

They watched only a short time before they both left.

Rahab sighed, relieved that they were gone. She felt pressure to please her father, yet knew she never could. That feeling drained her. She felt dirty in his presence.

Rahab turned her attention to the older man beside Joshua. His manner was orderly, calm, and worshipful. He burned incense and explained each sacrifice.

He sacrificed, not to petition their God to listen (He already did), but to show their love to Him. They worshipped in a way Rahab had never experienced.

She felt complete, like her unworthiness could be changed to something pleasing to this God. Her spirit soared as a bird freed from its cage to freedom.

The evening sacrifices had brought a sense of completion to the day. God had given them victory. The sun had set and the moon had not risen over the land yet.

The Lord had commanded burning the spoils. No animal was saved. No person was left alive. The city of Jericho had lived their own way and now they found that the Lord had no mercy for their acts against Him.

Joshua stood outside the camp, looking over the valley to where the city of Jericho had stood. He rested his hand on his scabbard, partly for reassurance, partly out of habit.

Joshua wiped his face with his arm, trying to clear the burning from his eyes. The cooler temperatures had helped settle the smoke, but it also brought a shower of ashes, coating everything with a fine black powder.

He stooped to wash by the water's edge, cleaning his hands of the battle and the ashes. He rubbed his arms clean and dunked his head in the water to wash the smoke from his hair.

How easy to wash away the physical grime of battle, but the images of wounded and dead men remained. Would they lessen with time?

When he finished, he stood, shook the remaining water from his hair, and replaced his cloak on his cooling skin. He faced what was once Jericho. "Cursed before the Lord is the man who builds this city of Jericho again. He will lose his firstborn if he lays the foundation. He will lose his youngest son when he hangs the gate."

A voice from the darkness surprised him. "But the Lord has spared one family."

Joshua turned to see who it was.

Salmon stepped from behind a tree. "Sorry, to startle you, Joshua."

Joshua laughed. "I should remember no moment in a leader's life is private."

Salmon nodded but remained quiet.

"You remind me of our problem."

Salmon walked beside Joshua and watched the glow of the city. "Problem?"

Joshua gestured to the camp of the harlot. "The harlot's family."

"Because they won't be circumcised?"

Joshua nodded again.

"We spare them from destruction, and yet they don't want to obey our Laws."

Joshua nodded.

"A problem indeed. But not the entire family.... I must confess." Salmon paused until Joshua looked at him. "I was in charge of burning the spoils. I spared a gold piece."

Joshua started to speak, but waited.

Salmon swallowed. "I gave it to the harlot."

Joshua bit his lip before speaking. He had watched Moses curb his own anger many times by biting his lip. He swallowed, tasting blood.

Salmon continued. "Wasn't the harlot delivered by the Lord's own Hand?"

Joshua didn't like the direction Salmon was going, but he nodded.

"Weren't we commanded to save the spoil for the Lord?"

Again Joshua nodded.

"She was part of the spoil God sanctioned for us to save. He has set her apart for Him."

Joshua knew of the Lord's mercy. Wasn't God merciful with him when he was afraid and didn't know how to lead this people?

But a harlot set aside for His use? He had told her that God would change her. But did he believe it? Maybe enough to become part of their people. He watched the city's glow. "Moses told me to number our days, that we may present to God a heart of wisdom." He sighed and turned to Salmon. "I don't know enough of God. I must seek His face."

Salmon stared into the dark waters, but spoke to Joshua, "The Lord saves those He chooses. Who are we to question Him?"

After Salmon left, Joshua considered his words. A harlot saved for God's use? He didn't think so. Salmon was becoming too consumed with this woman. Wasn't there a limit to whom God would use?

CHAPTER 7

The people moved over the plains of Jericho and camped in the foothills of the mountains to the west. The next city was Ai, built on a hill, surrounded by cliffs that hindered attack. Its fourth side, backed against the mountain, prevented any surprise attack. Their defenses were strong. Their position secure.

"A thousand may fall at your side." Joshua needed those words written by Moses as he waited the return of the spies sent to Ai. He heard their report in the Tent of Meeting with the other tribe leaders.

Ethan, one of returning spies, suggested, "It's a small city with not so many people. I'd say two or three thousand of our warriors will do."

Joshua turned to Hezron, leader of Manasseh's tribe. "Select 3,000 men from your tribe, Gad's, and Reuben's."

Hezron nodded. They had crossed the river ready for battle.

Joshua turned to the spies again. "How can we get inside the city?"

Salmon spoke, "Could we hide in the hills around the city the night before; then a few enter as merchants with a cart of produce to sell?"

Joshua continued with the plan, "The produce being more soldiers?"

Salmon nodded. "Exactly."

Joshua tapped the hilt of his dagger. "What sort of defenses do they have at the gate?"

Ethan shrugged. "Two guards? That's all I saw; did you see any more?"

Salmon shook his head. "Only two."

Joshua paced in front of the men. "How much cover did they have on the hillside in front of their gate?"

Ethan hesitated. "On the far hillside, there was a forest, but on the hillside leading up to the gate, not much. They had crops and grasses growing on terraces in the valley area where they could irrigate, but as we got closer to the city, it became steeper, and nothing but boulders would offer any protection."

Joshua continued planning. "How long would it take for us to climb the hill?"

Ethan looked at Salmon then at Joshua. "Would you be leading them, or someone else?"

Joshua raised his eyebrow. "You doubt that I can run as fast as someone else?"

Ethan looked down and mumbled, "The hillside is quite steep. It'd be easy to get winded, especially if a person isn't—"

Joshua stopped him. "I'll be in the second group advancing. So how much time?"

Ethan looked again at Joshua. He had a twinkle in his eye and attempted to keep a grin back. "Enough time to sing Moses's song of victory through once."

Joshua faked a stern look. Ethan was a good motivator, even if he didn't think he could run. "They should be moving as soon as the cart reaches the gate. The sun will be in their eyes as it peaks over the hilltop. What about sentries on the wall? Do we need to position archers for defending our attack?"

Salmon shook his head as he glanced at Ethan. "The wall wasn't wide enough. They depend on the cliff's sheerness to inhibit large numbers from scaling them."

Ethan added in an attempt at an apology. "Even I was winded reaching the gate at a walk."

Joshua nodded. "Perhaps you also should be with the second group that advances, and a younger man should be in the cart?"

Ethan sighed.

Joshua knew he had pushed his authority too far. Ethan was one of the older men, but not unused to the rigors of activity. He thrived on being in the center of action. That's one of the reasons Joshua chose him to spy out the lands. "Hezron will use 3,000 men from the three tribes and hide in the woods tonight."

Hezron nodded.

"Two merchants," Joshua pointed to two men, "will ride their cart into the city gate at daybreak, when the sun will be in their eyes. And the cart ... who has a cart small enough to maneuver that hillside, yet big enough to hold a few men?"

Eleazar raised his hand. "I do."

Joshua nodded. "How many men?"

Eleazar thought a moment, "Probably three."

Joshua turned as he paced. "That's five men who will disable the guards and silence any others who shout an alarm. Who should be in the cart?"

Several hands rose. Joshua selected the men.

Joshua fingered the hilt of his dagger. "Will five men be able to hold the gate open long enough for us to get inside?"

Salmon looked at Ethan. "Should be no problem."

Joshua repeated the plan, "So you will be reaching the gate at sunup."

Ethan added, "The cart should be coming from the north, not from our camp. In case someone is watching."

Joshua took his dagger out of his scabbard and unconsciously checked its point. "Good. The cart should leave tonight and circle to the north during the night, to be ready for its pre-dawn entrance up the steep cliffs." Joshua re-sheathed his dagger. "Any other considerations?" He looked around the group of grim-faced men. They were serious, but their eyes showed an excitement for the battle. Hearing no other comments, he added, "The 3,000 will meet tonight at the spring with waterskins filled before the moon rises. Anything else?" He looked around the room again and nodded. "That'll be all." He stopped them before they rose to leave. "Remember, victory is the Lord's."

They repeated his words in unison, "Victory is the Lord's."

This was the first battle they would execute without detailed plans by the Lord. Joshua was excited by the tactics developed as the leaders and spies spoke their observations. They were not just a people eating and sleeping together anymore. He could feel the camaraderie building as the men united to fight for their own land. They were becoming a nation under the Lord.

The night had been short. He stood before the three thousand men who had marched through the night, reaching the forest across from Ai in time for a brief break before the sun rose. They ate dried fruit, nuts, and bread before resting.

A stream meandered across the bottom of the valley, providing refills for their waterskins.

Now, Joshua stood before them, armed for battle and watching for the cart to reach the gate of the city. The sun would soon rise above the mountain behind them. His group of men shifted uneasily. The wait was always harder than the battle. The tenseness of nerves, muscles, and mind heightened as they all listened and watched, yet heard only silence.

Joshua squinted again, turning at a noise in the woods. He could make out the squeaking cart's wheels. It started up the other side of the cliff toward the city. The horse kept at a prodding pace. Joshua nodded, smiling. That was good discipline. Do not hurry. Do not push the horse too fast. As the cart reached the half-way mark of the hill, Joshua held his breath. The horse seemed labored. They slowed its pace. Was the weight of five men too much for it to pull up the cliff? It was taking longer than they'd anticipated.

He glanced at the horizon as it was beginning to lighten, becoming too light, too fast. Would they reach the gate in time for the sun to shine in the eyes of the gatekeeper and allow them entrance without peril?

Joshua looked at his men again. They were watching the cart too. Almost cheering it on with their gestures and unspoken thoughts.

All were ready. Maybe too ready. Some seemed to be on edge.

Joshua took a few deep breaths. Moses had always told him his men would mirror his attitude. If he was nervous, they would be nervous. Maybe what he saw was a pond's reflection of himself. He checked his belt's tightness and his sword's scabbard and drank a sip of water. Would he always feel the uncertainty of battle, even though God had promised victory?

He watched as some of his men sat and drank. Nervousness was spreadable, but so was confidence. They had caught it.

Joshua glanced at the hilltop. It was getting light before the cart reached the gate. The horse labored up the hill. Would the five men be able to hold the gate until the rest came? Joshua had deferred much of the plans to the spies who had seen the gate first hand. Was that a mistake? Second-guessing and doubts flooded his thoughts. That first group had to be at the gate shortly after the cart entered ... Joshua bit his lip in concentration. He fingered his dagger and looked over his men.

Waiting was hard, but the time for action had come, even if things weren't ideal. Even though the cart hadn't yet reached the gate, he gave the signal for the first group to climb up the cliff.

These men's lives were in his hands.

He felt that uncertainty. He suddenly knew these plans would not work. He didn't' know why he knew; he just knew. He glanced at the cart. It had entered the gate. Too late to call them back. He felt sick. The flatbread he had eaten while waiting in the darkness now churned in circles. Why did he feel such lack of peace? Shouldn't he just trust God's Words?

The first group was halfway up. They were no longer bunched as a unified force but were strung in a thin line as some were able to keep the fast pace and others could not. He needed those fast men up at that top quickly. Otherwise ... he shook his head.

He couldn't run that hill. He was relieved Ethan had suggested someone else lead. Yet he needed to be there. He bit his lip and tasted blood.

They would soon be in trouble if he didn't bring his men to help. He gave the signal, and his men started. Was he leading them to their death? He shook his head. Confidence. He must show confidence for his men to feel it. He glanced at the gate. He couldn't see the cart. It was inside. He breathed deeply. He was just nervous. God had given the victory. He must trust Him. But when the first group arrived at the gate, they were strung out too much.

His own group were becoming strung out. He tried to keep them bunched, but he was winded and couldn't keep up. The first group needed whoever could get there fast. He let them run at their own pace.

Joshua paused to catch his breath. He wasn't that old. The first group had reached the city gate. But the army of Ai poured out of the city. Ai had the advantage. Being above his men, they slashed downward with no effort, whereas his men must catch their breath from running and wield their swords uphill. And these people, though they may be few, were huge.

His men were falling, wounded and dying. He ran faster, but could only gasp for breath.

Where was the Lord?

Those of the first group who saw the army descend on them, fought until they were surrounded. Those who could broke free, turned from the fight and fled from Ai's army. They ran by Joshua with their heads down, as if they didn't see him.

Joshua watched as the surrounded soldiers fought bravely, but they didn't have a chance. His group would never make it to help them.

Ai's army turned to overpower his group. He sensed his men's uncertainty. Many looked to him for guidance. He didn't know what to tell them. Stand fast, while your brother runs? He could not. He turned with them and ran.

Ran.

Like a dog with his tail between his legs.

What had happened to easy victory?

The men of Ai chased them through the hills and into the plains. They caused the soldiers of the great God to flee.

Their enemy's victory shouts rang over the hills and down in the valley, echoing in Joshua's ears as he trudged back to camp. The great army of God returned to their camp defeated.

Joshua finally caught his breath, but not his calmness.

His people watched Joshua follow his soldiers into camp. They lined the pathways as his soldiers walked passed them. Their quietness rebuked him.

He felt shamed. Joshua felt his face flush. He rubbed his hilt, self-consciously. When he realized what he was doing, he dropped his hand to his side and clenched his fist.

They should have returned victoriously.

Moses had never retreated.

Why had God led them into defeat?

How dare God do this to him!

Joshua kept his head down and would not meet anyone's gaze. He strode through camp and stomped into the Tabernacle. When he entered, he fell before the Ark of the Lord, tearing his breastplate off, throwing it on the floor. He fell on his face before the Ark. "Lord, You told us You had given us the victory. You promised us this Land. Where were You today?"

He could still see the fallen men. They had trusted him. Their bodies lay still on the ground. Their blood poured out. Wasted.

He grabbed sand in front of him and threw it on his head. "Where were You? I was willing to stay on the other side of Jordan. But You brought us here.

"All the people of the Land will hear of this defeat. They will surround us and cut off our name from the earth. What will You do?"

The Lord commanded Joshua, "Get up! Why do you ask for My presence? Israel has sinned. Israel will not stand before their enemies with sin in their midst. Rise and consecrate the people."

Joshua sat on his knees. Sinned? What had they done? Hadn't they given God the spoils from Jericho's victory. But then he remembered Salmon.

Salmon had caused this defeat. He had given gold to that harlot!

Joshua stood before the Ark. He bit his lips in anger. "I will consecrate the people." But in his heart, he prepared what he would tell Salmon. No man would humiliate him before this many people.

But the Lord was not finished. "Bring each tribe before Me by lot. When I show by lot which tribe, bring each family. When I reveal which family, bring each household. When I choose the household, then I will show the man. His spoils will be burned. He and everything that belongs to him. He has disgraced Me."

Joshua nodded. He would obey. The lots seemed needless. He already knew who had taken the spoil. He waited for more words from the Lord.

He had none.

Joshua's anger at God was gone. He had found a new target and he would search him out, but first he must consecrate the people.

When Joshua stepped outside the Tabernacle, Hezron was waiting for him. "Joshua, I thought you should know. There were thirty-six men killed today in battle."

Joshua stilled his tongue, so as not to speak in anger to Hezron. He was not the cause of their defeat. He had fought beside him. Joshua swallowed and nodded.

The trumpets called the people before Joshua.

It was easy to stand before the people when they had victory. Today, when he stood before them, he saw families of the slain soldiers.

Their eyes were red with grief and accusation.

He bit his lip until he tasted blood. He felt his failure. He had led them into battle without the Lord. He raised his hands for quietness. "We must consecrate ourselves to the Lord. We have sinned. He will judge us tomorrow."

After standing before the people, feeling their disapproval and accusation, Joshua searched for Salmon. He would rid the nation of sin. He knew where to look.

He found Salmon at the Tabernacle, speaking with Eleazar. Joshua strode to him. "Salmon, a word with you."

Salmon closed his mouth in mid-sentence. He stiffened and stepped back. His eyebrows raised in question.

Joshua couldn't restrain himself. "We went to battle without the Lord. Sin is in the camp."

Salmon nodded. "I heard you at the meeting."

Joshua stepped forward. "Don't you have anything to confess?"

Salmon looked confused. "Confess?"

Joshua clenched his fists at his sides. Did Salmon sin and now deny it? No wonder the Lord said they would find the one by lot the following morning. "Does the harlot remind you of anything?"

Salmon looked at Eleazar, then back at Joshua. "We were just talking about their need to be circumcised. The father's sin should not be paid for by the entire family. The harlot has not lived under his protection, and the son is of age to decide on his own." Salmon looked at Joshua as if that would calm his anger.

Joshua let out a breath slowly. How could Salmon not confess his own sin? Did he have to remind him about the gold he had given to the harlot? He took another deep breath. Maybe it was better if the Lord accused him before the entire people. He would be an example to the people. "The Lord will reveal the sinner to all of us tomorrow."

Even with the setting of the sun over the foothills, across the plains from where the campsite sat, Joshua didn't feel the Lord's comfort. The colors spread across the sky behind the mountains, reminding him of the blood of his men as they had fled the battle.

He still harbored anger against Salmon for his humiliation. How could Salmon not feel his own guilt?

Dorona came and placed her hand in his. "Troubled by the battle today?"

Joshua turned from the colored horizon. "Thirty-six men are dead because I didn't seek the Lord before we left."

"Do you mourn the men or do you mourn your embarrassment?"

"Without my mistake, there would be no mourning."

Dorona rubbed his arm. "Is it a mistake when you did not know?"

"I did not ask to know." Joshua walked away from her. "When something went wrong, Moses knew it was the people's fault. I didn't blame the people; I blamed God. I questioned why He brought us here."

"You're not Moses. Don't try to be him."

Joshua looked toward the sun, but didn't see it. "I want to know God as Moses knew Him."

"Consecrate the people and find the one who sinned. Purge the evil from the people and move on."

Joshua sighed. "I know who is to blame."

"Then execute justice."

Joshua looked into her eyes. "It's Salmon."

She gasped. "What did he do?"

Joshua gestured in a sign of hopelessness. "Before we went to battle, he told me he had given gold from the Lord's spoils to the harlot."

"Why?"

"He said the Lord had given the harlot as part of the spoils of Jericho. The Lord had set her apart."

Dorona took his hand and looked into his eyes. "Salmon has a heart for people. He remembers the people, even when the Lord judges the sin."

"He must remember the Lord hates sin."

They stood in silence, watching the darkness overpower the colors of the sun.

Dorona finally spoke. "Is he wrong?"

Joshua reminded. "All the spoil was to be given to God."

"But wasn't it?" Dorona persisted.

"When the Lord told me, our people had sinned, I immediately thought of Salmon. How could it be anyone else?"

Dorona paused before speaking. "Let the Lord tell you. You may be surprised."

Joshua smiled. "I am always surprised by what the Lord does. Look at Jericho. Who would have thought that our shouting would cause their walls to fall?"

"Then don't step ahead of God, by judging a man before He does."

"Don't you think he's wrong?"

Dorona smiled. "I think you should wait for the Lord to tell you."

"How will I cast the first stone?"

"Why must you throw the first stone?"

"I am their leader. They follow me."

"They should follow God."

"They follow me."

Dorona stared over the plains. "Remember the thirty-six men who didn't come back. I would gladly throw the first stone if you were killed."

Joshua laughed for the first time all day. He squeezed her tightly. "Dorona, you help lead the people to greatness."

Dorona's chin came up. "Our Lord leads us to greatness. You are His instrument. But I will be His rock thrower, if I must."

Joshua arose early in the morning. A night's sleep had allowed his temper to cool and his perspective to mellow. He would miss Salmon's encouragement and his reminder of the people's needs. He looked over the plains of Jericho as the sun rose for the day. Even with the cloudless sky, he felt weighted down by what would take place today.

The Lord would purge evil from His people. He had brought them to their Land. He would help them conquer it.

Joshua walked passed Rahab's campsite. What had they thought of Israel's defeat yesterday, especially after the victory over their great city?

If they had not saved this woman, Salmon would not have given her that gold. They would not have been defeated yesterday. The seed of resentment entered Joshua's heart as he thought about it. He knew it was wrong. But he wanted to blame someone for the looks of anger the people showed toward him. How could he stand before the people and act like all was well, and he was in charge?

His time on the mountain with God that morning was forgotten. Instead he remembered Salmon and what he had done. He must prepare himself for what he now must do.

The trumpet called the people to the Tabernacle.

Joshua looked over the crowd. "Bring the leaders of each tribe." Jacob, their ancestor, had twelve sons. Each son became a tribe. The designated leaders from each tribe stepped forward, holding a flat rock. One side showed their tribe's ensign. The bottom of each rock was blank.

Joshua cleared an area in front of him. He drew a circle in the dirt with his foot. "Toss your stones in the circle, men."

All the stones landed with a thud and a puff of dust. For a moment, while they waited for the dust to settle, Joshua wondered if he would be held responsible for the gold given to the harlot, since he had known of the deed and had done nothing about it. He clenched his teeth unconsciously releasing his tension.

When the dust cleared, he saw one stone showed the ensign, all others were bottom side up. Joshua released the breath that he was holding. It was not from his tribe. He looked around the circle of men. He caught Salmon's eyes and held it for a moment before he spoke to the crowd. "From the tribe of Judah. All the families of Judah step forward."

The people shifted as heads of families from the tribe of Judah made their way to the front, Salmon among them. Each held a rock with their family name etched on the one side.

"Is this all the families?" Joshua counted them, then waited for Eleazar.

Eleazar counted the families listed on the scroll in front of him. "There should be twenty-four."

Joshua counted again. "Make the area bigger so that all may throw their stones at the same time." He waited as the people broadened the circle. "Toss your stones in the circle, men."

The thump in the dirt was louder.

The dust cloud took longer to settle.

When it had, Joshua read. "From the Zerahite family."

Joshua searched the faces of each family of Zerahite. He was confused. Salmon didn't come from the Zerahite family. He met Salmon's gaze across the circle. Salmon nodded to him and stepped away from the circle to allow the families of Zerahite to step forward. Was there a mistake? Hadn't Salmon withheld the Lord's spoil? Joshua coughed and continued. "All the families of Zerahite step forward." He shook his head. He had accused the wrong man. Joshua felt a rush of heat flood his face. He would have stoned a man who had done no wrong in the Lord's sight.

He breathed deeply, waiting for the men to settle around the circle. "How many households are represented?" He turned to Eleazar again. He was relieved for the pause, while Eleazar counted and answered. His knees felt weak and he leaned on his staff. He would have punished the wrong person. And Salmon was a dedicated man of God. Why had he doubted his integrity?

When Eleazar answered, Joshua was shaking. He spread his arms wider. "Make room."

The household of Zerahite came forward, and the crowd moved back.

Joshua counted them. "Show your rocks."

The men's rocks were inspected for their names on one side, the blank side on the bottom.

"Toss your stones in the circle, men."

Again the thud and the dust cloud rose. Joshua looked as the dust cleared. "From the tribe of Judah, the family of Zerahites, the household of Zabhi." Joshua picked up the stone and held it above his head.

He breathed deeply and wiped his sweaty palm against his cloak. "Now for the men." Joshua licked his lips. How quickly he had accused Salmon! If he hadn't obeyed the Lord in throwing the lots, he would have executed an innocent man. His insides twisted. The pressure squeezing his chest let loose and with it his anger. He felt chastened. He must depend upon the Lord for all wisdom. He turned to Eleazar. "How many men from this household?"

Again Eleazar answered.

"The men from the household of Zabhi come forward. People, make room."

The lot was cast.

When the dust settled, Joshua picked up the stone. He squinted to read the name. "Achan, son of Carmi, son of Zabhi, son of Zerah, from the tribe of Judah."

The other men shrank from the circle.

Achan alone was left, his hands clenched into fists at his side. He kept his head down.

Joshua looked at those who had stepped away from the circle. Hadn't Achan reported with Caleb about finding the king? Hadn't he looked Joshua in the eye the entire time the lot was cast? Achan was the last man Joshua would have accused. He swallowed. "My son, I beg you, give glory to the Lord. Tell me what you've done."

Now Achan looked down. "I've sinned against the Lord and His people. When we rushed the palace and found the storehouse of the king, I kept two hundred shekels of silver, fifty shekels of gold, and a mantle."

Joshua hung his head. "Where is it?"

Achan scraped the circle drawn in the dust with his foot. "Under my tent."

Joshua turned to Ethan. "Check."

While they waited for Ethan to return, Caleb came to stand beside Joshua. "Achan was with me almost the entire time." He shook his head. "I don't even know when he could have taken it."

Ethan returned with the spoil.

Caleb stared at Achan. "Why did you do it?"

Achan looked at his feet. "I wanted to provide for my family."

Caleb struggled to speak, "Didn't the Lord provide what you needed?"

Achan shook his head.

Joshua bit his lip. Had Achan just accused the Lord of not providing for him? "You have stolen what is the Lord's."

Achan mumbled, "The Lord has enough."

Joshua's anger grew. Not only did he deny God's provision with an attitude of unthankfulness, but he stole from God! "Who are you to decide when God has enough?"

Achan shrugged his shoulders. "I only took what I needed."

In that response, Joshua knew the sin was not just in stealing, but demanding from the Lord what was the Lord's. His voice broke when he said, "You stole from the Lord."

Achan pointed to the tent where the spoils from the battles were stored. "Look at all the spoil we brought back. God couldn't spare any?"

Joshua paced a few steps away from Achan. Not only unthankfulness but arrogance that he knew better than God. He thought he could take what was God's without a cost!

To some, it may seem so little, but Joshua knew those seeds of greed and pride were rooted deeply in Achan. Justice must be served.

Joshua turned to the household of Zabhi. "Gather all Achan's belongings, his livestock, his tent, and his family. Bring them to the valley of Achor."

Another thought troubled Joshua. Achan had flanked Caleb's side in the battle. Caleb could have been killed by his actions! "Why have you troubled us? The Lord will trouble you this day."

Achan looked at his wife, who stood behind him. He shook his head. "I only took what I needed."

Joshua thought of the Lord's commands. He remembered Dorona's words. The cost of disobedience was great. "Thirty-six men died because of your sin."

The people moved to the valley where they had gathered Achan's belongings.

As Moses had led by example, so Joshua now held the first stone. He would long remember that smooth stone that filled his palm. He threw it with his might. He heard the thud as it hit Achan.

Achan grunted in pain.

Joshua cringed, but bent to pick up another rock. Killing an unknown soldier was much easier than punishing a man he knew.

With each throw, he brought to mind the men who died because of this one's sin.

God was holy. He demanded obedience.

Joshua didn't understand the Lord requiring Achan's entire family to be stoned, but he would obey.

Even though he executed judgment upon Achan, Joshua also felt his own warning. He had not sought the Lord before battle. If he had, would any have died?

The sun grew hot.

Joshua wiped the sweat from his forehead, but he didn't stop until justice was complete.

The Lord gave commands, and He expected to be obeyed.

The price for disobedience had been paid.

Salmon drank from the stream, calming his thoughts after the stoning of Achan's family. Death of any kind was not pleasant. Salmon fought in battle because that was God's will. There were those who thrived in battle, as if they were meant for it, but not him.

He threw stones at Achan because that was also God's will. But he did not relish it. He liked to consider the Lord's care and His mercy, like with Rahab's family, rather than destruction. He glanced over at Rahab's family. How could they assimilate this family as their own?

"Shalom."

Salmon turned to greet Ethan. "It's hard to speak of peace after throwing stones."

Ethan stooped to wash his arms and head in the water. "Throwing stones makes me want to remember the Lord's Words." He knelt to drink, then filled his waterskin. "Even with water so close, I still feel better if I have my water by my side."

Salmon nodded. "We've been thirsty too many times not to remember how precious it is."

Ethan nodded toward Rahab's campsite. "You study their campsite."

Salmon nodded. "They remain separate from our people, even after their purification."

Ethan shrugged. "Our people are slow to accept differences. Remember Moses's wife?" Moses's wife, Zipporah, had been considered a foreigner by many, even after living with them for forty years.

"I told them of God's care and love. This is no way to show it."

Ethan gestured toward Rahab's camp. "They haven't chosen to believe our God. Until they do, it's good they're separate. At least we know they're not changing us."

Rahab's family watched the stoning of Achan. When they returned to their own campsite, Rahab pounded kernels of barley into flour. "The people are somber after the stoning."

Her mother coaxed the embers to life. "Death would be welcome."

Rahab stared at her mother. Didn't she want to be delivered? "Their rules protect them."

Galon settled against a cushion. "Protect against what?"

Her mother pointed to a black-and-blue mark on her arm, usually hidden by her tunic's sleeve. "Against this."

It looked like someone had twisted her arm. Rahab gasped and stood to look closer. "What happened?"

Her mother replaced her sleeve and laughed. She shook her head, dismissing Rahab's concern. "These people know what is right."

Rahab studied her mother with alarm. She looked at her father.

He appeared to ignore them. Her father had hit Rahab when she lived with them. Was her father beating her mother? She was so absorbed in her mother's bruises she almost didn't hear Galon.

Galon shrugged. "Rules don't protect, if you don't obey."

Rahab didn't understand all of their laws, didn't even know most of them, but she sensed a "rightness" in the punishment that brought accountability to their people. "Our city lost the sense of right, when we did what we wanted regardless of what was right."

Galon kicked a stone into the fire. One of the flatbreads that she was heating fell into the flames. "What's wrong with doing what we want?"

Rahab burned her finger, trying to grab the flatbread from the flames. She glared at Galon. What was wrong with him? Rahab hadn't lived with her family for years. Her father had sold her before Galon had grown up. Now she wondered if she even knew her family. "What you want is wrong."

Galon sat up. "You determine that? Who are you? Some woman nobody even wants."

His words stung. Rahab had been tossed aside by too many men to deny she felt like a used rag, but did her own brother not want her around? Or had the stoning caused him, too, to feel vulnerable and exposed to this people's Law?

She wiped the charred flatbread on a stone and threw it at him. "When you do what you want, you ignore that voice inside you that tells you what is right. Do you even hear that anymore? Or have you burned it like you've burned your flatbread?"

Galon caught the flatbread she tossed and threw it into the growing flames. He laughed and grabbed a cooked flatbread, stuffing it into his mouth. "If I don't determine what is right, who will?"

"Someone already has." Rahab tried to smack his hand as he took the flatbread, but missed. "These people have a standard of right, given to them by God. When it's disobeyed, there's a penalty. They have justice. Their rules don't change because a priest or king thinks it should. That's why they stoned that family."

Galon shook his head. "They stoned that family because they wanted entertainment. They don't allow drink, public displays of fertility, women in worship ... what else could they do, but sacrifice this family?"

Rahab opened her mouth to speak, then shut it again. She swallowed. "You think they did that for entertainment? It was judgment over disobedience! They were told not to take the spoils, and this man did. He stole from the Lord. Look what happened to his entire family because of it!"

She glanced at her father Was he listening? She thought about her own family's rebellion over circumcision and accepting the Law as their guide. What would happen to them, if they continued disobeying?

Galon laughed. "Have you listened to their laws? No man could obey all of them. If they stoned for every disobedience, they'd all be dead."

Rahab mumbled, "Maybe that's why our city is gone."

Galon's face turned hard. "And these people are perfect? I don't think so. Give them a little more time and by their own judgment, they'll all die. No man could obey these rules."

"Then why would their God give them?"

"To justify killing them." Galon laid his head back on the cushion as if ending the discussion.

Rahab asked, more to herself than to Galon, "What good is life, if we can't please this God?"

Galon opened one eye, taunting her. "To live like I want until I do die."

Rahab couldn't get the stoning nor Galon's words out of her mind. After making her family's meal, she couldn't even eat with them. Did Galon not want her around?

She felt for the gold piece she kept in her pocket. The spy's words had reassured her, "God has saved you and refined you. You are special."

Could a God Who demanded so much that He would stone His own people find value in her? Even when no one else did? She didn't think so anymore.

As she fingered the gold, she suddenly realized she too had stolen from this God. A sense of doom fell on her. Would she be stoned, too, before she even had a chance to know this God?

She wandered through camp, making her way to the Tent of Meeting. Who could she tell? She felt exposed as she waited outside the tent door, so she hid in the folds of the tent's opening.

Someone ran into her, then grabbed her.

She screamed and kicked.

"Steady. I mean you no harm. I thought I had plowed over you."

With the man's gentle voice, she stopped struggling and breathed deeply.

When she was standing steady on her feet again, she dared to look into his face.

It was the older man who blessed the people and performed the sacrifices. Around his eyes many wrinkles rose as he smiled at her.

Would he listen? She took a gulp of air, then plunged in to speak before she lost her courage. "I must speak with you about the stoning." She could no longer look into his kind eyes. She looked at her feet and lowered her voice. "I'm guilty."

At his chuckle, she looked at him. Was he mocking her? "During judgment, we are all reminded that we are unworthy."

He took her elbow, escorting her into the Tent. The folds of the doorway closed behind them. They stood alone in a big room. Curtains hung at various places where they could be pulled shut to make individual rooms. He led her to a cushion. "Sit down and tell me what this is all about."

Rahab took a deep breath. "The man stoned today was guilty of stealing from the Lord. I am too."

He seemed confused. "How did you steal?"

She reached in her pocket and brought out the gold.

It sparkled even in the dim light.

Understanding seemed to come. He laughed.

How could he be so cruel as to laugh at her disobedience, when they had just stoned a family for doing the same thing?

He took the gold and held it. "It's the Lord's."

She nodded. "From the spoils of my city."

He returned it to her hand. "And the Lord has given it to you."

Rahab shook her head. "The Lord didn't give it. A man did. I don't even know his name. I'm worthy of the stoning I saw today, for I have the Lord's gold."

He closed her fingers over the gold piece in her hand. "Salmon told me about the gold. He paid the temple to cover the gold that he had given you."

She stared at him, unable to speak. She swallowed and looked at the gold. "Why?" Then she realized why he had given her the gold. A dread came over her. "I won't make my living as I did in my city." She shook her head, dropping the gold as if it were on fire. "I can't go back to that life." She rose to leave.

He grabbed her arms, stopping her from darting from the room. When she didn't squirm, his smile returned. "Salmon didn't give the gold for your service, child. He gave it to show you God's love."

She leaned against the cushions behind her. "God's love? My gods only demand more than I could ever give. How could any god love?"

The man still held her arms. He leaned forward. "Our God spared you from your city's destruction. You are valued."

Her voice broke, "Even when no man wants me?"

The man smiled. "Man cannot see the value you have here." He pointed to her heart.

She leaned forward as he spoke, unable to believe. "Such a God would make me want to serve Him forever."

The wrinkles around the man's eyes grew as he smiled again. "That's the kind of God we have."

She raised her eyes to meet his. "How can I serve this God?"

The sun was sinking when Hezron leaned against a boulder. He watched the remaining embers that burned. They had finished stoning Achan, then burned the remaining spoils.

He had consented to taking only a few men into battle. He hadn't sought the Lord's counsel. He felt guilty for his part in the deaths of his comrades.

Judging another reminded him of his own faults.

Someone touched his shoulder.

He jumped, his hand hovering at his dagger hilt as he turned. He breathed deeply, then sighed in relief. "Shalom, Joshua."

Joshua nodded to the pile. "Be at peace. Perhaps if I were more like Moses who saw God, I would understand God's holiness."

"My grandfather used to tell me, 'If we could understand God's ways, then He would not be a God we would want.'"

Joshua grunted. "His ways are certainly not mine."

Hezron whittled on a small branch. He didn't enjoy executing judgment for sin. "When God has all the people execute judgment, we remember His consequences. But stoning the children is hard. I struggle, not with understanding His holiness, but accepting it."

Joshua leaned against a boulder. "Moses always asked God, even when he thought he knew the answer. I forgot to even ask. I'm afraid of what will happen to the people if I don't obey."

"You didn't fear the people today."

Joshua shrugged as he looked back at Hezron. "It was hard to see how his sin should also cause the death of his children, but he was responsible for training them. If he trained them by how he saw God's things, their hearts would not be towards God either. Like you said, it's not understanding God's holiness. I struggle with what the people think. What if, after they've had time to consider this judgment, they blame me? After all, I didn't consult God for the battle."

Hezron watched the smoke of the burning pile drift up to the clouds colored by the sunset. "Don't let fear of what people think, hinder you from doing what is right. Fear God Who will do right."

Joshua continued to look at the pile of boulders after Hezron walked away. The stars were starting to appear in the night sky, but he didn't notice. Hezron had said what he was afraid of. One man's sin caused all to suffer. How could he control the actions of every single man? How could he take the people into battle again?

Something shimmered on the other side of the mound of boulders.

He went to investigate, withdrawing his sword from its sheath as he walked. His breathing increased. He felt the hair on his neck prickle. What was it?

When he reached the side farthest from camp, he realized he was alone, in enemy territory, and far from shouting distance to camp. He swallowed the lump in his throat and kept walking.

The glow had grown from the size of a fist to a man. The glow radiated a whiteness brighter than the sun. The light appeared pure and holy, demanding attention.

Joshua stumbled. He looked away from the blinding light, allowing his eyes to refocus on his steps. He lowered his eyes so he wouldn't stumble, yet could watch the glow. The shine drew him.

A form appeared from the brilliance.

Joshua gasped and stopped walking.

The Lord materialized.

"My Lord and My God." Joshua fell to his knees, his sword dropping from his hand.

All Joshua's questions he had asked with Hezron and himself were forgotten. All his uncertainty about the people was gone. His longing to know all the answers was gone.

He didn't feel his own heart steady, nor his breathing calm. But he felt a rightness, a communion with God. All he did was worship. He focused on God and His glory. He concentrated totally on his Creator, his Promised Deliverer, his Provider, Him.

He didn't know how much time had passed. It didn't matter. He felt forgiven, complete, at peace.

He would never understand God. But he could trust Him. And he would accept what God would give him. No, he would give to God what God found acceptable. "What do you want me to do, Lord?"

The Lord spoke, "Don't fear. I've given you Ai. Take all the soldiers. Ambush them. Let no one live. The people may keep the spoil."

Joshua nodded. The matter of Achan and Ai was in the past, forgotten. God had moved on to the next thing. If God didn't dwell on Joshua's failures, why should he? God was gracious to him. He would lead him step by step.

Joshua could lead his men into battle again, if God was with him. He sat and nodded. An ambush would work. Take all the men. He grunted. They had only taken a few thousand when they fought in their own strength. He shook his head. If only he could undo his past mistakes.

Joshua remained on his knees long after the glow disappeared. He needed the Lord's counsel for each battle. He must remember that.

The following morning, after morning sacrifices, Joshua gathered the elders to discuss Ai. Joshua caught Caleb's glance across the circle of men. Caleb seemed to be bursting with hope. Joshua laughed. "What are you thinking?"

Caleb shrugged. "Let me take some men and leave tonight. We'll circle around to the west side of Ai, in the valley between Ai and Bethel and wait for your signal. When you approach the city in the morning with the rest of the people from the north, they will leave the city confident of victory as before. Flee. Draw them from the city. Then we, waiting in ambush, will take the city. The Lord will deliver it into our hands."

Joshua smiled. He and Caleb had spied out the Land. They had found courage together in what God would do. Tomorrow would be the same. "Are you listening to the Lord? That's what He told me to do."

Caleb shrugged. "He's ready for victory. We can do nothing less."

Joshua looked around the circle of men. "Let's petition the Lord for obedience tomorrow. He will give victory."

CHAPTER 8

The king of Ai listened as his messenger gave his report.

The messenger bowed. "The people from the desert sacrifice a group of people to their God. They don't burn them on altars, but stone them, then burn them.

"All the people help; no one remains in camp. They stone even their belongings and flocks. They do this without darkness, drink, or music. Their God demands much."

The king stood from his throne and paced. "We must give our gods more." He turned to his adviser behind him. "Vizier, you have a child. We must give our best to Baal."

The vizier turned pale. "My son is too big to enter Baal's arms."

The king waved his hand. "Make the fire burn hotter. Baal will reach his arms to all those who have an offering."

The vizier bowed his head, swallowing. "As you wish, sire."

"We must find more. If these people sacrificed many, we must have more." He turned again to the vizier. "Find at least a dozen high ranking officials who have children worthy to sacrifice. We must please Baal before battle." He turned to a messenger at his right hand. "Command the temple priests to prepare Baal for sacrifices. If their God doesn't require the cover of darkness for His pleasure, then we also will please our god in the light."

The king gestured to the messenger. "What battle plans are they making?"

The messenger bowed before him. "No one is sharpening swords or blades."

The king stroked his beard. "If they aren't preparing for battle, then we can attack when we are ready."

Another messenger entered, bowing. "King, I bring news from Bethel."

"What does their king say?"

The messenger stood from bowing on his knee. "He's sending his entire army to wait in your city until these people from the desert come."

The king rubbed his hands. "When?"

"They move tonight."

The vizier whispered to him. "Are we ready?"

The king scoffed. "This God's secret lies in getting close to the wall. We will not allow Him to come near. Our walls are on hills, too steep for them to climb. We will see them approach long before we must leave our gates. Before they even come close to the city, we will shake them away like the sand off our feet. Our people are safe."

Caleb and his thirty-thousand men had marched under cover of darkness, arriving behind the city where the mountain would screen them from Ai's view. The men were settling for a brief rest before morning. Caleb drank from a spring that gathered from the rains on the hills. The moonlight's rays gave enough light to silhouette the fortified city on the hilltop.

A twig snapped.

With his hand on the hilt of his sword, he asked, "Who is it?"

A messenger stepped forward. "The sentry sends word that Bethel marches tonight."

Bethel was the city north of Ai. Caleb looked to the north. "How many?"

"If this isn't every man from their city, I don't know how the walls contain them."

Caleb nodded and smiled. "Alert the men of quietness. Tomorrow when we enter Ai, we will also enter Bethel. Two cities taken in one battle. Truly, the Lord is with us.

"Report to Joshua of our plans to take both cities. We will split our men between them. But we will need all his men, once he signals. The Lord has given us the victory."

Israel's soldiers had moved their battle camp north of Ai on the hillside overlooking it. Most of the soldiers had already settled for the night. Hezron and his brother Madron sat by their fire. Hezron would take the first watch.

Madron finished his tea. "I sense a difference from the first time we marched against Ai."

Hezron wiped his mouth with the back of his hand. "This time, we have the Lord's blessing."

"These people are giants. Our fathers who spied out the Land were right. When we were fighting Ai last time, I came up to the soldier's armpit."

Hezron propped his sword against a stone by the light of the fire and ran his knife over its edge at an angle. "Maybe because our people had been slaves for so long, it stunted our growth." He laughed. "It gives a different perspective in battle when I swing my sword up to meet theirs, instead of down. Our training in the desert didn't prepare us for that." He concentrated on sharpening his sword at the right angle. After a time, he added, "But we have the swords of Egypt." Egypt had been a world leader, mining the ore and taking the best from other people. They heated bronze that didn't break under pressure of battle.

Madron yawned. "Wake me up for my watch."

Hezron nodded, not taking his eyes from his sword. "Tomorrow morning will come soon enough."

In the early morning, the king of Ai stood to be fitted in his armor. Sentries had informed him of the enemy's presence at the foot of their hill. He commanded his general, "Prepare the troops for attack."

His general hesitated. "Their numbers are greater than before, sire."

The king paused as his breastplate was tightened. "How many?"

"Five thousand."

The king knew he must appear confident. He adjusted his arm band strap, keeping his head down. "Bethel is coming?"

The general nodded. "They marched through the night. They arrived just before dawn."

The king lifted his arms as his sword was belted on. "Victory is secured. We have the advantage, being above them on the hill. We will cut them down as children before warriors. Sound the trumpets."

When the trumpets called the soldiers to attention before him, the king stood on the steps of his palace. He raised his arms and waited for silence.

The stirring stopped; the chatter quieted.

He paused longer than needed for his men's attention. "We win this battle, just as we won before, for the gods we serve."

The soldiers raised their swords and cheered. The cheering filled the streets and echoed from the walls.

The king waited again for them to quiet. He motioned to the guards. "Open the gates."

The men manning the gates pulled the draw-chains. The gates swung open.

The king pointed to the desert people who waited at the bottom of the hill. "Look at them. Fear keeps them rooted to the ground where they stand. They will fall into our hands without a fight. Forward, men, to battle."

His men roared as they poured from the gate like wine from a bottle.

They charged down the hill, where Israel waited. His warriors would overcome these little men of no worth.

Victory was sure.

They reached the bottom of the hill. The waiting army seemed to stand in fear of their approach. As Ai's army reached the bottom of the hill, Israel turned and fled.

The king smiled at the easy victory. This time they would follow them to their camp and take their spoil. He raised his sword and encouraged his men. "Onward. We have the victory."

They ran after them.

But as they chased the desert people, he heard a cry of a different kind.

It wasn't the sound of victory.

It sounded more of like despair, unbelief, shock.

The king turned from running after the fleeing army to look behind him.

Rising from his city was a cloud of black smoke. He stopped completely. How could it be? A sob rose in his throat. He swallowed. It couldn't be. They were winning . . . . That wine that had poured out from the gate, turned red; like with the color of his own blood.

Now the desert warriors, though small in stature, loomed over his soldiers, raining blows on his people as his own men fled for the hills. Without a city, what was to defend?

The king ran, not after the desert people, but after his own men, to hide in a cave.

The desert people pursued him.

He had lived in comfort. Temple worship allowed for much feasting and drinking, and so did being the king. The life of ease did not prepare him for running hills and wearing heavy armor.

The day turned hot.

His breathing grew ragged. He dared not stop and drink.

His men fainted around him.

The desert people gained on them. He turned to see his general struck down as he turned to defend himself.

The king hid behind a boulder, bending over his knees to gain his breath and wait for his side pain to ease. He removed his helmet to wipe the sweat that poured down his face.

He never heard their approach.

When he stood from gaining his breath and wiping his face, he looked into five enemy faces.

One soldier pointed a sword at his neck.

He dropped his head and sighed.

He surrendered because he had no choice.

The Lord gave His people victory before the sun passed its zenith. They now combed the cliffs for any soldiers hiding there. Joshua looked over the valley at the slain. The battle rush was over. He drank from his waterskin and wiped his sword clean in the grass.

Hezron brought the kings of Ai and Bethel before him.

They fell to their knees before Joshua. The king of Ai looked up at him. "Spare us. You have slain our people. We only remain."

Joshua removed his helmet and wiped his brow. He still held his sword. He put it back in his scabbard.

The king of Ai watched the gesture. His eyes lit with renewed hope. "I'll serve you."

All knew the Lord's words to spare no one. The Lord was holy. Sparing them would snare His people.

Joshua turned from the kings and pointed to the tree beside him. "Hang them."

The end of the day came as the sun sank over the hillside. The elders gathered around Joshua and reported their number of those destroyed.

Joshua recorded the slain in the book of their history. Twelve thousand slain from Ai. The city was burned. The people gathered the spoils of cattle and plunder.

Bethel had no recorded number, but the city was destroyed.

As the setting sun brought the darkness of night, Joshua looked over the warriors returning to camp. "Remove the kings from the tree and throw them in the gates of their cities. Cover them with stones so that no one will ever enter their cities again."

He called Eleazar to sacrifice.

What a difference obedience made!

It gave them courage over the following days as the people cleaned the land of the slain, burying them in caves and mass graves.

The congregation assembled on the hillsides around Ai for a special worship service.

Joshua and Eleazar stood on a terrace in front of the city of Ai, where all could see and hear.

Eleazar offered burnt and peace sacrifices.

Joshua read the blessings given by Moses from the Lord. The Lord had promised so many blessings. Whenever he pronounced a blessing, those on the hillside of Gerizim, north of Ai, shouted, "Amen." The hills rang with their voices as if the very rocks would speak His praises.

When Joshua read the curses, those listening on Mount Ebal, to the south of Ai, responded, "So be it." The curses warned of disobedience and its consequences. Even as their echoes poured back over the people, they felt the importance of obedience.

Joshua didn't stop until all the blessings and curses were read.

And the Lord was worshiped.

After the day of worship and the evening meal, Ethan rested in his tent.

Kamon shifted on the cushion to sit beside him. "What's wrong?"

Ethan laughed. "How do you know something's wrong?"

Kamon took his hand in hers. "You're quiet."

Ethan looked at the hillside where they had stood to hear the Law. "Are we missing something?"

"Why?"

"The Lord was so close to us in the desert. We gathered His manna. We drank from His waters. We followed His cloud. We saw His light at night."

Kamon laid her head on his shoulder. "Do you feel God has left us?"

"No, but ... He isn't visible."

Kamon leaned back and studied his face. "We've outgrown our childhood with God. God still leads us. But He wants us to stand for Him. Can we defend Him before the nations, without letting go of His Hand?

"Ethan, when is the battle the hardest?"

Ethan answered without having to think, "The waiting before the battle."

"That's where our people are. We've seen God in Egypt. We've known God in the desert. Now we must remember Him, when the tangible cloud and fire are no longer in sight, when victory seems sure even without Him, when you grow tired of fighting and want to be satisfied with incomplete victory, when you are waiting for victory...

"Remember Him."

Rahab and her family were permitted to participate in the burnt sacrifices and hear the words of the Lord. Rahab had stood in the back, high on the hill, watching when Joshua built the altar of uncut stones and Eleazar blessed their victory by burning sacrifices. She had listened as Joshua read the Words of their God. She stood amazed that their God promised so many blessings from the land, as if the land were theirs already. She felt as if a new life had been given to her.

But when Joshua had moved to the curses ... God said that the people who had been living in the land were an abomination to Him.

She shivered. No wonder her city had been destroyed! Her city had done all those things that would bring curses on these people.

She glanced at her father.

He had listened to the blessings, but when the curses came, he shook his head and left. Her brother and mother followed him.

She cringed.

As she listened to the Words of God, her heart grew heavy. How could she please this God when her past held such curses?

The worship was concluded. The people returned to their tents. Most had begun preparations for their evening meal. Hezron leaned over the fire for light, moving his whetstone across the blade of his knife. He always thought better when he did something with his hands. He tried to concentrate on the blessings God had promised, but memories of battle haunted him.

Madron, his brother, stretched his legs out before the fire. "How long before we're finished?"

Hezron pushed on the whetstone. "Fighting?"

Madron nodded.

Hezron shook his head. Their tribe had promised Moses they would fight until the land was conquered. Then they would return to their homes across the Jordan River. "It was a bold promise we made."

Madron rolled on his side and looked at Hezron. "I miss my family."

Hezron swallowed but couldn't speak. The times of waiting before battle were the hardest. Thoughts of home and his wife and child came to mind. He missed them, too. "Your wife's time is soon?"

Madron nodded. "She assured me when the baby was close she would move in with your family."

Hezron nodded. "That will be good for both families."

Madron put his arms under his head and looked at the sky. "Will my child even know me when I get home?"

Hezron paused in striking his sword. "It's easy to promise in the heat of a meeting when men make plans, but it's harder to fulfill that promise when waiting is long and our family is absent."

"Did Uncle Esmail ever leave his sheep?"

Hezron nodded. "One time, for our parent's wedding."

Madron nodded. "I wouldn't leave either, if I had the choice." He removed a flatbread from the coals without sitting up. "Don't you wonder at God, to want all the people killed?"

"I can't comprehend God's holiness. If I did, maybe I would understand the killing.

"Salmon told of Jericho sacrificing their children. Have you seen the women they rescued?"

Madron shook his head. "I avoid their campsite. I get this feeling of ..."

"Evil?" Hezron laughed. "The harlot's face was burned to appease their gods."

"What makes a people do those things?"

Hezron shook his head. "They don't know God."

Madron stirred the coals to heat another flatbread. "How can they find pleasure in such evil?"

Hezron wiped down his blade with a cloth and sheathed it. "God gives them up. He doesn't reach out to them. All goodness is gone."

Madron flipped the flatbread. "Want one?"

Hezron reached for one. He folded some meat cooked under the coals into the bread, took a bite and chewed. "Without goodness, there is only evil."

"Couldn't we ignore their evil? What harm would it do?"

"Why don't you just leave a wound alone on your ewe?"

Madron sat straight up, and raised his voice. "The fleece worms would lay their larvae in it. It would fester. I'd have to kill the ewe!"

Hezron nodded. "Same with evil. Evil doesn't just go away. It grows. God wants us to remove the evil."

"But to kill all the children?" Madron shook his head. "I have nightmares of their faces."

Hezron gestured toward Rahab's camp. "Do you want evil close to your family?"

Madron shook his head.

Hezron reached for another flatbread. "It also keeps God in our midst. If evil is present, how can His holiness be present?"

CHAPTER 9

News spread throughout the land of the defeat of Ai and Bethel. Kings beyond Jordan in the hill country and in the lowland and along the coast of the Great Sea toward Lebanon in the north heard it: the Hittites, Amorites, Canaanites, Perizzites, Hivites, and Jebusites. They counseled together against Joshua and Israel.

The city of Gibeon heard what the Lord had done in Jericho and Ai. The king called all his advisors. "What should we do with this people who mows down cities as if they were grass, leaving no one alive?"

He looked around the circle of his advisors. Their fearful expressions reflected his own feelings. "No one has any hope for our city?"

Mikar bowed before the king. "Oh Mighty King, if Jericho can be destroyed without a fight. Who are we to fight this God? But if the king is willing to live?" He studied the king.

The king nodded. "Go on."

"If the king is willing to live as a servant?" Again Mikar waited.

The king grunted, "Serving is better than death."

Encouraged by his response, Mikar explained his plan to the king.

As Mikar finished, the king smiled. "Brilliant. Go. Save our people from destruction."

God's people rested from their battle with Ai. Their campsite lay between the mountains of Ai and Bethel. Joshua could no longer see their tents spread out over the sand of the plains as far as his eye could see. Now, their tents wrapped around the foothills. The arrangement made him feel isolated from the people. He could only see the banner of his own tribe as he stood overlooking the camp. The other eleven banners were scattered around the bases of other hills. He must warn them of spreading themselves too far. They must remember that they were in enemy territory.

By conquering Ai and Bethel, they had split the land in half from the north to south. They had divided the inhabitants, preventing their enemies from consolidating against them.

Joshua had spent the day sharpening his sword and preparing his armor. He would soon send spies to see what city lay next.

Ethan entered his tent. "Joshua, messengers come from a far country to speak with you."

Joshua followed Ethan to the outskirts of their campsite. As he reached them, he felt confident. It was a small group, hardly worth noticing. He surveyed them.

One tall man, apparently the leader, stood with several servants. They were dressed in rags, as if many sandstorms had sucked their life from them. They bowed low before Joshua. "Excuse our appearance, oh great one of your people. We left our country many days ago, traveling far to speak with you about your God Who conquers all Egypt and the two Amorite kings. Your God must be worthy of victory."

Joshua motioned for them to rise. He felt uncomfortable having them bow before him. He was not worthy of praise. Where could he take them? He had no suitable place to hear their petitions. They were foreigners, after all. He couldn't take them to the Tent of Meeting, nor the Tabernacle. Even the harlot's family remained outside their camp. He swallowed. They were but a few. He could bring them to his own tent. He led the way and motioned for them to make themselves comfortable on his cushions outside his tent.

The servants knelt behind the one who had spoken.

The leader squatted with great difficulty against a cushion. "We've traveled long to hurry and welcome you." He stretched his legs toward the fire and sighed. "It's good to be off my feet."

Joshua saw the bottom of his sandals. They had no soles left. His foot was smeared with a salve, covered with dirt.

The man noticed Joshua staring and bent his leg under him. He shrugged. "I am sorry. My sandals were new when we left."

Joshua nodded. "So where do your people live?"

"We couldn't say, for the distance is great. But we welcome you." The man motioned for the servant behind him to bring his saddlebags closer. He unfastened the leather strap that fell off in his hand. He laughed and shook his head. "It was quite a trip!" He tucked the strap into his bag. He reached into the bag and removed a cloth-wrapped package. "We share with you what we have." From the decaying cloth, he unwrapped a piece of bread. He broke a piece from the loaf. It crunched loudly, pieces fell from his hand. He offered it to Joshua. "Accept it as our gift."

Joshua stared at the hard piece in his hand. It appeared as brittle as a vine shriveled on a dead branch. How could he avoid insulting the man, yet still refuse it? He swallowed, lowering his head quickly before the man noticed. "We have enough."

The man shook his head. He took a small piece and placed it on his tongue and chewed. "When we left, our bread was fresh. When that is all we have …" He let his voice trail off and he covered the bread as if embarrassed that he could offer such poor gifts. "Hunger will drive a man to eat anything." He finished chewing and swallowed.

Joshua hesitated. Their law didn't allow eating with foreigners. He felt his face flush. It seemed like a harsh law, especially as these were so needy. Perhaps he could offer food, without eating himself. He had already brought them into his campsite, another law that he had broken. He gestured to the flatbread Dorona turned on the embers by his feet. "Eat what we have."

The man licked his lips, studying the flatbread. "It would be good to eat something fresh." He grabbed for the flatbread, stuffing a huge bite into his mouth.

Joshua didn't want to tell the man that they must bless the food before and after they ate. They were so hungry, after all. Wouldn't God bless the food without his prayer? He pushed the bowl of meat and vegetables closer to him. He glanced at the servants.

Their eyes were fastened on the bowl as if it would disappear before they could have some. They watched, licking their lips and swallowing as their leader finished four flatbreads heaped with meat and vegetables.

Joshua watched him. This was the right thing to do. No one should be that hungry. He offered more until the leader pushed back from the fire and leaned against the cushions. "I could eat no more. Your hospitality is great. You honor us with such a meal."

Joshua gestured to his servants, their eyes seemed to bulge from their faces. They moved around their leader to grab what food remained, scooting back to their corner. They fought over what was left of the meal.

The leader looked at Joshua for the first time since he had started eating. He gestured to Joshua's place. "But you haven't eaten?"

Joshua replied. "Didn't Abraham feed the Angel of God without knowing it? It's the least we could do." And as he said it, he nodded. The Lord would bless this sacrifice, even if it wasn't total obedience.

Joshua hesitated. He could stretch the laws to feed these starving men, but he couldn't allow them to camp within their campsite. Sometimes, the words of God were hard to follow. He swallowed, trying to find the right words to make his explanation acceptable. "You can't stay inside our campsite for the night, for our God gives strict rules about our treatment of strangers. But you may rest outside of camp, and we'll talk more tomorrow."

The stranger stood with the aid of his servant and bowed low. "Don't trouble yourself. We're grateful for any hospitality that you show us."

Joshua was relieved by their willing acceptance of their law and regulations. He escorted them to the outskirts of the campsite. He watched as they pitched their tents for the night. His mind lingered on their reverence for him. He was, after all, the leader of a great people. He smiled as he walked back to his tent.

When he reached his tent, Dorona stood to greet him. She didn't say anything, but he felt her gaze. "What?" He looked at her face.

Dorona hesitated.

Joshua noticed her expression and sighed. He wasn't sure he wanted to hear what she had to say. Did he have to justify his actions to his wife? He was the leader of this people after all. He looked down at the embers of the cookfire. He remembered that he hadn't eaten. He wasn't even hungry now. Not after seeing how hungry those strangers had been.

He grew angry at her silence. "Don't you think I should have fed them?"

She shook her head.

"Didn't you see how much they ate?" He defended his actions. Why did she look at him like that?

She shrugged. "They were hungry."

He nodded, relieved that she didn't remind him of their law about strangers. His nod was premature.

She licked her lips and spoke, "Joshua, remember they are foreigners."

He pursed his lips to keep from saying something in anger. Why did every act of a leader have to be analyzed, evaluated, and judged—not only by the people but by his own wife? These foreigners were the first to treat him with the respect worthy of a leader of such a great people. Even his own wife didn't respect him like they had done. He turned from her and stormed from the tent without another glance back. He hiked the hillside and studied the campsite. He always gained perspective above the people, closer to God. He stayed a long time, remembering the stranger's words. But he wasn't closer to God.

The following day Joshua sent for the elders. They gathered at the Tent of Meeting and listened to the messenger's story. These far-away people were willing to be their servants. What more could they need?

The stranger pulled from his saddlebags a parchment. "We anticipated your generosity and your willingness to bring us into your service." He opened the scroll and spread it on a table before them. "Sign this contract between your people and our people. It guarantees our service to you and your consent to protect us in our need."

Joshua took the reed pen to sign the document.

The stranger retrieved the ink well from his sack, unsealed the top, and held it for Joshua's use.

After Joshua signed the document, he stepped back.

The stranger gestured around the room toward the other leaders. "It's not just from you, the great leader of this people that we would like this promise, but it's for all these leaders to sign. Isn't it a contract between your people and our people?"

Joshua nodded. He wasn't a king, after all. They ruled more by the counsel of elders than by his sole authority. He motioned for the others to sign.

They stood in line, each signing it.

When Hezron took the reed pen to sign, he paused to re-read the contract. "Where did you say you were from?"

The stranger smiled. "Didn't your great leader tell you? Don't our clothes speak for themselves? We have traveled far."

Hezron paused another moment and glanced around the room at the other elders. As he lifted the pen to dip in the ink, his hand shook so much he spilled the ink on the parchment. He wiped it with his hand.

The stranger hurriedly stepped forward and wiped the ink with the bottom of his torn tunic. "No worries, my friend. What is a mere stain with an agreement of friends? The words are still clear and the contract is still valid."

When all the elders had signed the contract and the ink had dried, the stranger rolled up the parchment. "We are your servants. You have only to request our help, and we will serve you." He bowed low and prepared to leave.

Joshua looked at the elders. "We can't send you away with nothing. What kind of host would we be? Allow us to fit you for your journey."

The stranger bowed. "You have already fed and refreshed us. We couldn't take more from you."

Joshua shook his head. "It's not enough. Your garments aren't enough protection for your journey." Joshua motioned for a messenger to come closer.

Joshua whispered to him, "Find some cloaks and tunics in the spoils that we took from the cities of Ai and Bethel. Make them a worthy gift from us."

Joshua motioned for another to prepare provisions and outfit better donkeys for their trip.

The messenger returned, carrying several changes for each person in their caravan.

Joshua smiled. "You have selected the best." He presented them to the strangers.

The stranger stepped back. "We couldn't take such fine garments. We are mere servants of yours."

Joshua laughed. "Shouldn't we care for our servants with our best?"

The stranger bowed and took them. "Your kindness is too great for us to refuse." Before they left, the stranger stood before the congregation dressed in the fine garments of their spoils.

Joshua introduced them to the people as an example of what blessing would come from the land when they obeyed the Lord.

They left, loaded with fresh provisions, silks, and better donkeys.

But Joshua had forgotten to seek the Lord.

Israel journeyed three days after making the covenant when they came to the cities of Gibeon, Chephirah, Beeroth and Kiriath-jearim, all on hills clustered in their path.

Ethan and Salmon were sent to spy the city of Gibeon. They reached Gibeon by mid-morning. Ethan grunted as he rested from hauling the vegetable cart. "You could lose some weight you know." He drank from his waterskin before lifting the handles to move the cart again.

A voice from the vegetables hissed, "You wanted to be the spokesman this time."

Ethan grunted, but lifted the handles of the cart and pushed it toward the gate. When he reached the gate, a soldier stopped him with a drawn sword. "State your business."

Ethan pointed to the cart and gestured to the vegetables heaped on it.

The soldier waved his sword. "You can't speak?"

Ethan nodded. He had forgotten about the pit in his insides that had stopped his mouth when they'd entered Jericho's gate. It was back again.

The soldier stabbed at the produce in the cart with his sword.

Ethan gasped. He must stop him before Salmon was stabbed. He dumped the cartload onto the road.

Salmon tumbled out.

The soldier grabbed Salmon before he could run and called to the other guards, gesturing at Ethan. "Seize him."

Two guards grabbed Ethan's arms, pulling them behind him.

Ethan's father had been a prisoner once, when the Amorites had invaded their desert campsite. His father's stories told of their cruelty to prisoners. Ethan had relished them as exciting then. Now, they seemed adventures of despair.

They tied his hands behind his back and took his cloak and dagger from his belt.

He felt exposed without his cloak. He felt defenseless without his dagger. But mostly he felt the pit of his stomach drop deeper. What would they do to him? Their evil did not inspire any kindness toward spies. He and Salmon were shoved into the palace and brought before the king.

Desert living had not prepared Ethan for the splendor of such a palace. He stood at the bottom of the steps before the king's throne. The glory of this king spoke of wealth, comfort, and control. Ethan squared his shoulders, causing strain on his tied hands. He resigned himself to what would come. Did greater wealth in evil hands bring greater cruelty?

The king watched them come. "Who are you? Why are you here?"

What could they say that wouldn't further threaten their lives? Ethan's tongue stuck to the roof of his mouth, and his lips felt numb. He licked his lips but couldn't find enough moisture.

Salmon cleared his throat. "We come in the Name of the Most High God to bless His Name."

Ethan breathed deeply. How could Salmon always have words for tough situations?

Another man entered to stand behind the king. He whispered in his ear.

Ethan started. Why did he look familiar? And that silk robe he wore ...

A foreboding, not based on torture, seeped over him. He licked his lips, but it brought no moisture to them.

The king whispered to a messenger who hurried away. He turned back to them. "Your leaders promised protection."

Salmon stepped forward to the lower stairs. "Our leaders would never offer protection."

Ethan tried to warn Salmon with a glance. He felt disaster coming. His insides quivered, and not from fear of this king and what he would do, although that feeling had been real a few moments ago. This feeling was the knotting conviction that comes when he disobeyed God.

Don't let it be so, his mind pled.

The messenger returned with a scroll.

As the servant unrolled the scroll, Ethan could not move. He recognized the parchment. There was that stain where Hezron had spilled the ink.

The king read from the scroll. "Your leader is Joshua, is he not?" He did not wait for an answer. He leaned forward. "Three days ago in your campsite, your elders signed a contract to protect us." He looked up from reading. "Here are the signatures of Hezron, Eleazar ... Should I continue?"

"Let me see that." Salmon stepped forward.

The king's messenger held it before them.

Ethan didn't need to see it. Ethan's unease escalated like the waves of Jordan in flood stage. He couldn't roll its waves back nor could he roll back time. His leaders had signed the contract, giving protection to a city they were told to destroy. He clenched his fists to restrain his anger.

God had promised total victory over all the cities.

The leaders had signed away that victory with a promise of peace.

These evil cities had already turned their hearts from God.

Israel hadn't asked God about the contract.

Salmon read the parchment before looking at the king. "What do you wish from us?"

The king smiled. "When we need protection, we'll let you know. In the meantime, return to your leaders and tell them this city is protected by their word."

Joshua paced outside of camp, waiting for Ethan and Salmon. He had been watching for them and noticed when they rounded the bend around the hills. He hurried to speak with them before the others did. He remembered the ten spies, at the time of Moses, who had turned the people's hearts against God, causing them to spend forty years in the wilderness. The people didn't need to hear this report until plans were made. He also remembered Ai and wanted to evaluate the situation before others intruded with their own battle plans. He approached them, smiling. "Shalom. You return early. You must bring good news." He looked at them, but they didn't meet his glance nor answer.

Ethan crossed his arms. His face was flushed, even his ears were tinged red.

Joshua sensed something was wrong. "What is it?"

Ethan commanded, "Bring all the elders, then we will tell you."

Joshua looked at Salmon.

He only nodded.

Joshua had grown accustomed to being treated as an important leader. Didn't even messengers from far countries acknowledge his leadership ability? He resented Ethan's commanding, almost condescending tone. "I don't want the people's hearts to melt in fear if you bring a bad report..."

Salmon shook his head. "We won't be the ones to upset the people."

Joshua glanced again at the men. What did that mean? He bit back an angry retort. Salmon was not one to upset anyone. Why would their report be bad? Hadn't God promised victory? He led the way to the Tent of Meeting without saying another word. But his mind moved between anger at their request and concern over what they had found. What had happened?

When the leaders gathered, Joshua could wait no longer. He raised his arms to quiet the group, then turned to Ethan and Salmon. "Tell us what you found."

Ethan glared at each elder gathered. When he met Joshua's gaze, his eyes were dark as granite.

Joshua bit back an angry command to speak.

Ethan bowed his head, attempting to control his anger. "Do you remember the men who came several days ago?"

Joshua's impatience grew. Of course he did. What did that have to do with what they had seen?

Ethan stepped toward Joshua. "Where were they from?"

Joshua swallowed. He could feel his insides tighten. A foreboding kept him from answering above a whisper, "They said they were from a far county."

Salmon persisted. "How far?"

Joshua licked his lips. They were suddenly dry. The strangers had avoided answering them when they had asked. Even Dorona warned him to reconsider, but he hadn't. He thought of the law he had excused when he had allowed them to eat at his tent. He had allowed them to speak to the elders as if they were welcome visitors. He hesitated. "They didn't say."

Ethan clenched his fists at his sides. "What can we do to them?"

Joshua stepped back from them. He could feel their tension. He wanted to defend himself. He felt his own anger building against them. Didn't all the leaders in the room sign the paper? But the words choked in his throat. Who had allowed them into their camp? Who had brought them to the leaders for consideration? Who knew better? The answers all fell on him. He felt the humiliation of his poor leadership. He slumped his shoulders. "We can do nothing."

Ethan's neck veins bulged. His voice was low. "You signed the contact with Gibeon and the three surrounding cities. They said we must protect them. Is this true?"

Joshua hung his head. He had led the people away from God. He had disobeyed. "What have we done?"

The silence in the room spoke more of all their embarrassment, dejection, and anger than any words could.

Ethan crossed his arms. "We stood humiliated before our enemies as they told us what our leaders had done to us. Who are we to trust?"

Joshua raised his head and looked around the room. Tears pooled in his eyes. "I never consulted the Lord."

Hezron stepped forward. "We all signed the contract. We are all guilty."

What could they do now?

Salmon spoke, "Let's seek God's counsel now. Maybe God in His mercy will give wisdom."

Ethan snorted. "Isn't it too late? How can God help us?"

Salmon looked around the room. "Even if He cannot undo what we've done, we must repent."

Joshua was the first to fall on his knees and beg for the Lord's mercy. The visitors' words had made him feel so important. He had been elated by their flattery about his great leadership. He had taken the credit for God's victory. He had excused his own disobedience of the Law and encouraged all Israel to give the Gibeonites aid. Now, because of him, God's people would be snared. Their hearts would be turned away from God.

What could be done?

After speaking to Joshua and the elders, Ethan strode out of the campsite. He looked toward the west, where the sun was falling behind the mountains. The cooling of the evening did nothing to still his heart. He stared long as the shadows deepened around the trees. He watched the shepherds bring their flocks closer for protection for the night. But the quietness of the night didn't reflect the stirring of his heart.

When a hand reached into his and squeezed, he was startled but not surprised. "Kamon."

"Your report caused great disturbance among the people."

Ethan took a step from her. "It didn't take long for the people to hear."

"Someone listened through the tent and made sure we all knew."

"That eavesdropper should have waited until his temper cooled before speaking."

She leaned against him. "Is that why you are here?"

He put his arm around her. "I'm angry with our leaders. God warned them not to sign a covenant with any people. The Lord already promised us the victory, but our leaders have taken that victory from us."

Kamon looked over the campsite. "Will it matter so much?"

"These people will always be an open sore.

Kamon shrugged. "The wound will heal."

"These nations give their all to their gods, even killing their children for their pleasure. We don't even consult our God. The heathens put us to shame." Ethan squatted beside her. "Their evil affects the way they view everything. They treat their women like animals. Look at the harlot's family."

Kamon wrapped her cloak around her tightly, against the chilling evening air. "I've seen the women getting water and firewood. The mother seems beaten and broken."

Ethan nodded. "The harlot listens to the Law. Watch her face. She seeks to know God. Salmon is drawn to tell her of our God." He reached to hold Kamon's hand.

"Don't let him go alone. I don't want him swept into their evil."

Ethan squeezed her hand. "I already told him. Her father hasn't even submitted to circumcision. We saved them from death. Circumcision should be a minor thing."

Kamon sighed. "If they mar their women, cutting off their own flesh should be easy. They don't help with fighting."

Ethan wrapped his arms around her. "Would you trust them in battle beside me?"

Kamon shook her head and looked into his face. "If Joshua can be deceived by these cities, Salmon can be deceived by this woman. She may be searching for God in a man who gives security. Warn Salmon not to be that man."

Ethan nodded. "I have. I don't understand Joshua. I respected him. He told of seeing God in person, not once but several times. But even he was deceived. How can anyone know?"

Kamon stepped away from Ethan. "An experience *of* God doesn't guarantee communion *with* God. Deception works because we don't really believe what God says. Joshua was deceived because he wanted to help the strangers. So did the rest of the elders. The strangers looked needy. Who doesn't want to help people? He didn't want to obey. Only later, when we see the results, do we see it for the disobedience it is."

When the other elders and leaders left the Tent of Meeting, Joshua fell on his face before the Ark. "Why can't I lead like Moses? Why didn't I seek Your counsel? What have I done to Your people by keeping a people alive who will cause them to forsake Your Word?"

After he had poured out his heart to God, he stayed on the ground and waited.

The room was silent.

Would God not speak to him again?

He trembled.

He must know what God desired.

He strained to listen.

And waited.

A beam of light slipped through the door's slit and shone through the cherubim's wings as they spread over the Ark of the Covenant.

Joshua remembered the glory they had seen in the desert. God had shown His glory in the clouds, and the earth hadn't been able to contain it. His glory commanded worship, submission, praise.

And God's glory was so much more than the gold sparkling on the Ark.

After Joshua's earlier frantic questioning, his breathing returned to normal.

The Lord was still present. His glory was here. He had not forsaken them.

He settled his heart to hear the Lord's Words.

"I am with you."

It was enough.

Joshua rose, dusted himself off, and returned to his tent.

Dorona helped take off his cloak. "Are you hungry?"

Joshua shook his head.

"I'll make you tea."

Joshua slouched by the embers, staring ahead. He cupped his hands around the vessel. Steam rose around his fingers. "Why didn't I seek God's counsel?"

"You're not the only one who signed the contract."

"But I was their leader. I persuaded the others."

Dorona persisted. "Did you repent?"

At his nod, she patted his leg. "Then it is done."

Joshua ran his fingers through his hair. "But the people will suffer the consequences."

"What did God tell you?"

Joshua sighed. "That He is with me."

"Then that is enough."

CHAPTER 10

Ethan waited outside the Tent of Meeting. He kicked at a rock wedged in the dirt by the entrance. He had been home several days now. His anger had cooled. There was nothing for him to do but move forward. But before he could move forward, he must apologize to Joshua. He waited, rubbing his sweaty hands down his cloak.

"Shalom."

Ethan raised his head at the greeting. "Joshua, be at peace." He looked at the ground again and swallowed. He raised his head and met Joshua's gaze. "I shouldn't have questioned your leadership."

Joshua squeezed his shoulder. "No, you were right. I don't know why I can't be like Moses and seek God first."

Ethan was relieved that Joshua understood. He also must speak to Joshua about another matter. He hesitated. He didn't want to question his leadership, but... "There's another problem ... talking about seeking God ..." He let out the breath he was holding. "The harlot's family ..."

Joshua nodded. "They don't submit to circumcision."

Strangers who lived with them were not required to be circumcised. Without circumcision, they couldn't participate in the Passover sacrifice, but they could still live outside of camp. But with the harlot's family, it wasn't just circumcision. Ethan shook his head. "They rebel against God and disdain His Law."

Joshua pointed inside the Tent of Meeting. Everyone else had left. Joshua settled against the cushions. "Should we have saved them?"

Ethan felt attacked. Was Joshua questioning his judgment? Or just saying out loud what Ethan had already asked himself? He clenched his fists. Had he shown mercy or weakness in sparing the harlot?

Against his doubts, he defended himself. "The harlot has a different spirit. She searches after God."

Joshua fingered his sheath. "Are those your words, or Salmon's?"

Ethan considered. "Salmon sees more than I, but I do see her desire to know God. You would have to be blind not to see it."

Joshua brushed the comment aside. "I fear her family may fall under God's judgment."

Ethan looked out the opening of the tent. "Must we wait until they harm someone before we do something? I want my family safe."

Joshua loosened his belt. "How are any of us safe? The Lord's presence hinders evil. His Word makes their actions uncomfortable." He paused. "But it may not change them."

Ethan squatted beside Joshua. He couldn't just wait for something wrong to happen. "I'll see if they are ready for circumcision."

Joshua nodded. "If they are not, we must judge them. God can make them either run to Him or run from Him."

Salmon sat before his campfire sharpening his knife. He needed to concentrate, he had already nicked his finger from allowing his thoughts to wander. How could he have signed the contract with Gibeon? He had felt uneasy, but had followed the others. He must think and not be a follower. Nicking his finger again, he sucked on it to stop the blood. This wasn't a task he should do without concentrating. He pushed his whetstone away from him in disgust.

"Shalom."

He looked up. "Be at peace, Ethan. You spared me from more bloodshed."

Ethan laughed and gestured to his knife. "It's not a task for the faint-hearted."

Salmon nodded as he put away his knife. "I can't keep my mind on it. You're just the excuse I needed before I really did some damage. What do you need?"

Ethan squatted beside him. "Come with me to the harlot's campsite. They don't assimilate with our people."

Salmon pulled his cloak over his tunic and tightened his belt. "Is it because they don't want to, or we won't let them?"

They began walking to the camp's boundary. "Thought maybe you could help me figure that out. Remember how they responded when we told them of their need to be circumcised?"

"Not all strangers have been circumcised."

Ethan nodded. "But it's just one more sign of their open rebellion."

"So what do you hope to accomplish by this 'visit'?"

Ethan lowered his voice as they reached the path to the harlot's campsite. "Wisdom."

"Is that why you've brought me?" Salmon chuckled.

"My wife told me to."

Salmon laughed. "Sounds like you already have wisdom."

They arrived, but the men did not acknowledge them.

Ethan looked at Salmon as if to tell him, "Didn't I tell you?"

Salmon nodded to the men. "Shalom."

They ignored him.

Salmon squatted down by the embers from their noon meal. Even as he did, the harlot came from the tent.

She bowed to both of them, surprised by their presence.

"Be at peace." Salmon didn't know what else to say. The men continued to act like he didn't exist. He could ignore them too. "Have you everything you need?"

The harlot looked for her brother or father to answer. When they didn't, she nodded.

Salmon turned and watched the men. He would speak as if they were interested. "We have spoken about the need for circumcision..." He didn't stand but made himself comfortable, as if he had been invited. He picked up a piece of wood by the fire and took out his dagger. He started shaving off the bark. "I used to think our rules were restrictive." He took a handful of the shredded bark and threw it into the embers.

Flames flared up.

He watched it for a moment before he went back to shaving off pieces. He glanced at Ethan.

Ethan had squatted behind the men, in Salmon's line of view.

Salmon gave a half-smile. If he had trouble, Ethan was positioned to help.

Salmon continued as if the men were listening. "I watched how other nations did things. It was tempting to want what they had. They did what they wanted. But as we conquered them, I learned our rules give us safety. Even our rules for sanitation. We can't leave our waste in our campsites!" He chuckled and glanced at the men.

Their faces registered nothing.

He shrugged and continued. He knew they heard. "But our camp, with so many people, doesn't have the filth those cities had. Their streets were filled with dung." He shrugged. "I can't tell you the reasons behind all the rules. But I know the God Who created us knows best what we need. As His people, I submit to Him to be happy." He had shaved the wood into kindling. He piled the kindling by the stone circle.

He stood. "We've come at a poor time." He waited a moment. It was like talking to a stick. How could he speak to their complaints when they didn't say a word? Then he remembered seeing only the harlot at the reading of the Law. He had looked for her and her family. Her family came initially, but now did not. "By your refusal to hear the Words of our God, you refuse to know Him. That is unfortunate." He shook his head. "Our leaders must discuss what must be done to assist you." He nodded to Ethan.

They walked out of camp and toward the stream.

Ethan shook his head. "You did not confront, but you allowed them to accept or decline with grace. I felt like punching them. They submit to no one."

Salmon shrugged. He had reached the water and knelt to drink. The water was cold. He wiped his mouth with the back of his hand. "They've lived with no rules. It would be hard to accept so many rules."

Ethan stood after drinking. "We did."

Salmon looked at their campsite. "We saw God deliver us from Egypt while we were young. We were fed by God's own Hand in the desert. We have no excuse not to follow His Laws."

Ethan shook his fist in their direction. "They were delivered from destruction! No one who was delivered like they were has any right to decide what rules they should follow. They should be begging to serve, not ignoring us as if we were dung at their feet."

As he was speaking, the harlot came down the path toward them. This wasn't the time of day when the other women came for water.

Salmon had been ready to return to camp, but now he stayed. Did she come now so other women wouldn't bother her?

When she reached the water, she was out of breath. "I must apologize for my family. They don't know your God."

Salmon nodded.

"I liked what you said about your God's rules. They give me security. They make me feel safe." She looked down the path she had come on, as if she watching for someone.

Salmon picked up a stone and skipped it across the rapids of the stream. It jumped almost to the other side. "Why does it make you feel safe?"

She seemed flustered now when he looked at her. She had watched him speak, but now she kept her face down, her hood over her face. "I don't have to fight evil alone."

What evil did she fight? "Why?"

She bent to fill her vessel with water. "Your God's Laws have consequences. You know what your God expects and what will happen if you don't obey. In our city, our gods and rulers changed laws anytime they wanted. I could never please them."

Salmon skipped another stone. Although the consequences seemed hard, their laws did give stability. But what evil was she speaking of? He looked at Ethan.

Ethan nodded up the path toward their people, as if he couldn't wait to return.

Salmon knew this would keep them longer, but he must ask, "Do our people bother you when you get water?" He gestured to her vessel. It wasn't the normal time to get water. Was she afraid to come when the other women did?

She seemed embarrassed. She shook her head, finally looking at him.

Salmon held her gaze. He saw fear in her eyes. "What are you afraid of?"

She shook her head and lowered her face.

Salmon must know what caused her fear. He squatted down to look directly at her. "Do you fear our God?"

She shook her head. "I could never fear your God. What I receive from your God is what I deserve." The harlot bit her lip. She picked up her vessel. "My family. They need this water ... I must go." She turned to leave.

In two quick strides, Salmon stood in her way. "What do you fear?"

She shook her head and stepped to go around him.

Salmon grabbed her arm.

He felt her tremble under his touch. Embarrassed he had been so bold as to touch her, yet knowing she would fly like a bird if he let her go, he released her arm and stepped back. Something in her face made him to ask, "Is someone harming you?"

She darted a look at him before lowering it quickly. She hurried past him. When she walked beyond his reach, she turned back. "The gold you gave me?"

Salmon had watched her with unease. How could he allow her to be in danger? Had the gold caused her problems? He remembered her reprimand when he had given the beggar the money. "Yes?"

"Your priest...told me you paid for it. Thank you."

Had someone tried to steal it from her? "It doesn't bring you harm, does it?" He studied her face. He was struck by her beauty, even with one side of her face so marred by scarring.

She readjusted the water. "No. Your God has refined me, like the gold."

Salmon smiled. "Then it has fulfilled its purpose." He stepped forward. When he saw her eyes flicker back down the path as if she would run, he stopped. "What's your name?"

The harlot shook her head. "Men only use my name for their advantage."

Salmon's smile faded. He had meant it as an innocent question. He could imagine what she had suffered. He was angry with what men had done to her. "Our people call you the 'harlot.'"

She swallowed and looked back at her tent.

He thought that she might run again. He weighed his words. "I'd like to correct them. Our God has called us by name. He already knows your name." He continued to meet her gaze.

She hesitated, shifting her hands on her vessel. "Rahab." And then she disappeared down the path.

Salmon watched her go, but he repeated the name in his mind.

When she was out of sight, Ethan coughed.

Salmon had forgotten Ethan was there. He cleared his throat and smiled weakly. He had been forward with the woman. He had wanted to protect her.

Ethan nodded toward her campsite. "She fears her family."

Salmon face hardened. He didn't like to think her family was what she feared. "What makes you think so?"

Ethan followed his look down the path to their campsite. "When we spied out her city, she wasn't skittish or fearful. She was confident, even courageous against the general. Remember how she confronted him?

"But here in camp, did you see how she watched her father? She sought his permission even to speak. She won't stand against her father because it would bring harm to her mother."

"The fresh bruises on her face?" Salmon had noticed them and wondered about them. The older woman had skirted around the campsite like a frightened dove. When he had glanced at her, he'd had to conceal his surprise at her face. They may not be worshipping their gods, but they continued to treat their women as an object to take out their anger on.

Ethan nodded.

Salmon continued, "In the desert, I watched an eagle's nest in the crag of a cliff. One beak rose above the edge of the nest to be fed. A day later, I saw two beaks. After a few weeks, I only saw one beak. I wondered what had happened to the second baby eagle.

"I climbed closer to the nest and found one of the fledglings outside the nest dead. Its neck had been pecked; then it had been pushed from the nest. It wasn't jabbed by the parents' big beaks."

Ethan hesitated, "You mean, the other fledgling did it?"

Salmon nodded. "The stronger baby kept it from eating. The parents stopped feeding it when it stopped begging." He shook his head. "We may never know what happens within another family's nest."

Ethan touched his dagger. "What about the fatal wound? Do we wait until there is one?"

Salmon looked down the path where Rahab had gone. "The fledgling is hungry and still begs. We can hope."

Joshua summoned the kings of Gibeon, Chephirah, Beeroth and Kiriath-jearim to the Tent of Meeting.

They entered and bowed low.

Joshua clenched his fists at his sides. "Why did you deceive us?"

The kings fell on their faces before him and the elders. "We heard how great your God is. You were destroying everyone. We feared for our lives."

Joshua breathed deeply, tempted to crush their fingers under his foot. He was angry at them for deceiving him, but angrier at himself for being deceived. How could he fix this mess?

"Do what you want with us. We will serve you."

Joshua paced before the elders and leaders.

Caleb stepped forward. "We have two and a half tribes that don't have their families with them. They must fight as well as fixing their own food and carrying their own water. Have these people serve them, so we can finish conquering the land."

Hezron spoke from the back of the men. "Because of their deception, can we trust them not to run to our enemies and tell our plans?"

Eleazar coughed. "In Moses's law, God directed a slave who served for life to have his ear pierce with an awl. If we do that to these men, they will be recognized by everyone who sees them."

Assents were heard and a consensus reached.

Eleazar added, "In order for them to live in our campsite, they must be circumcised."

Joshua nodded. Addressing the kings, he asked, "Would you agree to be circumcised? And have an awl pounded in your ear?"

The kings raised their heads. Gibeon's king spoke for all of them. "Whatever is good in your eyes, we will do."

Joshua declared, "It's been decided. You will haul water and cut wood. You will serve for life. Begin at once to pound the awl through your ears and be circumcised."

The first time Mikar had entered the desert people's campsite was to be treated as an honored diplomat from a far country. His deception had paid well. His city was saved. Now as Mikar attended the king of Gibeon from the camp of the Israelites, he felt the demands of these people as a heavy weight.

He had been the chief advisor to the king of Gibeon. He lived like a king without the accountability. But power could be deceptive. When Mikar advised the king, he held control over him. He thrived with that power. Although appearing to cater to the king's whims, Mikar didn't always think first of the king's best. Wouldn't the king be well cared, if his advisor lived well too? Wasn't his house the largest in the kingdom, other than the king's. Because he selected the king's servants, hadn't he also acquired the best for his own use? And controlled their loyalties? Because of his skills in negotiating, the king trusted him in all decision making. And so, Mikar had ruled the city behind the scenes.

Now as he watched his own king grovel on the ground before these desert leaders, he was relieved his position was not so obvious. He would bow to no man. Oh, he would give the appearance of servitude and humility, just like he had to his own king, but appearances are deceptive, just like power.

He would use servitude to rise again, not as king of Gibeon's right-hand man, for that would make him nothing more than a slave in this new situation. But he would rise as an advisor to this new people. Wouldn't they need to know how to control his city they now held as servants?

But in the process, he would find those still loyal to the old ways, and train them to be ready for his uprising. He would ultimately be king himself.

As he evaluated this people from the desert, Mikar straightened his shoulders and stood taller. This people ruled by elders. He could easily sway a group. Wasn't that like mob rule?

But what concerned him most was the absence of temple worship. Not that he believed the gods could be appeased. Wasn't he like a god, and didn't he, like the gods, delight in the dancing, drink, and sacrifice? He could never get enough. His appetite was unquenchable. He thought over the past sacrifices. He must have more.

Yet even as he considered the sacrifices, he realized these people knew not how to sacrifice with such pleasure. They had no gods of stone that would look upon their sacrifice with pleasure.

This God seemed to want His people, not to worship for their own pleasure but for His own. What a selfish God they had! Demanding His own pleasure above His people's!

The sliver of light that pierced into Mikar's heart to show him the God Who demanded him to change was squelched by his own darkness.

He shook his head.

And now his rulers had consented to circumcision. That would greatly influence appeasing their gods in sacrifice. He would find a way to avoid circumcision. He, like the gods, depended upon his function and enjoyment. There were ways to serve without abandoning his enjoyment. He would find them.

He followed the group of kings from the surrounding cities as they left the camp of the people. They were discussing ways to ensure proper fulfillment of their requirements: the awl through their ears and circumcision.

He fell behind them as he continued his own plans of usurping control. He noticed a group of the tents separate from the others. He gestured to them. "Why are they set apart from your people?"

Hezron, who led them from their campsite, explained, "That's the harlot's camp."

Mikar stopped walking. Perhaps these people weren't what they seemed. If they sanctioned a harlot, maybe not in camp, but on the outside of camp, maybe their laws weren't as restrictive as he thought. "The harlot's camp?"

Hezron hesitated, "We saved them from Jericho. They don't mingle with our people."

Mikar studied their camp. He noticed the woman working around the campfire. She was beautiful. "But they are allowed to live?"

Hezron shrugged. "For now."

Mikar craned to study the harlot.

She glanced up and saw him staring.

He smiled. She was beautiful, but marred from temple use. He raised his eyebrows.

Her face flushed, and she looked down quickly.

Mikar nodded and smiled. Another plan formed in his mind.

He had gained power by counseling his king. By deception, he had saved their lives, advising submission to Joshua's whims. Wasn't servitude better than death?

But circumcision? Mikar would not submit. He would not mar his body for this God. That was for women and children.

When Mikar returned to his city after the kings consented to Joshua's demands, he sent a messenger to Jerusalem demanding Sudru, his brother, to visit. He paced his chamber waiting, planning, and watching. When he arrived, Mikar embraced him. "You came."

Sudru shrugged. "You told me to."

Mikar unfastened his dagger and sheath from his waist and threw them onto his cushions as he sat down.

Sudru watched out the window. "The city is quiet."

"The men heal from surgery."

Sudru raised one eyebrow. "All the men?"

Mikar shrugged. "Surgery or death."

Sudru poured himself a drink and sipped from the vessel. "But not you?"

Mikar removed his dagger from its sheath and ran his finger over the sharpened blade. "I hid."

Sudru laughed. "What would make Gibeon's mightiest man hide?"

Mikar stopped moving his finger and glared at Sudru.

Sudru's smile vanished.

Mikar spat out the next words as if he could spit out the people who caused his servitude, "See my ear?"

Sudru gasped. "You are their servants?"

The silence in the room only magnified the scorn of Mikar.

Sudru studied his brother. "You bow to no man. What happened?"

"Look at all the mighty men of Jericho. They are gone. The wealth of Ai is no more. These people burn through this country like an unquenchable fire, leaving nothing when they are done. What city was next in their path?"

Sudru shrugged. "So why are you alive?" He settled beside Mikar on the cushions.

"We deceived them."

"How could you deceive this God?

Mikar suppressed a smile. "They did not consult their God."

"But they will keep their word?"

"They are men of integrity."

Sudru laughed. "That is a rare find around here. Perhaps..."

Mikar gripped his dagger to hold it more securely. "It is because they are men of integrity we are saved. In spite of what their God wanted."

Sudru stood once again and paced. "What did their God require?"

"Circumcision."

Sudru gulped. "No wonder the city is quiet. How will you please the gods at the temples?"

Mikar shook his head. "There will be no more sacrifices, except to their God."

"If Jerusalem did that, the people would riot."

They fell silent.

Sudru finally broke it. "Why aren't you circumcised?"

Mikar smiled, but it did not reach his eyes. "If I can deceive them once, I can again."

Sudru smiled. "You are the schemer." He sipped from his vessel. Walking to the window, he turned back. "How would you protect my city?"

Mikar concentrated on the edge of his dagger. He looked up. "I'm done planning for cities. I plan for myself."

"What about family?"

"Family? I have no need for family." Mikar raised his dagger and threw it at his brother.

The dagger landed with a thud behind Sudru's head in the wall.

Sudru's eyes widened. "You missed." He stepped toward Mikar. "Have you ever missed?"

Mikar shrugged. "When I choose." He pulled another knife from his tunic's pocket. "Perhaps I should plan your death before your destruction comes."

Sudru slid his hand up and down his cloak's pocket. "How did you get my dagger? You would kill me in your own house?"

Mikar repositioned his grip and smiled. "How often have I told you, don't trust anyone? It pays not to get too close to any one, Sudru. As to my house ... what house? I'm a servant now; I own nothing." Mikar aimed his knife at Sudru.

Sudru shifted toward the door.

"Leaving ... so soon?"

Sudru stopped shuffling. "You always planned well."

Mikar's back was to him now. He laughed. Standing he faced Sudru. "Ready for my plan?"

Sudru nodded. But he still glanced at the door.

"Tell your king defeat is sure. This God gets what He wants. But," he paused to make sure Sudru was listening, "the people are not as strong as they think. Their leader asks others to tell him what to do. Their elders follow an old priest. Their youth are anxious to finish fighting and to compromise."

Sudru stepped toward Mikar. "What can Jerusalem do?"

Mikar shrugged. "Think of something."

Sudru stepped closer. "What can I do?"

Mikar turned his back on Sudru. "I figured out what to do when everyone else submitted to circumcision."

"Are you suggesting that I, the general of Jerusalem's army, hide in the hills?" Sudru almost laughed.

Mikar turned back to glare at him. "How badly do you want to live?"

CHAPTER 11

After leaving Mikar's house, Sudru could not beat his horse into running fast enough to Jerusalem. When he reached its gates, he commanded the guards to open them. How long could their city exist without opening its gates for its people to work their fields and care for their flocks outside their walls? How long could they forestall the coming destruction from a people that believed in one God Who demanded total surrender?

After entering the city streets, he slowed his horse to adjust to the crowded street traffic. When he arrived at the palace, he felt for his dagger, now back in his hidden pocket, and entered the king's chamber. He bowed before the king.

"What have you learned about Gibeon?"

"Gibeon will not be destroyed."

King Adoni-zedek stood. "They had victory over these people who cover the mountains?"

Sudru shook his head. "They deceived them. They were promised life for their service. They are even now healing from circumcision."

The king stood before him. "Gibeon did not battle?"

"No."

"All the men were circumcised?"

"Yes."

"What of their mighty men?"

"Everyone will serve as slaves."

"Without a fight?"

Sudru nodded.

King Adoni-zedek paced. He held his fists clenched tightly at his side. "What right does Gibeon have to live?"

Sudru shrugged.

"We will fight Gibeon."

"But what of their mighty men?"

The king stopped his pacing and smiled at Sudru. "Didn't you say, 'all were circumcised'? They must heal from their discomfort."

Sudru smiled.

The king turned to a messenger. "Contact the kings of Hebron, Jarmuth, Lachish and Eglon. Tell them we march in two days against Gibeon. We will show them what happens when they do not fight against foreigners who do not worship our gods."

Mikar woke the king of Gibeon in the night. "Oh King armies of the hill countries advance against us. Before morning, we will be surrounded with no escape."

The king of Gibeon sat, now fully awake. "What countries?"

"Jerusalem, Hebron, Jarmuth, Lachish, and Eglon."

The king lay against his cushions, the pain of moving evident on his face. "Send a messenger to the camp of Gilgal. Tell Joshua they must save their servants, lest we perish."

Mikar nodded. "But will their God fight for us?"

The king glanced at his armor hanging on the wall. He thought about his mighty men, still healing from surgery. "He will have to."

Joshua had watched the stars come out for the night. The Lord was leading this people. They were conquering the inhabitants of the land. He could not hurry it along.

He returned to his tent and blew out the candle. The smoke lingered in the air as he remembered the fire by night that led the people through the desert.

Before, the people were content with food, water, and shelter. Now, they needed so many things. They were getting restless.

Tonight, Dorona had asked him how long before they settled and finished fighting. He wondered too.

He lay beside Dorona on their pallet. He heard her deep breathing. Some of his men were separated from their families, with the barest of necessities, so they could travel lightly and quickly. But families separated created problems. Another reason why he would like this mission finished.

He shut his eyes, wishing it was just as easy to close his thoughts to all the questions. Before he drifted into sleep, he heard his name.

He rose on his elbow. "Yes?"

"It's Ethan."

Joshua rose from his pallet and tied his cloak around him, stepping outside his tent.

"A messenger from Gibeon just arrived. Five kings of the hill country of the Amorites are marching against them to surround their city. Their men are still healing from circumcision. They beg our protection."

Joshua ran his fingers through his hair. "Sound the battle cry. We will march our men through the night to meet them in the morning. We will only move the soldiers, not the main camp."

Ethan nodded.

Even as Joshua returned to dress inside his tent, he heard the Lord, "Do not fear. I have given them into your hands. Not one shall stand before you."

Joshua heard the trumpet blow. He hugged Dorona and marched away in the middle of the night.

CHAPTER 12

Adoni-zedek, king of Jerusalem, surveyed the plains covered in mist. His general, Sudru, stood beside him. His warriors stood behind him ready to fight. He turned to see the other kings, fanned over the valley with their armies. Who could stand against them?

He sounded the battle call and charged toward Gibeon.

But before they reached Gibeon's walls, an army rose out of the fog in the valley and blocked them.

Overcoming his surprise, he continued his advance, raised his sword and attacked.

Swords clashed.

Men fell.

They battled to gain Gibeon's gates.

Their enemy was short, but agile and fast. They blocked their way on every side.

The sun tried to shine that morning, but the cloud hung heavy and thick. The sky grew darker as the morning continued. A wind picked up that swept through the valley like a giant broom scattering sand. Then the wind suddenly stopped. The king paused in the calmness. It was a quietness that brought uncertainty, like a pause before danger. He looked at the sky. The clouds were black, allowing no light to filter through them. As he studied them, hail the size of a man's fist, began to fall. He raised his shield and bent his head down.

One hailstone hit Adoni-zedek's shin. His leg buckled and he fell. He crouched under his shield for protection. Hail pelting his shield made his head ring. How could they fight in this?

His men turned to flee.

He tried to stand, but stumbled. "Stand firm. Fight."

One warrior, running from the fight, answered, "I'll fight any man. But I won't fight a God Who rains boulders from heaven."

Adoni-zedek raised his shield to see the battle. His men lay scattered, not from wounds made by swords, but from hail sent by this God!

He waited alone. His army had already fled. He stood, his shield raised over his head. He limped up the mountainside to hide.

Halfway up the hill, he spied a bush. Was that an opening behind it? He half limped, half dragged himself until he reached the bush. There was a hole big enough for him to crawl through.

He took one final look around the mountain. The battle had moved beyond where he could see. He squatted and pushed the branches away. Squeezing through the opening, he entered the darkness, tugging his shield behind him. It scraped the walls as he pulled it in, causing dirt to fall partly over the entrance of the hole. It would help hide him, as long as the dirt didn't fill the hole and bury him alive.

The cave was cooler. He leaned against the stone wall and breathed deeply from his climb. He drank from his waterskin, allowing the water to drip down his throat, saving as much water as he could for later.

He could relax here. He was away from the hail. This was no battle against mere man. This was a battle against God. How could a man kill God?

After settling, he listened. He could hear breathing that was not his own. He wasn't alone. He drew his dagger and strained his eyes to see in the dark. "Who's there?"

"You are Adoni-zedek, King of Jerusalem." The man whispered.

"Who are you?" Adoni-zedek turned toward the voice.

"Hoham, King of Hebron." He sighed.

Another voice from deeper in the cave startled Adoni-zedek. "I am Piram, King of Jarmuth."

If the kings had found the cave so easily, were they safe from the desert people?

Light pierced the cave's opening as the bush was pushed away and another crawled in, taking precautions, and moving far within the cave.

Adoni-zedek allowed him to gain his breath before asking, "Japhia, King of Lachish?"

The man started, but then swallowed slowly. "Yes, your voice tells me you are Adoni-zedek, King of Jerusalem."

"Yes." Adoni-zedek thought of leaving the cave. It couldn't be so safe, if four hid within. He crawled to the cave's mouth. The clouds had lifted and the fog had risen. But it was still hailing.

He looked over the edge of the path. The battle had moved away. Only the dead or wounded remained that he could see.

There was nowhere else to hide.

He crawled back to rest his head against the wall.

He stretched his leg and felt where the hail had gashed his shin. Feeling blood, he groped in the dark to tear off a strip of his tunic, wrap it around the wound, and tie it securely.

He dug some honey dipped figs from his pocket and chewed them, savoring each one.

He would wait to leave.

Water dripped from the bush by the cave's opening. He could still hear the hail hitting the bush and the ground outside the doorway.

Another person crawled into the cave.

Adoni-zedek squinted to see his form. He was a big man. Only one could fill that form. "Debir, is that you?"

"Adoni-zedek, you are here as well?"

Adoni-zedek whispered, "We are all here. The cave must be an obvious hiding place. Your men, did they hold them?"

"Didn't have a chance. I arrived from Eglon only to watch my men fall to their death."

There was silence then.

He didn't hear when the hail stopped, nor feel the sun when it dried the storm's drops. He felt alone.

This God wanted them destroyed.

Adoni-zedek had challenged God to fight, as if he could fight a God and win.

He wrapped his cloak around him more tightly, not for protection from the dampness of the cave, but for security from his thoughts.

Another man entered the cave, carrying a torch. "What have we here?"

Adoni-zedek fingered his dagger, ready to throw it.

Another entered. "Hezron, the battle rages farther south."

Hezron shined his torch into the dark corners of the cave. "It's a shame to leave the battle to guard these—block off any escape. We'll deal with them when the battle is done."

They backed out of the cave.

Adoni-zedek heard them roll boulders over his only escape. He watched the light from the cave's entrance disappear, like being buried alive.

He crawled toward the back, feeling the wall and dragging his legs.

"Don't bother looking." Piram said. "The cave ends where I sit. There is no other way out."

"Are we buried alive?" Japhia asked, his voice broke as he spoke.

Adoni-zedek crawled back toward the opening. "Their God cannot win." He pushed at the boulders in the opening. Even if all of them heaved with all their might, the cave was closed like a tomb.

Japhia said, "Maybe if we called out to Molish, he would spare our lives."

Adoni-zedek smiled in the darkness. He knew where Debir, king of Eglon, sat. He had not heard him move. Adoni-zedek crawled to him. If anyone could guarantee fertility from the gods, Debir could. He disrobed and prepared to make the gods happy.

They could not tell when the sun set. For there was no light at all, only five kings in their own darkness, worshipping themselves as gods, and denying the God Who would soon show justice.

Sudru had fought beside the King of Jerusalem. His men, startled by the desert people's presence, had merely defended themselves. The fog settled over them, hindering visibility beyond a sword's thrust in front of them. Battle sounds were muffled to the point he wondered if he was by himself. Or had the battle stopped? Sudru couldn't tell.

Out of the fog came a soldier, his sword extended.

Before Sudru could raise his sword to defend himself, the soldier sliced through his armor.

Sudru felt the stab of pain as the sword entered his trunk and sliced upward. He doubled over in agony, his sword falling from his hand.

The soldier moved on.

Sudru felt the blood leave his body as he crawled on hands and knees under the cover of fog. He left his shield in the dirt. It's weight too heavy to drag. He crawled over men, dead or wounded, scattered over the ground. His wound leaked a trail of blood.

Others called for help, water, mercy or just groaned for death to come soon.

He ignored their pleas as he sought to hide.

He had scoffed at Mikar's words, "I hid and I'm still alive." Now those words were what Sudru would live by. Somewhere to hide.

He moved from the battle.

When he heard voices, he hurried to find concealment, more than what the fog could offer.

The voices seemed closer in the fog.

He felt bark and knew he had reached a tree. He was sweating, his breathing coming in great gasps. He leaned against the trunk and gasped when he fell into it.

The tree had been struck by lightning years ago, leaving a hollow base.

He squeezed further into it. The opening was barely big enough for him to enter, but once inside formed an area large enough for him to sit with his knees cramped against his chest.

He stilled his breathing, leaning against the inside of the trunk, and closed his eyes. He could stay here as long as he needed. He was safe.

The voices passed by him.

He went unnoticed.

He sipped from his waterskin to wet his dry lips.

Crawling had taxed him. He felt his wound and pulled his hand away sticky and gritty.

The quietness inside the trunk of the tree was like a hollow jar, sealing any noise of battle away from him. Fighting seemed distant, unreal.

His thoughts floated and swirled.

He was safe....

Suddenly he was jolted alert as the tree shuddered.

The wind shook the tree as if it would pluck it out by its roots and toss it.

Something crashed into the tree. Were they attacking the tree? He peered out the opening.

The fog had been replaced with darkness. Ice chunks, as big as his fist, hit the ground outside. They pelted the tree. How can anyone run from a God Who controls what falls from the sky?

He sighed as the pain in his side returned.

What had made him think he could fight against God and win?

Israel had marched through the night, over narrow pathways, dark, swampy undergrowth, and high hills. As they neared their destination, no moon was visible. Clouds covered its light. They had arrived to confront the cities of the north who threatened Gibeon.

The sun tried to rise, but its shine was obscured by the clouds.

Joshua's men prepared for battle, refilling their waterskins, adjusting their sheaths, and eating their flatbread standing.

Joshua stopped before a running stream to refill his waterskin.

Ethan knelt beside him. He pointed at the water, tightening the string on his waterskin. "The water is stirred above our men. See how it flows muddy? Others must be upstream."

Joshua nodded. "Tell the men to be quiet."

The men were tired and hungry. They had no time to make flat bread for their journey. The sparse fruit and nuts they had found in vineyards and orchards along the way would not sustain their strength for a long battle. Would his men have the strength to fight?

He called Salmon and Ethan to his side. They had spied out the city and its surroundings before the contract with Gibeon had been recognized. "What can you tell me about a plan?"

Salmon raised his eyebrows and took a deep breath. "The hillsides around the city could offer our archers and sling throwers great cover, if the fog wasn't so thick that they can't see the valley..." His voice trailed off as he looked down the streambed.

Joshua followed his glance and could only see a few feet in front of him. He nodded.

Ethan shrugged. "If we'd just present a unified front line around the base of the city's gate, they would not see us. The surprise would be great."

Salmon nodded. "For all of us."

Joshua laughed, but without humor. "Surprise it is then. Any other considerations that you can remember from the terrain?"

Ethan thought for a moment before adding, "There are many caves in the hillsides, but with the fog we shouldn't need to consider hidden archers ... maybe when the fog lifts, we could use them to conceal our own."

Joshua nodded. "Form a barrier along the north-facing side of the city of Gibeon. Stretch out our line to keep anyone from reaching our flank. Emphasize quietness. While this fog muffles noise, it also distorts the location of the sound. Tell them to be ready."

Ethan and Salmon nodded and left to issue the command.

Then Salmon rejoined his men to organize them in their respective place in the line.

Joshua inspected the line, walking the distance from its left flank to its right. He nodded to the leaders as he passed them. Only seeing them as they appeared out of the fog by his feet. They were a somber group, quiet and waiting. He seemed always to be waiting. That was the hardest part of any battle. During the action of battle, he had only to react; waiting gave him too much time to think and second guess and wonder if he had considered everything. That was when he had to remind himself what God had already told him, "I am with you." He nodded. He knew it. He believed it. He fingered the hilt of his sword.

He strode back to his position in the middle of the line-up and had just taken a good, deep breath, when out of the fog the enemy appeared. Before he could sound the battle cry, he heard their yell for attack. One soldier came at him. He had only enough time to swing his sword in defense, before the battle consumed him. He focused on the next man. And the next.

Time seemed to stand still, as one soldier after another attacked through the fog.

The wind picked up, and it was all he could do to stand straight and remain fighting.

The wind didn't last long.

Suddenly the stillness came again.

Joshua paused between fighting to look at the sky. It was thick with dark clouds hanging low over the ground. That moment of quietness from the wind gave him a feeling of something ominous yet to come.

Lightning bolted through the sky. In that brief glare of light, Joshua saw the battlefield already littered with men.

Thunder rolled, sending tremors across the ground.

Then the hail fell.

It was unlike any hail he had ever seen. Joshua had been a young man during the plague of hail in Egypt. But even those hailstones could not compare to these. These were boulders falling from the sky.

Joshua raised his shield to protect his head.

The battle between the armies had stopped.

Everyone raised their shields for protection against the God of the sky.

The opposing army ran, unwilling to fight against such a God.

Joshua laughed. "If God fights for us, who could be against us?"

Beside him, Ethan struck a soldier trying to escape the hail. He finished another who had tripped on his own sword.

"Joshua!" Salmon ran to him, panting. "Not one of our men has been hit with the hailstones."

Joshua looked around him. "God not only slays our enemies, but also protects His own."

Salmon pointed toward the cliffs where the soldiers had hidden. "The enemy is fleeing. We won't be able to destroy them all before the sun goes down, and we can't chase them into the night."

Under the cloud cover, the day had passed quickly. When darkness came, they would have to stop. "We must fight until we can fight no more, whether our strength fails or the sun sets."

Salmon slowed to walk with Joshua while he caught his breath. "Then I'll need God's strength."

Joshua nodded. His men had found strength to fight all day. "Remember how Moses told us that God bore us on eagles' wings and brought us to Himself in Egypt? He has done the same today."

Salmon laughed. "I could use those wings now, for the day has been long."

Joshua nodded. "The night longer."

Salmon looked to the western sky, where the sun was shining through the dark clouds before it dipped behind the mountains. "Then He must stop the sun, for we must see."

Salmon began to run again to catch up with his men.

After Salmon left, Joshua looked again at the sky. If the sun would stay a little longer, his men could find their enemy hiding in the hills.

Would God hear such a request? God had sent the hail when his men had no strength to fight. Didn't God want these people destroyed? He would ask.

Joshua knelt on the battleground. He raised his face to the sky. "O sun, stand still at Gibeon. O moon, in the valley of Aijalon do not move."

The Lord heard and granted His servant's request.

The sun stood still.

The moon stopped.

And Israel avenged their God.

The battle was over. God judged the Ammonites of Canaan, who had tried to destroy God's people but couldn't.

The Israelites rested from battle, camping in the valley north of Gibeon.

As Joshua strode through the camp, he didn't feel tired. He had marched through the night, had fought through the extended day, and now night had fallen again. But he was energized. God had heard his request and honored it. He had asked for the sun to stand still and it had. He didn't understand why God would listen to him, but it was obvious God wanted His land purged of sin.

Walking through the campsite, he noticed a Gibeonite lounging with his own men. Wasn't he that deceiver, whom he had fed at his own tent? He approached their fire. "Who are you?"

The man sat up, and appeared to hide a smirk. "Mikar, sir."

Joshua bit back his anger. He pointed to the water vessels and to the stacked wood by the fire. "Fill these water vessels and bring more wood."

Mikar rose, taking his time, to obey. "There seemed to be enough already."

Joshua fumed inwardly. Hadn't even God listened to his request? But this Gibeonite thought himself above Joshua and questioned him? Joshua tipped the water vessels over with his foot. The water poured out of the vessels and puddled underneath them. "It appears that you are wrong."

Joshua raised his eyebrows to Medad, one of the leaders, lounging around the fire.

Medad smiled. "I'll keep him busy."

Joshua nodded. "See that you do." He moved on through camp. Why did the interchange with Mikar anger him? Did it remind him of his own failure to obey God? Why had God even listened to his request?

Joshua finished walking through camp, subdued. His exuberance over the victory, and the fact that God had heard his request for the lengthened day was dimmed by his own failures. He did not sleep well.

In the morning, Hezron reported to Joshua. "Are you ready to go to the cave of the kings?"

Joshua finished his mouthful of flatbread and wiped his hands on his tunic. The night had been short. He had fallen into bed long after the stars finally shone. His last thoughts before sleeping had been to obey God more fully. Now, he looked with longing at the flatbread heating on the stones before his fire and the vessel of tea in his hands. He took a final sip and placed it by the embers.

Hezron lit a torch from the fire's embers and led the way up the hillside to the cave.

As they went, Joshua called some of the soldiers to join him.

The rush for victory was over. The thirst for God's justice had abated. He wished complete destruction wasn't necessary. Killing in the rush of battle, he could do. Judgment that came after the battle was harder. He didn't relish confronting the kings. God had already given the victory; this was just sealing it. He must obey.

When they reached the cave opening, Joshua motioned to the servants from Gibeon, "Uncover the opening."

They removed the boulders from the opening, revealing a passage large enough to crawl through.

Hezron took his torch and stooped to enter. He had barely reached the inside of the cave, when he backed out immediately.

His face was pale.

Joshua grabbed the torch from Hezron and started to enter. "What is it?"

Hezron gripped his arm and shook his head. "You don't want to see."

Joshua studied Hezron for a moment. He turned and motioned the Gibeonite servants with him. "Bring them out."

They dragged the kings through the cave's opening and dropped them at Joshua's feet.

They were naked. Their bodies bled from cuts inflicted as they had called in worship to their gods.

Joshua turned from them and walked down the path. He retched, losing the flatbread he had eaten. Wiping his mouth, he returned to the kings and his mighty men.

Adoni-zedek stood. Blood still flowed from his many cuts. "I bow to no God of yours. My god gives me pleasure."

By their own wickedness, the kings made his next command easy. Joshua motioned toward the soldiers. "Mighty men of valor step on their necks."

As the soldiers stepped forward and saw the kings, they hesitated.

"Don't fear or be dismayed!" Joshua encouraged. "Be strong for the Lord fights for you."

They threw the kings to the ground and stepped on their necks.

Bones cracked and air wheezed from them.

Joshua stepped forward and stabbed them.

The wheezing stopped.

He wiped his sword on the grass beside the pathway.

Joshua pointed to the valley. "That tree, the one struck by lightning, hang them there." He turned away. He felt the shame of their sin. He wiped his hands on his tunic again as they walked to the tree in the valley. He wanted to bathe himself to clean away their filth. But they were not finished.

The Gibeonite servants carried the bodies to the valley.

The men of might hung them there.

All those in camp saw the wickedness of the land.

They praised God for the victory. He was just.

The rest of the day was spent searching caves and hiding places to ensure their enemies' destruction was complete.

Then, after God's people had conquered all the men who were caught outside the cities, they went after those who had fled to the fortified cities had refuge.

The city of Makkedah was captured. Its king was killed.

No one in the city survived.

Over the following weeks, they would continue to the five cities and conquer each city.

As the sun fell over the horizon, Joshua called again to the mighty men. "Remove the kings' bodies from the tree. Throw them into their cave. Cover the opening, so nothing will dig them out."

The five kings of the Amorites, who thought they could win against God, found they could not.

Thus, the five men, who worshiped their own bodies and whatever gave them pleasure, found pleasure did not follow them.

The five men, who wished for life, met their death and the only true God.

The hollow tree was dark, but light seeped through the crack and Sudru could tell it was day. Was it only yesterday he had been in the thick of a battle with God and man? He had escaped death through battle and hail. Was he now safe?

He must have dozed; for when he opened his eyes, he remembered his pain. He tried to stretch his legs but found they were too cramped. He tried to bring feeling back into his toes by wiggling them, in spite of the confined area.

He heard voices. And stopped moving.

"Five cities against our people ... the Lord gave us the victory."

"Hand me that cord, will you? This one is heavier than three combined."

Sudru tried to concentrate over his pain. He remembered the battle. Not really a battle, but a judgment from a God Who owned the skies. So the enemy had won. He had done well to hide. Mikar's advice had helped.

What were they doing? He leaned forward to watch through the tree's opening.

A man was bending over a crumbled heap.

That crumbled heap was the body of his king.

His body was marked, as for worship. His wounds still oozed.

What had sacrifice done for his king? Nothing!

This God of the desert people had sent hail to help His own.

What help had his own gods given him? None!

Sudru sighed in disgust. His gods were nothing.

His hiding place had been so grand when he first crept into it. It had sheltered him from the hail and protected him from soldiers. Even when the wind had gusted so strong he thought it would whip the tree right away from him, it had stood fast.

But now, he listened as these desert people made camp around his tree and hung the five kings on its branches. What a shame they had lived, if they must die in such shame. Their gods had not heard their pleas, even though they had sought the gods pleasure as they waited death.

They had denied the one God, Who held their lives in His Hands.

Sudru was sickened by it all.

He listened to their report of complete victory.

He tipped the final drops of water from his waterskin into his mouth. The water was warm and tepid. He swallowed, watching the shadows of five bodies swinging from the tree's branches.

He held the single drops in his mouth as if he could make them last. When he finally swallowed them, he sighed and shifted. He brushed his hand over his wound, feeling the stickiness. It still seeped. He closed his eyes again. He felt hot. His wound ached. His body was weak.

Before nightfall, he was aroused again as he heard them cut the ropes that held the bodies swinging from the tree. The bodies dropped in front of his opening. He winced at the sight of their swollen, protruding tongues and their eyes bulging from their heads.

He lowered his head and tried to swallow, but his mouth was too dry.

Someone gave the command to throw their bodies into a cave and cover it.

Sudru was anxious for them to leave, but they spent another day, burying the dead that were strewn around the open field.

When his city finished a battle, they did not honor the dead. They didn't honor their living bodies; why would they honor a dead one? They left corpses to rot in the sun where birds could pick out their eyes and animals could gnaw on their bones. What honor did a body deserve? Did this God command such respect of a body, even a dead one?

Sudru longed to stretch out his legs. He tried to make enough moisture to swallow. He couldn't. He had lost much blood.

He stayed long after he heard the army break camp and the last soldier leave.

His life had been spared.

He remembered his brother's words, "I hid, and I'm alive."

He laughed.

He was still alive.

Barely.

He closed his eyes.

God was also still alive.

Who was this God Who won every battle against all odds, Who killed all these people and left nothing behind?

Sudru did not open his eyes again.

But he did meet this God.

The battle may have ended, but the duties of the campsite didn't stop. Although he had not submitted to these desert people in circumcision, Mikar acted the submissive servant now.

Medad, one of the desert people's leaders, called him over. "Get wood and water for camp."

Mikar nodded and turned to obey.

Medad stopped him with another word, "And help bury the dead from the battlefield."

Mikar groaned inwardly. Already the heat and insects were finding them. Soon the animals of prey would, too.

The battle had not gone well for his brother's city.

As Mikar cleared the battleground, he searched the faces of those he buried, looking for his brother. He had not found him.

Had Sudru hidden as Mikar dared him to? Mikar had been cruel when he last spoke to Sudru. He cringed even now as he remembered. He would not have hit his brother with the knife. But he knew Sudru's pride. He was the general. Generals didn't desert in battle. But Mikar knew that unless he had deserted, Sudru wasn't alive.

If Sudru was alive ... with Sudru's expertise in battle, and Mikar's planning ... they could defeat these desert people. They could round up soldiers from all the cities and form an army no God could defeat.

Mikar was beginning to believe Sudru had escaped death. Then he came across the tree. The five kings had been hung on it for a day. He had avoided the tree until they had removed the kings and thrown them into a cave. Seeing the kings only reminded him of their defeat.

These desert people thought they were so much better. They had been exhausted from their night march to arrive here before the five cities fell on Gibeon. If their God hadn't thrown hail, there would be no victory for them. They were weak.

Now, as the desert people had moved to destroy the cities whose kings had come to fight, Mikar felt drawn to the tree.

Its branches were full of life, in spite of the beating the hail had given it.

He laughed. His own death had been close. His deception had earned him life.

He smiled. He had deceived this God for the salvation of his city. He would outwit Him again.

He squatted by the crevice of the tree, wishing he could be assured his brother was alive.

Something shiny from inside the trunk reflected the sun's sinking light. He stuck his head into the trunk's hole.

And found his brother.

Mikar touched Sudru's leg. His skin was cold, but not yet rigid.

Mikar backed out of the hole and stood. To have looked the last two days for his body and think he had made it, only to find him dead was disappointing. But Mikar wasn't surprised.

Sudru hadn't planned well. To hide in a tree that would be used to hang his own king?

Mikar laughed and shook his head.

Sudru never did plan ahead.

Mikar hurried to catch the carts loaded with supplies going to battle against the cities.

He would do better than his brother at defeating this God Who demanded circumcision of him.

CHAPTER 13

Eleazar, the priest, stood before the people. "Our God in His mercy has spared our nation from this wickedness. The Law is God's grace keeping us from becoming like these people."

He read from the Law of Moses, "You shall not give your offspring to Molech. I set My Face against that man who gives his offspring to Molech. Put that man to death.

"You shall not lie with a male as one lies with a female; it is an abomination.

"You shall not have intercourse with any animal for this is an abomination. Defilement.

"Do not defile yourselves. You are My people. Obey My commands to show to the nations that I am God."

Eleazar finished reading the Law to the people.

The people returned to their tents.

After changing from his priestly robes, Eleazar left the tent. The light was fading as the sun was setting and the coolness of the night was sinking over the campsite. He thought only to return to his fire and the warmth of a cup of tea when he saw a bundle on the ground.

He squatted beside it.

The bundle was a woman, crouched and weeping.

He touched her arm. "Are you hurt?"

When she raised her head, he wasn't surprised to see the harlot. "What troubles you?"

She took several gulps of air and wiped her face with the back of her hand. "The reading of the Law ... is that for your people only or for all people?"

Eleazar spoke. "All people fall under the Law of God."

She bit her trembling lip. "Then I am undone."

"We are all undone when the Law becomes part of our life."

She shook her head. "I've killed ... my baby."

Eleazar had lived long enough to know that some things weren't as simple as they seemed. He remembered the words that he had read to the people. "You offered him to Molech?"

She could only nod as she hid her face in her hands.

He thought for a few moments. "Who made you?"

Her shoulders slumped. "I fought the general. He hit me. I remember falling. I must have hit my head on the way to the floor." Her voice broke. "When I woke, he had taken my son away."

Eleazar squeezed her arm. "Then you did not offer your child; the general did."

The harlot raised her head and looked into his eyes.

The anguish he saw wrenched his heart. Sin affected more than the one who did it.

She shook her head. "After I could stand, I ran to the temple. I arrived in time to see fire and smoke pouring from Molech's hollow body. My son fell into Molech's arms. I could do nothing but watch. My baby disappeared from my sight. But I still hear my baby's screams every night . . . No God should forgive that."

Eleazar held her. "The God of mercy can heal all wounds." He hesitated. "Our God does not condemn you for another's sins. The general has paid the price for his wrong."

The harlot still cried. "And what of my life? My father sold me to another who tired of me. I have lived by satisfying men."

How would she have survived otherwise? Eleazar shook his head. "You are weighed down with sins that are not your own."

"But I pay for it, every time someone looks at me. They see who I belong to. The gods have marked me as theirs. Yet they do not love. Isn't this cause to weep?"

Eleazar stood and looked at the distant mountains. He could only nod his head.

"But I chose to continue that life. It was my wrong as well. And it follows me here. Even your people call me 'the harlot,' though I've done nothing here to encourage that."

Eleazar nodded. "Moses told us, 'Be sure your sin will find you out.'"

"So what do I do with my sin?"

"You have seen our sacrifices?"

Rahab nodded.

"Our God has provided a sin sacrifice. Unique from all other sacrifices. Instead of giving the lamb's meat as a sacrifice, the Lord commands the blood of the spotless animal to be poured out. The blood takes care of the sin."

"Will this blood take away my guilt?"

Eleazar smiled. "The Lord has provided two sacrifices. The blood of the sin sacrifice takes away the sin, but the guilt sacrifice takes away the feeling of wrong."

"But does your Law apply to me?"

"God is not just for us. He is the God Who created the world, all men."

"Your God would accept a sin and guilt sacrifice from me?"

Eleazar smiled and nodded. His wrinkles lit up his face.

"But I have no animal. My father would never allow me to take what is his ..."

Eleazar placed a hand on her shoulder. "The Lord provided for those who couldn't bring a lamb. He said a pair of turtle doves could be used."

Rahab's eyes filled with tears. "But I have none. I am undone and cannot even pay for my guilt and sin. Must I die in my sin?"

Eleazar paused. The sin offering worked because of the blood that was shed. But the Lord knew of all the people's need for their sin to be removed. "The Lord provided a way."

Rahab looked into his eyes.

Beyond the anguish of her sin, he could see a glimmer of hope and trust. He praised his God for providing a way for all people everywhere to come to Him. "The Lord provided a grain substitute."

"But there is no blood..."

"God wants all to come to Him and find forgiveness from their sin. No one is to be left out; not even the poor."

She looked down. "Even though I'm not one of your people?"

Eleazar squeezed her shoulder. "God accepts any who bring the sacrifice His Way."

"Could I do that now?"

Eleazar nodded, his eyes filling with tears. Here was one whose heart was open for God to use.

She ran to bring the offering.

Eleazar put on his robe again and sacrificed for Rahab.

When Eleazar had finished offering the sin and guilt sacrifices for Rahab, she took a deep breath. "There's so much evil around me, I don't know how much is in me and how much is outside of me."

"Are you looking to God?"

She seemed startled by the question. "Yes."

"The sacrifice is enough." Eleazar smiled. "When you see God, He shows your unworthiness, but He also shows His mercy."

"I see my unworthiness. But when will I see His mercy?"

"When you believe what He says about you is true."

"I am unworthy."

Eleazar nodded. "But do you believe He has saved you because He loves you?"

Her mouth opened but she didn't speak.

Eleazar repeated. "When you believe that, you will see His mercy."

CHAPTER 14

The people came to the Tent of Meeting to have disagreements solved, to be judged and to hear the Lord's Word read. Today, the leaders of all the tribes would judge the harlot's family. Since they were not from any tribe, all the tribe elders would judge them.

Joshua sighed. He had allowed this family to rebel against the Law long enough. He raised his arms to get their attention. When the room quieted, he pointed to Rahab's father. "This man refuses circumcision, yet desires fellowship with our people." Rahab's father interrupted. "I don't want fellowship with you."

Joshua raised his eyebrows. This meeting would not go smoothly. "If you aren't a part of our people, then the judgment of your city will be upon you."

He stepped toward Joshua. "Your laws are restrictive. I don't want your deliverance."

Perhaps he misunderstood. Joshua rephrased his words, "So you would choose death over obedience to God's laws?"

"I find no pleasure in your God."

How could someone choose death rather than obey God?

Joshua remembered Elizur. He had been stoned for gathering wood on the Sabbath. He had died angry at God. Rebellion hardened his heart, so death was more pleasing than submission. Joshua shook his head. He could understand wanting his own way. Didn't he also struggle to obey? But to choose death over life? He had hoped this family would submit. He had also wanted this meeting to progress favorably. "I'll give you the decision tomorrow."

Rahab's father stepped forward. "I won't change my mind."

Joshua bit back an instant response and smiled, but he knew it didn't reach his eyes. Such arrogance. No wonder the Lord wanted these people removed. "We'll seek the Lord."

The Jericho man pressed, a smirk crossing his lips. "Whose words do you obey when you don't agree with this God?"

This man questioned his actions! His defiance demanded proof, as if he needed to be shown what was so great about their God, as if God needed to prove it to him.

Joshua stood firm. No man had any right to question God.

But even as he considered, he felt rebuked by this foreign man. His disobedience with Gibeon, and his lack of seeking God's counsel at Ai flooded his thoughts. Hadn't he also questioned God?

Dorona's words came to his mind, "You're forgiven. Move on."

He looked around at the leaders before replying, "I obey when I don't understand."

"Sounds like a servant to me."

The man had a cocky response for any defense he could find. And why should he even defend himself to this man? Joshua bit his lip, remembering that's how Moses's curbed his anger. He smiled. "That's what I am."

"Won't catch me being one."

Joshua glared at him. His arrogance brought out his cockiness. With this attitude, he would never submit to anyone's authority. "Aren't you a servant to your own desires?"

He shrugged and sauntered out of the tent.

No one said a word.

Joshua was supposed to be the leader, but with this entire discussion, he felt like a child on the back of wagon, rolling downhill uncontrolled. He threw his shoulders back and looked around the room. How could he control this meeting now? His gaze rested on Rahab's brother. Here was another problem. He sighed. "Do you agree with your father?"

Galon stepped forward. "I stand with my father."

Rahab's mother grabbed his arm. "No! Don't choose ..."

Galon flung her arm off. He raised his hand and struck her, then seemed to remember where he was. He looked around the room at the men watching, dropped his hand, and stalked out.

Rahab's mother looked at Joshua. She dug her hands into her pockets, as if she could hide within the folds of its material. "I can't live without him."

It was the first-time Joshua had seen her face. She had always kept it hidden in her hood. It wasn't marred by a fire brand, like her daughter's, but it was bruised. What evil had happened here at their campsite under his leadership?

Rahab touched her mother's arm. "But you would be free of his abuse."

"He loves me."

Rahab grabbed her mother's shoulders and shook her. She raised her voice, as if she could make her mother believe the words. "He loves you when he beats you? That isn't love. You could live like God meant you to live. You could be treated like a person, not someone's dog."

Her mother didn't say another word, but scurried from the room.

No one spoke as the tent flap fell closed.

Joshua definitely felt like a child in a run-away wagon. This evil had happened under his authority. How was he to direct this people to remember God, when they wouldn't even acknowledge Him as God? He stared at the tent flap and thought about what had just happened. The father wasn't the only one abusing her.

Rahab faced Joshua and the elders. She sighed. "I'm sorry for bringing my family to your people. Your God is just. He will do what is right."

Joshua shifted to address the jury. What was justice?

Rahab took a deep breath. "May I address one more issue?"

Joshua nodded for Rahab to continue. How much more could this get out of his control?

"Your law speaks of death to those who offer their offspring to Molech. I am guilty and worthy of death."

How much evil had they brought into their camp by rescuing this family? With all her speeches about serving God, Joshua hadn't expected this. He swallowed and looked at the elders.

Some showed a hardness, as if they expected it.

Others looked shocked.

His gaze stopped at Salmon. He looked concerned. Would he be biased in his judgment?

How should he proceed?

Before Joshua could respond, Eleazar stepped forward. "If I may, Joshua?"

Joshua stood back, relieved to allow Eleazar to intercede.

Eleazar escorted the harlot in front of the elders. "Tell the entire story, child."

Joshua studied Eleazar. How did he know about her?

Eleazar put his hand on her shoulder and nodded.

She swallowed before raising her head. When she did, she kept her gaze on Eleazar, as if gaining strength from him. Her eyes welled with tears as she retold her story. "My father sold me to a man who soon wearied of me. To live, I pleased men. The general came. I had his son.

"The king demanded sacrifices.

"After beating me, the general stole my son.

"I ran to the temple in time to see him sacrificed." She bowed her head and wept.

No one spoke.

Eleazar turned to Joshua. "We have much to seek the Lord about, do we not?"

The harlot and her family left the Tent of Meeting, but the elders did not.

Eleazar faced the men. "Where shall we start?"

Joshua swallowed, relieved Eleazar was directing the meeting. "The head of the household does not submit to the Law. He deserves death."

Eleazar explained. "Circumcision is a minor issue here. He rebels against God and His Law."

Their voices rang with one accord. "Stone him."

The answer was clear.

"Now his son."

Eleazar explained. "He is of age and able to make his own decision and so must be judged separately. He refuses to submit to our laws."

Joshua looked around the circle, acknowledging the nods.

A voice rang out, "Stone him."

"Are we all agreed?" Joshua allowed a sufficient pause to allow for disagreement. Then confirmed the judgment.

Eleazar nodded. "Now for the wife ... she seems to go along willingly with whatever her husband or son does."

"Could she have stopped him?" Salmon interrupted. "Did you see her face? If she tried to stop it, she would have been killed."

Medad, a leader from the tribe of Asher, argued. "She's her husband's property. She is guilty."

"Remember Achan. He was stoned with his entire family. Shouldn't we do the same here? Then the entire problem would be over. After all, his daughter's a harlot."

Salmon looked at each elder. "His daughter doesn't live under his protection. Didn't you listen to her? She was thrown out of his house. She shouldn't be judged by her father's sin."

Ethan stepped forward. "The harlot saved us, giving us valuable information, not only about Jericho, but about all these people that live in this land. We have promised her deliverance."

Medad snorted. "We gave her deliverance, and this is what she's done with it."

Eleazar stepped forward. "Her sins were prior to knowing our God. She has offered the sin and guilt sacrifices. The Lord has already taken care of her sin."

Joshua studied Eleazar. When had this happened? Joshua asked, "What does the Law say regarding the wife?"

Eleazar spoke with assurance. "She should be stoned with her husband."

Joshua glanced at Salmon.

His face was pale, but he nodded.

Joshua confirmed. "She is stoned with her husband and son. Any other discussion about the wife?"

No one spoke.

Joshua looked down and adjusted his belt. He felt the tension shift in the room. He would rather do battle on the field, than fight for justice in the Tent of Meeting. Tempers were growing hot and swords must stay in their sheaths. He shifted his waterskin at his waist before looking around the room at each leader. "Now, the harlot..."

Salmon corrected. "Her name is Rahab. She is no longer a harlot."

Eleazar nodded.

Joshua cringed. He should have made that distinction, but everyone referred to her as the harlot.

Hezron asked, "If we stone her family, she will have no protector. She will be alone. Won't that invite men to abuse her again?"

Medad spoke under his breath, "If any man would want used property."

Salmon took a step toward him. "She couldn't choose what family she was born into, just as you couldn't. But she has changed her actions, as you can control your tongue, or—"

Eleazar raised his arms. "Men. Much happens in a family that we'll never understand. She must be judged apart from her family since she is of age and not under her father's protection. However, we should not judge based on the problems that will result, but on what is right and wrong, according to what the Law says."

Salmon asked, "What has she done?"

Medad questioned, "She's guilty of not reporting her family's evil."

Eleazar stood. "She reported it."

Joshua stared at him. When? Why hadn't he heard of it?

Eleazar continued. "She has wept over her own sins and the sins of her family. She has offered sin and guilt sacrifices. But she doesn't understand the mercy of God, Who covers her sin."

Medad shook his fist. "But sacrifices don't cover a sin worthy of death."

Salmon countered, "When was the last time you wept over your sins?"

"I can't recall killing my son."

Eleazar interrupted. "We judge on what was done, not on the response afterwards."

Salmon asked, "Doesn't the Law give provisions for killing accidentally? Aren't there cities of refuge to be assigned for those accidental deaths?"

Medad retorted "Sacrificing her son is hardly accidental."

Salmon countered, "She didn't choose to do it. The general did."

Medad shook his head. "She's lying anyway."

Salmon's punch came quickly.

Medad's head rolled back. He stepped forward, his eyes hot with anger. He wiped his bleeding lip and glared at Salmon. "What is she to you? Do you visit her at night?" He paused, then sneered. "Or did you only visit her when you were away from camp doing God's service?"

Ethan stepped between them, holding Salmon back. "This won't help her."

Eleazar waited until Medad stepped away from Salmon. "Should she be held by laws that she didn't know at the time of her action? Were we judged for breaking the Sabbath when we labored under Egypt's bondage? Of course not. But when God gave the Law, then we were accountable for it."

Medad stepped forward. "But this is murder. All people know it's wrong."

Joshua raised his arms. How could they find unity?

Moses always went before the Ark to speak with God when he didn't know what to do. But this seemed to be a decision that must be brought before the elders. Did Joshua have authority to judge her, or should it be by the elders' consent?

This family was causing division among the elders.

Before the council could hear the Lord's Words, they needed to calm down. "Let's ask the Lord."

Medad muttered as he fell to his knees. "Why ask the Lord, when we already know what should be done?"

Each prayed silently.

Joshua's plea was for unity. They couldn't fight the nations if they were fighting each other. An army is only as strong as the thread that holds them together. If this decision tore their leaders apart, they would see the results in the next battle.

Joshua remembered Achan's lesson. Sin in the camp would affect the battle's outcome. He couldn't ignore it. But what was the answer?

Joshua remembered the harlot's question the first time he met her. She had asked whether God's change would hurt. Salmon had said she searched for God. Even today, when she had confessed, Joshua sensed in her a spirit hungering after God. Almost like Moses ... he shook his head. No, she was far from Moses in her thirst for God. No one could compare to Moses's desire for God. But he admitted that her heart wasn't hardened against God.

She almost seemed a victim of the evil, unlike her mother who succumbed to the wrong. Rahab worked to rise above the evil and conquer it. He shook his head. It was hard to believe. She was a harlot after all.

He heard Eleazar rise to his feet.

Joshua's questions hadn't been resolved. If anything, he was more in a turmoil.

Joshua looked at the elders' faces.

Some smirked to each other as they whispered and nodded toward Salmon.

Others showed anger.

Some even remorse.

None showed peace.

Joshua sighed. This was not the unity they needed. "Tomorrow we stone the harlot's father, mother, and brother, who would not submit to our laws."

He paused and looked around the circle. "In the case of the harlot, we cannot execute someone without God giving us peace about it. We'll discuss this another time, when tempers have cooled."

Mikar was cleaning the leather bridle of Medad's donkey when a messenger summoned Medad to the Tent of Meeting. Mikar swiped his rag into the sheep fat and smeared it over the leather, but he wasn't paying attention to the sheep fat nor the cleaning of the leather. Although Medad's servant, Mikar did not plan to stay one for long. He was not use to servanthood, nor would he become used to it. Hadn't he been the king's chief advisor? No, his service now was nothing more than a stepping stone to get back into power.

He wondered why the messenger had called Medad. Only major issues required all the leaders to be called. Were they preparing for battle again?

When Medad stomped back to his tent and threw his cloak on the ground beside his cushions, Mikar offered Medad wine.

Medad grabbed the vessel, muttering under his breath about a harlot.

This was more than Mikar had hoped. He squatted at Medad's feet. "The meeting didn't go well?"

Medad stared at him, as if seeing him for the first time. He settled against his cushions. "It's that harlot. She's brought trouble ever since she came. Our council's divided, and we can't get rid of her."

"Why is she here?"

Medad shrugged. "Our spies claim she saved them. I think they used her services and feel guilty."

Mikar nodded. Hadn't he learned as the king's counselor that sympathy prompted more secrets? "She worked the temples of her city?"

Medad nodded.

Mikar shrugged, as if it didn't matter to him. But he seethed inwardly. How could one who sacrificed to the gods, so quickly turn from them and follow this God? No one forsook Molech without punishment. "Then she's either a traitor to her gods, or a deceiver to your people."

Medad leaned forward and pounded his fist on the ground. "That's what I told them. She lies!"

Mikar knew she wasn't lying. She had forsaken the gods. If beautiful women didn't appease the gods, then his pleasure at their sacrifices was stolen from him. She had no right to do that. He hated her for it. She must be taught a lesson. She would be sacrificed for the gods' pleasure and his. "Master," Mikar waited until Medad looked at him. "I can solve your problem."

Medad leaned forward. "How?"

Mikar shook his head. "It's better you know nothing. But trust me. You won't need to judge her in your courts."

Medad considered.

Mikar waited. There was more than one way to gain power and position. He might not be a Jew, but he could influence a Jew for his own ends and the ends of the gods. And he would find his own pleasure satisfied, even in the campsite of a Jew.

Medad smiled and nodded. "Let it be done."

CHAPTER 15

The next morning, Salmon stood outside camp with all the people. Joshua called on the people to execute judgment. He threw the first rock at Rahab's family who stood facing the people.

After throwing a few stones, Salmon moved away from the people. When he saw Rahab's anguish, he paused. Salmon couldn't understand God's holiness, but he did recognize the need for obedience. Rahab's family had been given ample time to follow God's rules. Hadn't he been angry at their insubordination when he had spoken to them? But he felt for Rahab's mother. Although her dedication was admirable, was it love for her husband or fear?

The son's actions in front of the assembly had been revealing. The mother's bruises had come from more than one man's beatings. He remembered Rahab's fear of her family.

He sighed.

This just showed how the entire city of Jericho had treated people. They didn't respect people as created by God. He shook his head. When man did what was right in his own sight he treated his fellowman with disdain. They became nothing more than animals.

In contrast, by obeying God, man's value was elevated. Because he was God's, he had worth.

Salmon's heart went out to those who did not know God. He thought of Rahab. She had come to know God, probably even better than some of God's own people. She searched for Him. He had watched as she listened to the Law being read. She drank it in like she couldn't get enough of God. She listened, not just with her ears, but with her heart. God's own people should be shamed by her thirst to know Him.

Salmon had watched all this from afar, mindful of Ethan's caution, but desiring to know her.

Now almost in contrast, Salmon watched the others executing justice. Their expressions revealed much of what was inside them.

Joshua threw stones, not out of malicious intent, but out of obligation to see God's holiness preserved. He obeyed, but found no pleasure in it.

Salmon's respect for Joshua's leadership grew.

Out of the corner of his eye, Salmon noticed Medad. He threw stones as if he enjoyed it.

Salmon shook his head. Some men always enjoyed lording over others. He must watch himself next time they met. It may make a difference with how Rahab would be judged.

A rock hit Rahab.

Salmon stepped toward her and blocked any others. "Stand back farther from your family." He glared at Medad. It had come from his direction.

Medad shrugged and smiled.

Salmon seethed, biting his tongue to keep from responding. Medad's former insinuation came to mind. Would someone always think ill of her?

She backed away from her family to stand beside him. Rahab acted as if she hadn't even felt the rock. She kept her hood over her face. She looked so helpless. So small. So alone.

The people jeered and taunted, "Foreigners ... idol-worshippers ..."

Salmon clamped his jaw shut. He wanted to stop them. Wasn't watching her family's punishment enough?

Rahab's head remained bowed. Her shoulders shook as she silently cried.

After the rocks were heaped over their bodies and God's justice had been met, the people began to leave.

Medad walked by Rahab and Salmon. "Your turn will come, little harlot. You'll get your justice."

Rahab seemed not to hear.

Salmon stepped in front of her and glared at Medad. "Do not judge before God does."

Medad smirked. "We don't need God to show us sins that are already obvious."

Salmon clenched his fists at his sides. What had he told himself earlier? He must remain calm to help Rahab. Smashing Medad's smile from his face would not help Rahab. He breathed deeply and heard Medad chuckle as he left.

Rahab stumbled to her camp after the stoning. She sat by her cooking fire, staring into its dead embers. She had held herself together at the stoning by reminding herself it was a sacrifice she must make to this new God Who could not allow evil in His midst.

She felt empty. Her city was gone. Her family was gone. Everything she knew was gone.

Even though she had feared making her father angry, his presence hindered others from bothering her. She had been alone in the city. But she could bolt her door and not let men in. Here—she glanced back at her tent—she had no protection from any man. How would she be protected now?

Her thoughts shifted to her brother. He had been hitting her mother. She hadn't wanted to believe it. She had tried to ignore the feelings she had when she was around him. But she had watched him strike her mother in front of all the elders.

When she had listened to the Law, her family had stayed behind. While she was gone, new bruises had shown on her mother. What had happened when she'd been away? She shook her head. Maybe she didn't want to know.

Thoughts of her mother made her tears flow again. Why couldn't her mother stand against her father and brother? Could she have changed them? Rahab snorted. No one could change her father.

He had died for his desires. And her brother was hardened just like him.

So, with her family's death, she had gained release. The oppression had lifted. That presence of evil had disappeared. Her father's displeasure with her was gone. She could breathe. Like a bird set free from its cage. She could fly.

What would she do with that freedom? How would she live? She only knew one thing. She would never return to that life.

What else could she do? If God allowed her to live.

She shook her head.

"Why do you shake your head?"

The man's voice startled her. She wasn't alone. She looked around her, afraid. Her father hadn't been absent long before the men started to come. She grabbed a fist-sized stone by her cook fire and looked for the speaker. She saw Salmon squatting in her tent's shadows. How long had he been there? She relaxed her grip on the stone. "I didn't know anyone was here."

He shrugged and smiled. "I came to make sure you were all right."

She stirred the ashes with a stick and placed leaves over the embers. After the embers smoked, she moved a vessel over the coals to heat water. She crumbled the dry tea leaves into a vessel. She almost laughed. She was doing what her mother would do. Whenever her mother didn't know what to do, she would offer food. Then she realized her mother would no longer cook with her. She felt the loss again. She lowered her shoulders.

Salmon didn't say anything more.

She worked in silence. Fidgeting with the fire to heat the water. The water boiled.

She poured one vessel and handed it to Salmon and fixed another for herself. Rahab moved, now conscious of his presence.

Her hand bumped her tunic's pocket. The gold piece felt solid and reassuring. The priest had told her that Salmon expected no service for the gift, but she knew man's ways. Now, she realized why he was here. She felt her cheeks flush.

She studied him, even with her head bowed. If she still lived in the city, she would think nothing of offering her services to the spy. He was kind, thoughtful, protective.

But now, she had come to know this God. She had sacrificed for her sin and guilt. The priest had told her God would be satisfied. She couldn't return to what she had been before....

But maybe someone like her could not be accepted by this God. Maybe her life must remain as it was in the city. Would it be so bad with Salmon? Her cheeks flushed at the thought. She took a deep breath to gain courage.

She fingered the gold. It meant more to her than just what it could buy. It reminded her of her worth ... before God. She didn't want to return it, but she could not serve Salmon's wants. She swallowed before handing the gold back to him.

He looked at her extended hand. He reached to take what she offered. When she dropped the gold in his hand, his eyebrows raised. He took her hand in his.

She trembled at his touch.

He gave it back. "It's yours."

Rahab shook her head. "I won't perform the service you desire."

His eyebrows raised. "What service?"

Rahab gestured to her tent. "I seek to please God and not man."

Salmon looked at the tent. His eyes widened, realizing what she meant. He shook his head, dropping her hand and backing away from her. "No! I'd never pay for your service ... I mean, that's not what the gold piece was for ..." He looked around, trying to find the words to explain. Finally, he held her gaze. "I'm here so you're not alone in your grief."

Rahab nodded. And replaced the gold piece in her tunic's pocket. She could keep the piece. She was relieved. But was he only waiting until she had finished grieving? She must be strong to keep her resolution. When she looked into his eyes and saw his kindness ... he would be harder to refuse a second time.

No man had ever refused her service. No man had ever cared, if she grieved. She had learned to hide her feelings.

She turned from his glance and sipped her tea, trying to still the unrest he had caused. She didn't understand. What did he expect from her? Why didn't he leave?

She grabbed a handful of grain from a jar and pounded it with a pestle and stone. Feeding her brother had always been the answer to his needs. "You must be hungry."

He stood behind her.

She tensed. She didn't want to see when he hit her.

He touched her shoulder.

She winced.

"Rahab. Look at me."

He had used her name.

Why had she told him her name? No man used her name without wanting something.

His voice was low and urgent. "Look at me."

That's what the general would say before he asked her to work the temples. But these desert people didn't have temples. She steeled herself to deny him again and raised her eyes to meet his.

His gaze surprised her. He didn't look with intensity and desire. Or even demand. His eyes held pain. "I won't hurt you."

She dropped her shoulders. She was wary. She had heard that before. What did he want?

He cupped her face, as if he were holding a fragile butterfly. "Rahab. I'm not hungry ... unless you need something to eat. I'm here to grieve with you."

She shivered at his touch. What kind of man was this? She had known man's anger. She'd been hit by many men. But this... tenderness, gentleness...was that what this God gave to a man?

His voice broke, "How can I help you?"

She closed her eyes. She felt lost and afraid. She was alone. And when he touched her with such gentleness, she felt undone. How could he help her? She didn't know where to begin.

He still held her chin.

Sighing, she shook her head. "It's only a matter of time."

His voice was not more than a whisper, "Time until what?"

"Until your people stone me." She found courage to look at him again.

He clenched his jaw.

She cringed. Had he forgotten what she had done? He had heard at the elders' meeting. He knew what she had done. He would regret delivering her from her city's destruction. Now he would beat her.

He pressed his lips together but still held her chin. His tone deepened, "My people do not understand God's mercy."

"Mercy?" She didn't understand that either.

"You shouldn't be held accountable for a law you didn't know. You shouldn't pay for a crime you were forced to commit. The leaders must decide. But I'll do my best to show them you don't deserve judgment."

She gasped. Why would he do that for her? "But what about God's rules?"

"God already delivered you from the city, didn't He?"

She nodded.

"Eleazar mentioned you offered the sin and guilt sacrifices."

The priest had performed the sacrifices. "Shouldn't it remove the guilt?"

He smiled. "Do you believe you're beautiful?"

She stepped back. Did he mock her? She was no longer beautiful. Not with her face marred by a brand.

He laughed. He lifted her face so she would look into his eyes again. "You are beautiful."

She stepped back again. She knew where this was going, and wanted no part of it. "I once was, but it was a curse. I am no longer."

He shook his head. "No beauty is a curse."

She couldn't believe that. Her beauty caused men to use her. If she had been ugly, she would not have attracted the attention of cruel men who had money but no heart. "By my beauty, I survived."

Understanding seemed to come to him. His smile disappeared. "I've brought you pain." He dropped his hands to his sides. "You can be beautiful without feeling beautiful, can't you?"

She considered. She didn't know where he was going with his question. She didn't want to be trapped. She nodded hesitantly.

He took a step away from her.

She relaxed. She could think now.

"But that doesn't remove the truth that you're beautiful."

She tensed again. What did he want? No man cared what she thought. They came for night action or a listening ear. They didn't expect her to think. What did he want her to say?

"Truth doesn't change." He persisted. "Same with the sin sacrifice covering your sin. The sacrifice covers your sin, whether you feel it does or not."

She searched his face. He was answering her earlier question. He wasn't expecting something from her. A weight lifted. The sin sacrifice didn't remove the guilt until she believed the One Who accepted the sacrifice. That's what the priest had been trying to tell her. "How do you know God takes away the sin?"

He smiled. His eyes twinkled and softened his features. "That's where trust comes in."

"Trust?" she sighed. Trust made her vulnerable. Men used her when she trusted. She had trusted her father but learned it was better not to. She had trusted the man who paid her father, but he had thrown her on the street when he tired of her. She had trusted the general, but he had scarred her face and her heart. Could she trust this God?

He read her confused expression. "Trust is a gift from God. God plants the seed. He keeps His promises, and that seed grows."

She had already seen what He promised about her city came to pass. She could believe this God. But how could anything from God grow inside her? "What if the seed is trampled, so that there's nothing left?"

Salmon smiled, sadly. "In the desert, God led us by His cloud by day and His fire by night. He was always there. I came to know this God by looking to the cloud for reassurance. Like a child holding his father's hand learns to walk."

"Where is He now?"

Salmon shook his head. "When we reached our Land, His cloud and fire disappeared, and now we cannot see any sign of His presence, but He is still with us."

Perhaps if she could see this God, she could trust Him more. "Why won't He let you see Him?" Rahab's voice trembled.

"God has told us He is with us. We show our trust by believing His Word."

Rahab wanted to trust this God. "But what about my sins?"

Salmon stepped back. "When I disobeyed, my father corrected me. But I was still his son. Nothing could take that away. He restored me to fellowship. That's what God does when I've sinned. He disciplines. It's painful. But then He reminds me of Who He is and who I am to Him."

Her father had never shown that love. He had beaten her when she didn't meet his wishes, and he made no effort to restore relationship. Could this God care that much?

The sun was setting.

Her hands trembled as she drank from her cold tea. It was one thing to believe God had taken away her guilt and sin; it was another thing to feel it. Must she trust before the feelings came?

This God had saved her from destruction. He had accepted her sin and guilt sacrifice; the priest had said so. Why shouldn't she trust Him?

With the setting of the sun, the darkness crept over her campsite. The darkness brought a closing of one phase of her life, a phase of fear of distrust, because she'd had no one trustworthy. Now she had found Someone Who was worthy of her trust.

She shivered as the darkness brought cooler temperatures.

Salmon took off his cloak and wrapped it around her.

She smelled the wood smoke and man-smell on it. Even as she settled into the warmth of his coat, she grew afraid. Would he now expect her service?

She could probably trust a God with her sin sacrifice better than she could trust a man with his passion.

He looked around the campsite, then at her. "You'll be safe?"

She nodded. What choice did she have? She had nowhere else to go. Did he have a plan?

He studied her for a moment, then nodded. "God will be with you," and he left.

She breathed a sigh of relief, yet felt disappointed that he had not stayed.

After Salmon left, Rahab prepared for sleep. She could serve this God. She would trust this God.

He was with her.

Not like her father who made her afraid when he was nearby and always watched for her to make a mistake. God Who was pleased with her sacrifice and ready to forgive.

What had the priest told her? Once she understood her unworthiness, she would know His mercy.

God, in His mercy, wanted her.

Wasn't that the seed Salmon told her about?

Something good could grow in her, planted by God. She would allow God to make it grow. He would be pleased.

As she went to sleep, she touched her chin where Salmon had held her. His touch had been gentle. No man had looked at her with such tenderness.

She longed to be worthy of this God, but also worthy of a man who knew this God, a man like Salmon. With these thoughts, she fell asleep.

When she awoke, the night was moonless. The blackness kept her from seeing anything.

She listened for what had wakened her. Sounds seemed louder now that she was alone. She sat up, holding the blankets under her chin.

She wasn't alone.

A hand groped for her mouth and covered it. She tasted wood smoke, grease and horses. "Do not scream. The gods do not like a traitor."

She hit, kicked, and struggled.

The more she fought, the tighter he held her.

His hand slipped from her mouth.

She screamed.

He struck her chin.

Her head jerked back, and she remembered nothing more.

Joshua lingered at the Tabernacle after the Sabbath sacrifices. How would Moses have answered the dispute with the harlot? Moses didn't rule by vote of the elders. Moses would have just stated the Lord's decision. He made it seem so easy. But Joshua did not speak with God face to face, nor was he the only authority. They ruled more by the elders' counsel, than by his final authority. Would God give unity in their decision? God had directed the lots for Achan's judgment. Should he do it by lot?

Eleazar was leaving, after changing from his priestly robe and breastplate.

Joshua fell in step with him as he walked to his tent.

"What's on your mind?"

Joshua sighed. "We never settled the issue with the harlot."

Eleazar stopped walking. "You still call her that?"

Joshua shrugged.

"You sway the elders by your choice of words. Don't you remember God's mercy for your own shortcomings at Gibeon?"

Joshua looked down but defended himself. "She's a harlot. Her sin is great."

"All done before she knew the Lord's Law."

"Do we excuse murder because it's in the past?"

"Joshua, you're being ridiculous. Why does she bother you?"

"She belongs nowhere. She causes problems."

"She belongs nowhere because all she knows is gone. You should be showing mercy—do you forget we were strangers and slaves in Egypt?"

Joshua sighed. "But she is marred."

"That's not why she irritates you."

Joshua raised his voice, "Then tell me, why does she bother me?"

Eleazar stopped walking and waited until Joshua looked at him. "She threatens you, Joshua.

Joshua laughed in disbelief. "Threatens me?"

Eleazar continued, "You are threatened by someone, who is not a Jew, who searches for God with her whole heart. She reminds me of Moses, wanting to stay on the mountain top where God is, but stuck here with us evil ones."

"Us—evil ones, Eleazar? We are God's chosen people."

"Yes, Joshua, evil ones. She feels the evil more than anyone else, because she spends more time searching to know the God of glory."

Dorona leaned against Joshua as he lounged after the noon meal. "What's bothering you?"

He wrapped his arms around her. "The harlot—Rahab. We haven't decided what to do with her."

"Why must something be done with her?"

"She killed her baby."

She gasped. "How could a mother do that?"

Joshua stretched out his legs. "The general offered her baby to their gods."

"She allowed that?"

"He beat her. She ran to the temple in time to see her baby burned."

She shuddered. "What's to decide?"

"Whether to stone her."

"Why? For being beaten by a man and having her baby stolen from her? Joshua, that doesn't make sense!"

Joshua slouched against his cushions. "There's also her family's sin ..."

"That wasn't her sin. She lived with an evil father, while everything she knew was destroyed by a God she had never known. Joshua, what's to decide?"

"When you put it like that, nothing." Joshua stretched. "When I listen to the leaders, I lose focus. I make a better general than I do a judge."

"You want justice, but you also want everyone to agree. You can't have both. It's good for you to struggle. The battles give you no challenge."

Joshua shook his head. "Even with victory, there's much to decide and plan. Don't think I do nothing in battle."

Dorona laughed. "I clean your tunics and cloaks after the battles. The mud, sweat, and blood I must scrub tells me you do plenty. I know you fight for our people."

Joshua hugged her. "I fight for you."

Dorona sighed. "Camp is different without you. The people seem ... less settled."

"God certainly is with us in battle. After Ai, I've learned to wait for His assurance before I take my men into battle. But I count on God protecting you here, too."

Dorona shifted. "It's not that God isn't with us, it's more like half of me is missing."

Joshua squeezed her. "God made us one. We can't be apart without feeling a hole. Bone of my bones, flesh of my flesh. I feel it too."

"You're busy swinging your sword, saving your life. I stay behind and wait. There's not much to do. It's not the same without you."

She shifted against him and held a vessel to drink. "When will we settle?"

Joshua sighed. "We have divided the land in half. We must conquer the south, then move to the northern lands."

"Where would you like to settle?"

"Anywhere you are, I am home."

Dorona leaned on his shoulder. "After wandering for so long, don't you want to be able to see the same mountain range out your window every time you rise in the morning?"

"Unexciting, don't you think?"

Dorona squeezed his knee.

"I'm a general of the army. What will I do in times of peace?"

"Do you think all the battles will be fought?"

He shrugged. "Does evil go away?"

"Your wisdom will be important for the people."

Joshua watched the fire flare up, then settle again. "Do you think they'll listen after they're settled?"

Dorona smiled. "Who else will remind them that God is with them?"

Joshua thought again about the harlot. He shook his head, and corrected himself—Rahab. "The people remind me of what is urgent. You remind me of what is important. I must not let the urgent get ahead of the important."

Salmon approached Ethan's campsite just as the sun was setting. "Shalom."

Ethan wiped his hands on his tunic as he stood. "Be at peace."

Salmon stood beyond the fire's edge. "I have some questions for you."

Ethan walked with him to the outskirts of camp.

It was quiet except for the water gurgling from the spring.

Salmon sighed. "How can you make someone trust?"

Ethan brushed his hands down his legs. "Why do your men follow you into battle?"

Salmon laughed. "I wonder that myself."

Ethan laughed, but shrugged. "They wouldn't if they didn't trust you. You've proven to them that what you say, you will do."

He watched the sun sink below the mountain ridge. "This wouldn't have anything to do with a certain harlot, would it?"

Salmon looked at Rahab's campsite. "All the men in her life have failed her. Her view of God is warped by the evil she has known. She has trouble trusting God."

Ethan knelt down and drank from the spring. "She hears the Law. She will come to know the God Who gives the Law. He is trustworthy."

Salmon studied her campsite. "I need to protect her."

Ethan wiped his mouth with the back of his hand. "That need to protect is given to us by God. We protect our people. I would give my life to protect Kamon. That goes back to the Garden, where God gave woman to man to be his helpmeet."

"I need a helpmeet."

Ethan laughed. "Haven't I told you that? Don't allow her beauty to draw you into accepting her past. She has scars that hinder her from being your helpmeet."

"She doesn't have that lost look that so many of the women we've conquered have."

Ethan nodded. "True. But she's still stained."

Salmon had stopped listening. There was no smoke from her cook fire; no movement around her tent. "I didn't see her this morning at the reading of the Law. I should check on her."

Ethan studied her tent. "I'll go with you."

As they approached her tent, Salmon heard a moan. He ran to the tent. "Rahab?" Hearing nothing more, he stepped inside.

It took a moment for his eyes to adjust to the darkness. He saw her uncovered, bruised body in the corner of the tent.

Salmon grabbed a blanket and covered her. He knelt by her head, pushing back her hair. "Rahab, who did this to you?"

She moaned.

Salmon raised her head. "Ethan, bring me water."

After moving the water toward Salmon, Ethan knelt beside him. "I'll get Joshua."

Salmon dipped a cloth in the water and stroked her face. "Bring Hannah, also. She'll need a woman to help with what has happened."

The day following the Sabbath, the elders met at the Tent of Meeting.

When Salmon entered, the room became quiet. He glanced around the room. Why had they stopped talking? He shook his head.

Joshua raised his arms to start the meeting. "Men, we are here to decide about the harlot."

Eleazar coughed.

Joshua corrected, "Rahab."

Medad said, "She should be stoned."

Joshua raised his eyebrows and spoke loudly. "The harlot, Rahab, was beaten and abused last night."

Medad shook his fist at Salmon. "We'd have no problem if she had been killed with her family."

Salmon felt the hair rise on the back of his neck. "She didn't cause the problem. She was molested in her own tent."

Medad stepped forward. "She probably offered her services to him."

Eleazar walked between the men. "I've offered the sin offering for her sin. She is saved by our promise and kept by the protection of the Law. We will not speak of stoning her for things done prior to coming to live with us. We will not discuss her past again."

Salmon sighed. Eleazar's leadership and explanation of the Law kept the judgment from getting personal. Salmon had nothing he would add.

He looked at Medad.

Medad scowled.

Salmon knew that he wasn't happy with the decision, but he could do nothing to change it.

Eleazar turned back to Joshua. "As to the other problem. She needs protection, for an unmarried maiden does cause problems in camp ..."

Salmon stepped forward. Hadn't he promised her that he would help her? How could she trust God if his words meant nothing? This was the only way it could be done. "I'll protect her."

Several snickered.

Medad voiced his complaint. "You would forsake the commandment about adultery?"

Salmon shook his head. He cleared his throat and raised his voice. "I will marry her." He waited for someone to offer another solution.

No one said anything.

Salmon saw Ethan open his mouth and then shut it. He knew what he'd say.

Ethan whispered, "With her background?"

Salmon nodded. "Do we believe God's mercy? Or do we just talk about it? If God has forgiven her past, shouldn't we?" He looked at each of the elders.

Some wouldn't look at him.

Others stared at him in disbelief.

He avoided looking at Medad's face. It would only make him angry.

When he saw Ethan's expression, it looked like resignation, maybe even acceptance. He didn't know for sure.

What was he supposed to do?

No one else gave any suggestions.

"How much does the sin offering cover?" Salmon spoke faster as he continued. "I believe God covers all her sin. She is no longer a harlot. She's clean by the mercy of our God. I will marry her tomorrow, if she is willing."

Eleazar looked around the elders' circle. "Then let it be done."

The meeting had dismissed and everyone had left. Salmon stood outside the Tent of Meeting, staring off at the mountains. What had he done? Had he been moved to such passion as to make a covenant before God, without asking Him?

He was deep in thought, when someone touched his shoulder. He jumped.

"It's just me."

Salmon looked at Eleazar and nodded. "Shalom."

"Are you at peace, Salmon?"

Salmon shook his head. "My heart feels like an eagle, trying to soar in a box. I've made a life changing decision without consulting God."

Eleazar shook his head. "No, you were ruled by passion to do what is right. You saved a woman to whom we promised salvation. By your protection, you honor that promise. You are a man more worthy than the rest of us."

Salmon shook his head. "Then why do I feel so afraid? I shake more than I do when going to battle."

Eleazar laughed. "Those already married have stood in your sandals and trembled. We had only to ask the woman's father for permission. You have declared your heart to the entire congregation without knowing her heart. That is cause to tremble. But go, ask her, with the sanction of our God."

Salmon walked to Rahab's campsite, practicing how he would ask her. Nothing seemed right. The more he practiced, the more unsettled he became. He knew this was the right thing to do. But it wasn't just right, it was what he wanted to do.

On the other hand, she wasn't ready to marry. She could barely stand his presence, let alone his touch. He had felt her tremble when he had merely touched her shoulder or her chin. She had even winced as if he would hit her. How could they come together as man and wife when she had such fear? And that was before her attack; now what would she be like?

Even if she was able to trust God, would she be able to trust a man?

Before he found answers, he reached her campsite.

Phinehas stood at the outskirts of her camp. Phinehas, although a priest, had learned doctoring skills in Egypt. He and his wife, Hannah, had come to stay with Rahab as she healed. "Shalom, Salmon."

"Be at peace. How is she?"

Phinehas lowered his voice. "Her body's broken but her spirit fights."

Salmon nodded. "May I speak with her?"

Phinehas nodded to where she lay by the fire.

Hannah sat with her. She moved as Salmon approached.

Rahab's face was swollen. Bruises covered her face and neck. Her eyes were closed.

Salmon knelt by her. His voice broke, "Rahab."

She opened her eyes. They were slits between her swollen cheeks.

He took her hand. "I've come from the elders' meeting."

Her eyes widened. Her chin trembled.

He saw her fear. He patted her hand. "There will be no stoning."

She closed her eyes. "Perhaps stoning would have been better."

Salmon swallowed, finding it hard to know what to say. "Life is not always pain. Remember the gold." He licked his lips trying to will back the tears that were pooling in his eyes. "Your gold will still sparkle. You are God's."

She did not move.

The silence was long.

Salmon had trouble watching her pain.

She licked her lips. "Did I not trust enough?"

Salmon sighed. He looked at her face, all bruised and battered. Her body was covered, but he had seen enough yesterday to know it was bruised today. Whoever had done this to her would pay. Judgment would come. He would make sure of it.

His hand trembled as he stroked her hair from her forehead. How could he assure her of God's presence after this? "Before our God delivered us, our people suffered in Egypt. Suffering made us ready for Him. It made us look to Him."

Rahab swallowed with difficulty.

Salmon brought a vessel to her lips. He held her head up so she could drink.

She sipped before falling back against his arm. "Then I'm ready for Him. I see Him."

Salmon put the vessel down beside her on the ground. How could God allow this? How could he help her to trust? His mind whirled in circles trying to make sense of this suffering. He hadn't really heard what she said. Then her words registered. "What did you say?"

She smiled, repeating, "I see Him. He's holding my hand."

His example of the father teaching the toddler how to walk ... holding his hand. Salmon felt ashamed he hadn't believed his own words about trusting God.

Had she taken God at His Word? He looked at her.

She seemed settled, at peace.

She had conquered her battle with trust, while he floundered like a swordless warrior, hoping he could make her trust. Why hadn't he trusted God with her trust? He realized what she said and laughed, but it died quickly in his throat. "But I didn't protect you..."

Rahab shook her head. Her face winced in pain by the effort. "God protected."

Salmon was confused. How could she think God had protected her when someone had done this to her?

"I didn't feel a thing." She laughed, then grimaced by the movement. "Man has hurt my body before. But God holds my heart."

Salmon squeezed her hand. He was surprised when she didn't pull away. She may think God had protected her, but he did not. How could God protect her and allow this to happen? Salmon would see this man die. "I didn't protect you ..."

"God was enough." She licked her lips. "I will trust this God Who wants me to know Him."

Salmon sighed. He had practiced and planned how he would ask her. But now he found his courage failed. She trusted. Where were the words he had practiced? "In the elders' meeting, I promised to protect you."

She didn't say anything. Did she hear him?

He swallowed, thinking of how to explain. This was more difficult than he thought it would be. He seemed to be just blundering. Why was this so hard? "My protection comes with a condition."

She licked her lips. It looked like it pained her to keep her eyes open, but she watched him.

He lifted her head and brought water to her lips.

She sipped from the vessel. It seemed to tax her.

He wiped her mouth. "I must marry you tomorrow."

She closed her eyes and trembled.

He saw her tears, slipping out the corners of her eyes. Her consent meant everything to him. Salmon leaned forward until his face was close to her. "I wouldn't make you my wife in the true sense, until you could trust me." He was babbling now, and he knew it.

Ethan had warned him of his emotions with this woman, but he hadn't suggested any other way to protect her.

Salmon had doubted Eleazar's words about his passion, but now he knew it for what it was. He wanted this woman, not just for her beauty, but for her thirst for God, for her hunger to know Him. He lifted her head. "Look at me, Rahab."

She winced, but opened her eyes.

He saw such pain, it frightened him. "Do you find me so despicable you could not want me?"

Her tears were falling faster now.

He traced them with his thumb, trying not to touch her bruises. He couldn't wait for her answer.

She swallowed. "When you grow tired of me, you will regret your decision."

Salmon struggled to tell her what she meant to him. "You're not some dog to be discarded when I tire of it, Rahab. You would be my wife. Like Adam in the Garden needed a helpmeet, I need you by my side."

The sun glistened off a rock nearby and shone brightly. That reminded him of her gold. "Let me see your gold."

Her eyes widened. "I couldn't find it after ... after he came."

He shook his head. He hadn't meant to bring her more pain. He held her hand. "Does the gold ever lose its worth?"

She shook her head, but winced with the pain it brought.

"Neither will I grow tired of you. You are more precious to me than gold."

She choked. "Why?"

"God has saved you. You've been through the fire. And the fire has made you shine."

"Won't your people reject you like they've rejected me?"

Salmon shook his head. How much hurt could one person hold? "You thirst to know our God. It convicts them. They don't like it.

"God separates those who love Him and those who don't. If you are rejected by my people because you thirst for God, I want you standing by my side."

Even as he tried to find words, he knew he loved her. If he told her, would that convince her, or make her withdraw? How many other men had told of their love yet it meant nothing but rejection later? Would she believe him? "Rahab ..." He licked his lips. "I love you."

She closed her eyes.

"Would you marry me?"

Her hand shifted in his. Her face turned ashen behind the bruises. She wouldn't open her eyes.

Would she consent?

The moment seemed longer than any battle he had ever fought. Yet more important than all other battles put together.

She opened her eyes and looked into his. "Yes."

It took a moment for him to realize she had answered. The eagle trapped in the box had been set free. It was soaring. Soaring far above the clouds. He smiled. "Tomorrow, then."

The morning came. Had Rahab only dreamed of Salmon asking her to marry him? She shook her head, feeling the pain that the movement brought her. Maybe the herbs Hannah gave her for pain made her dream strange thoughts.

Hannah slipped inside her tent and sat beside her. "Salmon will be here shortly. Phinehas didn't think you'd be able to stand too long. I found one of your silk tunics for you. Are you strong enough to stand and put it on?"

Rahab hadn't dreamed Salmon asked to marry her. She couldn't focus. Her thoughts spun in circles.

When she tried to stand, Hannah caught her before she fell and helped her to sit. "I feel so shaky."

"Your head wound is deep. Just sit." Hannah slipped the garment over Rahab's head. "The green sets off your eyes. Let me fix your hair."

"Salmon feels obligated to marry me."

Hannah brushed Rahab's hair from her face. "I saw how he looks at you. Rahab, look in his eyes. They show his heart."

"But why would he want me?"

Hannah laughed. "He sees a beautiful woman who is seeking to know his God. Why wouldn't he want you?"

Rahab could think of many reasons...her past, her family, her lack of knowledge about his God. "I can't marry him."

Hannah squeezed her. "He's not like those you've known. He'll protect you. He'll keep his word. Trust him. You have promised him."

Rahab had promised him. Why had she trusted a man again? The words were no more thought, than she smiled. Trust again. God was making her trust Him and His people. What had she told herself before ... trust with her heart and allow her feelings to come later. If she must do it with her God, then she must do it with Salmon. But would that be enough?

Eleazar entered. "Shalom. You are feeling better?"

Rahab nodded. "Be at peace."

He patted her hand. "You will be at peace when Salmon comes."

He opened the tent flaps to make room for the gathering.

Others soon arrived. They eyed her as if she was some piece of meat hanging at market.

Rahab shivered.

Hannah patted her hand. "Salmon is an important leader. Many wish him well."

Rahab didn't think they wanted to wish Salmon well. They took advantage of this opportunity to gawk at the harlot from

Jericho. She thrust her shoulders back and sat straight. She would show a front of courage and grace she didn't feel.

More people came, allowing only standing room.

She began to doubt if Salmon would even come. Did he really want to marry her?

When the campsite was filled beyond what she thought it could hold, Salmon called at the door.

Hannah explained, "It's our custom. The groom comes to the bride's home to request marriage of her father."

She had no father to grant permission. What was she to do?

Eleazar stood and answered.

Hannah leaned closer to whisper. "Eleazar wanted to do this for you. He hoped it was acceptable?"

Rahab didn't know what to think. The High Priest was willing to act as her father? If Salmon accepted her and the High Priest took her as his own, what did it matter what others thought?

Rahab clasped her hands in her lap and waited.

Hannah smiled. "Here's where we couldn't keep with custom. For you would walk with Salmon to the wedding ceremony and all the people would join you. But, in your condition ..." She looked at Rahab and shook her head. "Instead, Eleazar will perform the ceremony here, and you must keep your strength."

Rahab glanced at Salmon as he entered.

He didn't seem to notice all the people crowded in her tent. He looked for her and smiled. He looked at her with...what?

She knew the lust of men at the temple; but this look, although intense and possessive, did not make her feel like she was undressed by his eyes. She felt herself valued. Her face hurt as she smiled back.

He knelt by her pallet and reached for her hand.

His hand was warm, strong but gentle.

She stood.

Eleazar started instructing on the marriage vows.

Everything blurred. Her head felt light. She could feel the room spinning. She was so hot. The silk material smothered her. Had she tightened the belt too tight? She wiped her forehead and tried to focus. She saw two of Salmon, swimming before her face. Her legs felt numb. She swayed.

Salmon caught her as she fell.

Then all went black.

When Rahab woke, she looked around the tent trying to remember what had happened. She remembered the crowd. People staring at her, evaluating her worth. Her thoughts swirled like some moth in the lantern's light. Had she dreamed her wedding?

She closed her eyes and tried to focus.

Voices broke her concentration.

"I warned you about her beauty tempting you." That sounded like the other spy.

"Ethan, her beauty didn't tempt me." That was Salmon's voice, she'd recognize it anywhere. He sounded weary that he must explain. "I am honoring my word."

Ethan sighed. "Saving her, yes, but marriage? Couldn't you have kept your word in a less dramatic way?"

"You didn't offer any other solution in the meeting."

"Would you have listened?"

"No."

There was silence.

She hadn't dreamt the wedding, but had Salmon only married her to honor his word?

"She has many scars. Can she give you an heir?"

Salmon sat near her. "She must heal. I told her I'd wait."

Ethan sounded frustrated, "Until ...?"

"She is ready."

Ethan sighed. "Salmon. Marriage isn't some agreement between merchants. You are joined by God to be one."

"I know. We will be."

In her mind's eye, Rahab could see Salmon's lips tighten shut. He had worn that expression when her family wouldn't listen about circumcision. He had looked angry then. Rahab almost smiled at his stubbornness. He was defending her! Her heart soared. This was a man she could serve.

Ethan's voice lowered. "But she may never be ready."

"That's the risk I take, isn't it?" Salmon's tone seemed to end the conversation.

Rahab shifted on her pallet and groaned. Everything hurt. Her chest felt like it had been sat on by a camel. Her insides where she would receive seed for a child felt shredded. Could she give Salmon an heir? Or had the thief stolen what service she could give Salmon?

"I am here, Rahab." It was Salmon's voice, gentle, almost pleading.

She groaned again but her thoughts wouldn't focus. She drifted back to sleep.

The next time she woke, she heard clanging. What was that?

"We leave for battle."

Was that the spy? Her thoughts swirled above her head. She tried hard to focus.

Salmon answered, "I promised to protect her."

"She can stay with Kamon. She'll be safe."

Who was Kamon? Rahab shifted. Just to move, hurt. She groaned.

They stopped speaking, suddenly.

She felt like a spy, able to listen, but unable to hide.

After a pause, she heard clanking again. She recognized it for what it was ... armor.

The spy's voice lowered, "Your men need you."

"The Lord has given the victory with or without me." That was Salmon.

There was a long pause. Rahab wished she could see their expressions. Her eyes felt heavy.

Their silence meant more than any words.

Did Salmon resent her already?

"Wouldn't you do the same, if it was Kamon?"

"But Kamon wasn't a ..." Ethan stopped himself. His sigh was loud. "I would."

There was a long silence.

Ethan shifted, his armor jingled. His response seemed resigned, "Meet us when you can." Then she heard him leave.

She forced her eyes open.

Salmon met her gaze. "Feeling better?" His voice was gentle, as if the stern conversation had not taken place.

She smiled. Her face's swelling had gone down. She could open her eyes without her cheeks hurting.

"I'm sorry to rush the wedding ... the leaders demanded that you be protected."

The leaders demanded ... to fulfill his duty ... was that what made him marry her? If he did it out of obligation, he would grow tired of her, just like the others.

She closed her eyes. The joy of the wedding was replaced with a heaviness of being trapped by a marriage of obligation. She wouldn't give in to his need for intimacy. Perhaps the marriage could be ended. She didn't want that, but nor did she want Salmon to marry her out of duty.

"Drink this, Rahab." He helped her drink.

He sounded endearing, not like he was annoyed or wanted something from her. Would he soon resent that she kept him from going to battle with his men?

"How long have I been sleeping?"

Salmon smiled and fixed her cover. "Long enough to make me nervous for your return."

She closed her eyes again, already tired from thinking. But even as her thoughts drifted, she knew she didn't want him to leave ever again.

Rahab healed. But with her healing, she sensed Salmon's restlessness. He was attentive to her needs. Always thoughtful, but when he didn't think she watched, he would gaze toward the south.

Rahab could stand it no longer. "You want to be with your men."

Salmon sat beside her, eating their evening meal. He turned his gaze from the south. "I want you to be strong and heal."

"I'm better." She tried to sound strong. She didn't want him to leave. What would happen when he was gone? Yet, if Salmon didn't go, he would resent her if anything happened to his men. "Go, be with your men."

Salmon studied her. "If you stayed with Kamon, you wouldn't be alone. You'll like Kamon. She's like a sister to me. I'll introduce her to you."

Rahab finally convinced Salmon to join his men in battle.

But she didn't know he would leave such a hole in her heart when he left.

Rahab moved her things so she could stay with Kamon while Salmon was gone. Salmon had spoken so highly of her. When she reached Ethan and Kamon's tent, she was surprised by its size. It was bigger than Salmon's, almost by twice. Salmon wasn't much for elaborate housekeeping.

She had smiled at the feminine touches Kamon had added even in the primitive housing. The herbs, drying at the back corner of the tent. Even desert flowers in a vessel by the cook fire.

Kamon showed her to a partitioned section of the tent that would be her private quarters. She laid her cushions and blankets down, completing her move.

Even as Kamon directed her to the room, Rahab felt a cold reception. Although Kamon had been friendly with Salmon before he left, she didn't seem too welcoming of Rahab. It wasn't that she said anything unkind, but Rahab sensed a feeling of unacceptance.

Rahab squared her shoulders and hoped the days without Salmon would pass quickly. Maybe she wouldn't have to stay too long here.

Instead, the days passed slowly. Rahab found herself, watching for the dust in the horizon, signaling Salmon's return.

Rahab was scrubbing a blood stain on one of Salmon's tunics. She glanced at Kamon. Kamon had been teaching her the laws for the women. "My city didn't have all these rules ... it shows me how much God cares for you."

Kamon squeezed the water out of her cloak. "What was your city like?"

Rahab stared ahead, but didn't see. In her mind's eye she saw her day-to-day existence to survive in Jericho. She didn't want to remember those things. But then she thought of the markets. Her mouth quivered into a smile. "At the market, I could see all sorts of silk garments, hanging like flowers in a beautiful bouquet, waiting to be worn. If the merchant looked the other way, I could touch their soft, shimmering fabrics hung at eye level, as if a special garden was planted just for the rich.

"All sorts of sweets were displayed: honeyed figs, dates, and nuts, yet I could only dream of the taste. It made me wish for a life I didn't have. A life of ease, where I could do whatever I wanted."

Rahab paused, shaking her head. "I could see into the lives of the rich, but never taste its pleasure."

Kamon sighed. "The colors alone would be worth seeing."

Rahab didn't want to give a false impression, so she continued, "The rich weren't without their pain. Rich men were still discontent. They came for my services and never paid well, but expected me to give what they thought they deserved. Those men beat me the most. So, in riches, there was pain." Rahab shook her head. "They could buy anything, but it didn't make them happy. Their riches couldn't get them what their soul needed."

Kamon sighed. "You are like Salmon. You see into the hearts of people."

Rahab shrugged. She was encouraged by Kamon's comment, for she had felt a kinship with Salmon. He sensed what people felt, not just what they said.

Kamon's interest also helped to make her want to continue talking. It was not often she could share her thoughts with someone who listened.

Salmon was a good listener too. But this companionship with a woman was different. Maybe if she had been closer to her mother, or even had a sister ... She sighed, wishing wouldn't change anything.

Rahab continued, "I was alone in a crowd. People surrounded me, but no one cared for me. I was beaten close to death a few times by men, but none of my neighbors would have known if I died. Everyone lived for their own pleasure."

"If everyone could do what they wanted, why weren't they happy?"

Rahab snorted. "We did what we wanted ... but didn't get what we wanted out of it. We thought it would make us a happy people. But we weren't. Like my dad. He was a slave to his own desires. He died pursuing happiness but getting none. Life was meaningless, pleasing himself. His desires were never satisfied. They grew and consumed him. It drove him to his death." Rahab swallowed the lump in her throat. She shook her head and didn't finish.

Kamon had stopped washing and stared at her. "Seems a sorry life."

Rahab shrugged. "It was expected."

"Why?"

"In my city, no law told us we had broken any rules. Without rules, we did no wrong. We could do anything we wanted. We sought pleasure under the guise of appeasing the gods. Those gods didn't care what it cost. We did what we wanted ... but not really."

"Ethan described the people as having a hollow look in their eyes, like they weren't home."

Rahab nodded. "Now I know we were made to please our Creator. When we don't, we hurt. We had pain, but no relief. Like our heart was cut out, but we still lived. The pleasure we sought couldn't make the hurt go away. We tried to ease the pain without God." She shook her head. "We could only numb it."

"Like?"

"I drank. I started when the first man threw me out of his house. I was twelve years old at the time. Rejection hurt. Drink helped me forget. Especially when I had to give to other men and knew it wouldn't last.

"Women, who worked the temples all the time, took herbs." Rahab shrugged. "Any way to escape pain.

"My people didn't know your God. But apart from God, nothing's enough. Without God's rules, I became an object of someone else's desires. But with God's rules, I have worth, ... value."

Rahab gestured around her. "Why does this God want to know me?" Her voice broke as she swallowed. Tears filled her eyes.

Kamon had stopped working to listen. She held the damp cloak in her lap. "Rahab. You value what our people take for granted. We have this God, yet we don't recognize Who He is and what He has done for us. We complain about the rules He gives, instead of thanking Him for protecting us from what you endured. You shame us by your worship.

"When Ethan and Salmon brought you to our camp, Salmon was drawn to you. I could see it by the way he watched your camp, as if he was your assigned protector. I warned him not to allow your beauty to allure him." Kamon laughed. "Little good that did him."

Rahab licked her lips. Was that why Kamon had kept her distance? Her beauty had again been a curse. She shook her head. "And now?"

Kamon looked up with tears in her eyes. "It was not your outward beauty, although I know that would attract any man, but your inner beauty. You see God in everyday life. And you draw me to want to know God better.

"Before, I looked at the rules and saw only what my eyes told me. You have shown me to look beyond what I can see, to the more important, unseen things ... to see God."

When the first dust cloud from the warriors was sighted, news spread through camp like a sand storm. All the women ran outside the camp to greet them. The reunion of couples and families was a sight of joy and excitement. Some couldn't wait to share news, telling everything that had happened in the time they were separated. Others, by the intensity of their expression and the squeeze of their embrace, told of feelings deeper than any words that could be spoken.

As men found their families and ambled off to their own campsites, Rahab watched from a distance. She spotted Salmon, almost at the beginning, with his men. His head towered above the rest. But still she didn't step forward. What kind of reception would Salmon give her? What if he didn't want her anymore? She waited in the background as couple after couple left. She stepped behind others, watching him.

He searched the crowds, anxiously, his eyebrows scrunching as he peered at faces.

But still she hid. Why? She didn't know herself. Had she imagined his care for her before, and now she would see it as nothing? Would he remember his promise after the long separation not to touch her? Would she expect him to keep it?

The crowd had thinned.

She almost felt guilty for making him wait so long.

Most had returned to camp.

His expression showed concern and almost panic as he searched for her. He saw her. His face lit into a smile.

She could hardly keep the smile from forming on her own face.

He approached her at a run.

She stood waiting.

When he reached her, he stopped, almost tripping over his feet to stop in time. "You are well?"

She nodded.

He seemed not to know what to do with his hands. He had reached out when he first came close to her, but had dropped them, as she continued to stand and watch him.

"No harm came to you?" He bowed his head to study her face carefully.

"No harm." She shuffled her feet. She felt awkward after watching the other couples embrace, yet she stood back from him.

He smiled. "I missed you." His voice broke.

The intensity in his eyes frightened her. Her tongue felt swollen as if she'd gone without water. She could only nod.

"Let's go home."

She felt guilty by what she knew he wanted. Couldn't she have allowed a warm greeting? But she couldn't bring herself to be touched.

Over the days Salmon was home, she relaxed in his presence and grew to expect his caring manner. She didn't have to please a man to keep from starving, like she had lived before. But she found she wanted to please Salmon. When he commented on how good her flatbread tasted with the herbs she had added, she made them like that again. When he thanked her for the drink she brought him, she wanted to fill it whenever he emptied it.

Instead of feeling like a servant because he demanded, she wanted to serve because he appreciated what she did. She was learning to love Salmon by serving him. Was she also loving her God by pleasing Him?

Salmon honored his promise not to touch her.

By withholding affection, Rahab thought she would stay safe. She would hold her feelings close inside, so when he tired of her and threw her out, she would not hurt. She sensed his tension and frustration at times, like he wished he hadn't promised not to touch her, but she would not allow him. Wasn't this what God wanted, for her to feel safe?

CHAPTER 16

Joshua and his men were traveling south. When they reached the southern tip of the Amorite's territory, Joshua allowed his men to rest. He sent out scouts.

He lounged by his fire, stretching his toes toward the flames as the evening coolness came. It felt good to sit and remove his sandals and wiggle his toes. He massaged his calves. Hiking over the hills reminded him that he was not a young man.

His sword seemed heavier, the deeper they hiked into Amorite territory.

He fingered a fig from a pile before him.

Ethan squatted beside him, helping himself to one of the figs. "Two cities have joined to fight against us. Fighting with swords is difficult on the hills, especially with how tall these people were. There's no room above them to make a stand."

Joshua chewed slowly. The enemies' height was always a consideration. Hadn't the original twelve spies told of the giants in the land? If he could put his men on hills, they would be striking down, a position with an advantage. But even with all the hills, there was no way to position his men above their enemy. "What about their archers?"

"They're skilled in long-distance shooting. They post their archers on hills and shoot down. They don't miss."

Joshua nodded. "Could we outflank them?"

Ethan shrugged. "They are far behind the lines of men."

That would rule out getting on the hill and striking down. "How do we get close enough to fight?"

Ethan shook his head. "I don't know."

In the morning, Joshua stood before his men. The short night had brought no answers. It didn't matter how many battles they had won; each battle brought new problems. This one was no different. With some battles, he felt confident in what his men could do, but with this one ...he shook his head. He had no answers.

He waited to hear the Lord's words, reassuring him of victory. That would be enough to command his men to begin. Then the spirit of the fight would possess him and he could fight.

Today, he felt no confidence of victory. He heard no voice from the Lord. The seed of doubt slid into his being and made him hesitate. Was there sin in the camp, like at Ai? Should he lead his men into a battle where they could not win?

He looked behind him. His men stood ready. Because of the narrow valley, only a few could enter at a time. He looked at the hillsides. Boulders could conceal Amorite archers who would mow his men down in waves as they ran through the valley, even with his own archers defending his men from the hillside on their side. Could he send them through that passage knowing their lives would be lost?

Joshua re-settled his sword at his side.

He still didn't hear a word from the Lord. Should he wait?

The men were getting restless, expecting him to give the charge to battle.

He looked at the sky. He missed the cloud they had followed in the desert. It had seemed so easy then. He licked his dry lips, hoping he could swallow. He removed his waterskin and sipped. The water was still cold from the springs.

Waiting was hard.

He heard the rustling and activity from the Amorite camp.

The Amorite trumpets called them to charge.

The earth vibrated with their pounding feet.

But still Joshua remained where he was. Waiting.

Then he heard another noise.

It wasn't the Lord's voice.

It wasn't the sound of thunder, but it roared, filling his head. Before him, between his army and the Amorites, a black cloud rose from the ground, surrounding the advancing enemy.

Joshua stared. What was fire? He smelled no smoke. It seemed alive in its movement, as it swallowed the progressing army. He braced himself, waiting for the enemy to reach them.

As the enemy advanced, so did the swarm, for that was what it was.

Joshua could now hear the buzzing of the hornets as they attacked the enemy. He motioned for his army to kneel and watch as the Lord gave them the victory.

The Lord drove the Amorites to their knees with His swarm of hornets.

After the swarm of hornets had lifted, Joshua and his men followed in its wake.

Soldiers, stung on the head, had died instantly. Those stung in other places were disabled.

The Israelites ended their suffering.

God had given the victory.

The battle was over. They were clearing the battlefield. Ethan called to Salmon. "Here's another one."

Salmon helped Ethan carry the body to the common burial cave. "I came upon a man who asked me to listen to his story before I killed him."

"What did he say?"

"The man's family was originally from Sodom many years ago, before the Angel of the Lord destroyed that city. Their young daughter had given a piece of bread to a poor man. In punishment, the people smeared the girl with honey and exposed her to a nest of hornets. She died. The girl's family left the city after that, but the story has been passed down through their generations."

Ethan pointed to another body to move. "Now it ends with this man dying of a hornet's sting, too ... But what a sad story. I can't understand that kind of cruelty."

Salmon paused before entering the cave to put down the body. "Maybe that's why God destroyed Sodom."

Ethan squinted as his eyes adjusted to the darkness of the cave. "Remember Jericho's beggar?"

"How could I forget?"

"Maybe that's why our land is ready for us. Do you think it would have been ready forty years ago, when we first sent spies into the land? Or was the people's sin not yet enough for God's judgment?"

Salmon put the body down. "Makes me wonder about the days of Noah. Eleazar and I were talking about those times. The wickedness was so great God destroyed all mankind except eight."

Ethan surveyed the battle scene for more bodies.

Seeing none, they covered the cave's opening with boulders to keep animals from bothering the grave.

Ethan dusted his hands, stepping back. "After seeing God's judgment, why do we try to run from Him?"

The days were long as Rahab waited for Salmon to return. She couldn't complain, for the entire campsite of women waited for their men's return. Their lives held by that thin thread connecting their hearts to those who fought.

Rahab had tired of waiting in camp with little more to do than getting water and making food. She had grabbed her basket and told Kamon she would gather herbs outside of camp. How could she guard her feelings, when she couldn't wait for him to return?

Kamon joined her.

They wandered southward, hoping to catch a glimpse of any dust swirls that might indicate the army's return. They worked in silence, each lost in her own thoughts. The distance had lifted between them after Rahab had shared about her city. A new sense of openness had developed.

Rahab licked her lips before breaking the quietness. "Salmon mentioned that he married me to be his helpmeet. What does that mean? I hope it's more than just cleaning his clothes and making sure he's fed ... even though I'm willing to do that."

Kamon laughed. "Sounds like a pet dog...feed, water, and take him outside the camp. Salmon needs someone to make sure he eats, that's true. That man would forget to eat, if someone didn't cook for him. But, yes, being his helpmeet is more than that." She selected some sage and added it to her basket. "Do you know his dreams? What he longs for?"

Rahab bowed her head and fingered her basket of herbs. She knew what he longed for. She had not allowed him to touch her yet. She needed time. And she must guard her own feelings.

The silence seemed awkward, especially after she had shared so much before. Rahab felt like she must say something. "I can't imagine any man really sharing his dreams." She shrugged.

Kamon nodded. "It took a while for Ethan to share with me. But when he did, it was like he exposed his soul. Men must appear tough and confident, as part of that warrior image. But really, they're fragile. Squishy with a hard shell." She laughed. "They expose that fragile part only to someone they trust."

Rahab didn't like where this was going. She had squelched her feelings as a way of retaining some control when the men came to her. Control gave her power. If she didn't allow Salmon to touch her, she controlled him, and her feelings stayed safe.

She never wished for another man to be near her. Her father had chased away any desire for that! To trust a man, impossible! But her memories took her to a night, not too long ago when a certain spy promised her deliverance, then proved trustworthy. She shook her head. Salmon had weaseled into her heart and found a way to make her miss him. How had she allowed that?

Did she really want to know his dreams, if it required her to be vulnerable? Maybe she could be content with cooking and cleaning. She interrupted. "In my city, no one trusted anyone. I learned to hide my feelings."

Kamon sighed. "Hiding your feelings makes you think you have power, but it's only through vulnerability that a couple becomes one. Intimacy allows your man to be real; it exposes a man's soul."

Kamon said it with such directness, not accusing. Did she know of Salmon's promise not to touch her until she was ready? Rahab shook her head and tried to listen.

"When the world fights against him, he must be strong and unmovable. By being his helpmeet, you provide a secure place where he can be weak and exposed. You support him, so he can fight the world again."

Rahab felt her face flush. She wasn't the helpmeet Salmon needed. In fact, after fighting the world's battles, he had to fight his temptation not to touch her. She was making it harder for Salmon. How could she redirect the conversation, where she wouldn't feel guilty? She hesitated, hoping this new question wouldn't make her uneasy. "What made you know you could live with Ethan?"

Kamon hesitated, weighing her response. She picked at the herbs in her basket. "It wasn't a question of whether I could live *with* Ethan."

Rahab nodded. Putting up with someone's idiosyncrasies only told of your forbearance. Look at her mother, putting up with her father's beatings.

Kamon repeated her statement. "It wasn't whether I could live *with* Ethan. It was more a question of whether I could live *without* him."

They fought their way northward from the southern point of their land, conquering as they went. No survivor was left. From the hill country of the Negev to the lowlands, all were destroyed. They arrived back at their campsite in Gilgal after many weeks.

Joshua released the soldiers to return to their families.

Ethan had found Kamon in their tent. He held her close for a long time. She felt thinner than he remembered. Had she lost weight?

Although his days had been filled with moving camp or battles, nights without her had been long. He breathed her hair. "I missed your smell."

Kamon laughed. "How do I smell?"

Ethan smelled again. "Of rosemary soap ... baked flatbread, wood smoke and sometimes slow-roasted lamb."

Kamon pushed against his chest. "Sounds like you're hungry."

Ethan hugged her tighter. "I can eat anytime. Let me hold you."

"You are fine?"

Ethan nodded. "God was with us in every battle. He held my hand at night and fought beside me every day. He gave peace I couldn't understand. A calmness that even the danger of battle couldn't take away. When Joshua says God is with us, I know it."

"What were the people like?"

Ethan straightened. He stared at the back of the tent, but didn't see it. "It's different killing a soldier in battle than a woman and her child."

"Did it get easier?"

Ethan sighed. "As I entered city after city, house after house, and saw their faces—Kamon, you can't imagine the brokenness of those people. The men use their women as if they were animals. The women gave themselves in sacrifice to anything the gods and their priests told them.

"Their faces had no expression, like they wore masks without life. Their eyes looked like they had no soul. Could someone live and yet not feel? Some didn't even show fear when death was close. It was like all hope was gone."

Kamon shivered. "Rahab has told me of her city. How would anyone come back from such hopelessness?"

Ethan shrugged. "Look at Rahab. She searches for God. Perhaps that spared her from that look of emptiness and hopelessness."

"How do you not grow hardened?"

He cupped her face in his palm. "We obey God. Does obeying God make my heart hard or strong?" He shrugged. "We worked with God in judgment. It seemed a mercy to kill them. I killed and wept.

"I keep my dagger with me all the time, even under my pillow at night. I am lost and naked without it. I have nightmares. I fight in my sleep to protect you from the evil I see during the day."

Kamon tried to step back, but he held her.

"The intensity in your eyes frightens me."

Ethan laughed, dropping his hands. "Your godliness kept me focused. I couldn't wait to return to you."

Kamon shook her head and stepped from him. "You are hungry. I'll get your meal."

When Ethan had entered the tent, Rahab grabbed a vessel and almost ran for water. Seeing Ethan and Kamon's affection made her uncomfortable. Her parents had never shown affection. She still wouldn't allow Salmon to touch her. Was it out of fear? She stayed safe with what she knew, rather than be vulnerable with what she didn't know.

When Salmon found her at the stream, he was winded. He blew out a few short breaths. "Where were you?"

Why was he so concerned? "I came for water."

His intensity frightened her. He seemed angry. He had never been angry at her.

She backed up, afraid of what he would do. Why was he bothered when she hadn't been at the tent?

When the general had returned from battle, he had acted as if he owned her. Now she looked at Salmon. Is that what he thought?

He backed away from her and paced. "When I didn't find you, I thought ..." He shook his head.

What had he thought? She stepped toward him, waiting for him to continue.

He did not. Instead, he grabbed the vessel she had filled with water. "Let's return to our own tent." He didn't wait for her answer, but strode to their tent.

She walked behind him. She wasn't sure she wanted to follow. Had she really missed him when he was gone? She wasn't sure, now that he had returned. Should she prepare her things in case he threw her out of his tent? When they reached their tent, would he keep his promise not to touch her until she was ready?

Rahab could resist his affection and withhold what he desired. But did she really want that? Was it fear of hurt or desire to control that made her decide?

She remembered pleasing him with just a meal. He had been appreciative. Thankful. Was she right to withhold what should be given to her husband?

Salmon would not take what she didn't willingly give.

She controlled at least one man who could have taken something from her. She liked that feeling. It gave her strength. Power.

But with that feeling, she remembered God. Would God be pleased?

She shook her head. She must stay safe.

CHAPTER 17

Jabin, the king of Hazor, stood over his table, surrounded by the kings of the north. Seated around him were Jobab, king of Madon, as well as the kings from Shimron, Achshaph, the north hill country, Arabah, the Canaanites, the Amorites, the Hittites, the Perizzites, the Jebusites, and the Hivites. Jabin raised his vessel and gulped its contents. "You all know why we're here. You've heard of this people from the desert who destroyed Egypt, Jericho, Ai and the southern region of our land. They are moving here. Not to visit, but to take our land.

"We do not consider Gibeon, the deceiver, who played them for a fool and won. But now, who are they? Servants! Carrying their water and wiping the desert people's noses. Is that what you want to do?"

Shouts of "No!" was the unanimous response to his question.

Jabin continued, "How many kings, rulers, princes, and officials do we have here? Look around you." He paused to allow them to look. "At least twenty."

The king of Madon stood. "They have Egypt's armor and swords, pulled off its army when it washed ashore from the Reed Sea."

King Jabin shouted louder. "They have Egypt's armor, but we have chariots and horses. We can mow them down before they even lift their swords."

Jobab, king of Madon, raised his vessel. "They have only one God. One God against our many. What happens if we catch their God sleeping? He must sleep sometime, doesn't He?"

Shouts of consent filled the air as they drank from their vessels and made plans.

"Before we meet by the waters of Merom for battle, let us sacrifice to our gods."

Jabin led them to his temple where he brought more women and men to please the gods in honor of his guests. Orgies were in full display and spirits were high as they planned their victory.

Joshua led his men north. They followed the Jordan River where the path was easier, until they reached the Sea of Chinnereth, the lake to the north. They veered east around the lake, following its beaches and pathways.

Then the rains fell.

Joshua pulled his hood farther over his head to keep the rains from dripping down his back. He had castoff his armor, protecting the leather straps and iron edges from the damage the rains would cause. He glanced back at the carts, drawn by oxen and donkeys, pulling their supplies ... and now their armor. He kept his sword, dagger, and knife within hand's reach.

Joshua's men were tired. They had rested from their southern battle campaign long enough to give God praise and grow restless; then they had moved to the north.

The rest now seemed forgotten.

Joshua's time with Dorona never seemed enough. Each time he left, it seemed harder than the last.

When would they settle? He shook his head; he was thinking like the people. He must focus on the next battle.

They rested for the noon meal, long enough to make something hot to drink. His men needed it; maybe he needed it more. Joshua squatted by the fire, nursing the warm drink between his hands. This dampness made it harder for him to ignore the pain. He massaged his fingers as the heat of the vessel eased away the numbness. Their stiffness, especially after a day of battle, sometimes made his hands ache through the night. Probably caused by swinging the weight of the sword all day.

He watched the fire's smoke as it rose to meet the clouds that hung low, holding more rain.

Salmon and Ethan approached his fire. Ethan took a vessel, pouring himself some hot water.

Joshua acknowledged them with a nod.

Salmon's eyebrows raised when he saw the fish cooked by the embers. "May I?"

Joshua nodded. He waited for them to settle. He had sent them to scout the land.

Salmon took a piece of fish and chewed. "This is good."

Ethan cradled his tea in his hands, allowing the steam to rise into his face. "It's colder here. Their soldiers wear leather boots. I almost wanted to steal them off their feet. These sandals aren't meant for rain."

Joshua stepped closer to the flames, realizing with their reminder of the cold, that his feet were cold. He wished they would chew faster and gulp their tea. He didn't want to hear about cold feet and good fish. He breathed deeply, telling himself to wait patiently. Why was he so impatient for the news?

They were coming to the end of the battles. They would soon be able to settle. He was anxious to return to Dorona. He calmed his thoughts to wait for their news.

Ethan shifted his feet, wiggling his toes before he squatted beside Joshua. He drank from his vessel before taking a stick from the fire's edge. He drew in the damp ground. "We are here." He glanced around him and lowered his voice. "After this small rise is a plain where waters gather from the mountains in the rainy season. They are camped here." He marked above the plains with an "X."

Salmon squatted on the other side of Joshua. "The enemy has accumulated numbers far surpassing anything we've fought before."

Joshua swallowed. He shook off the rain that dripped from his cloak's hood and took a drink from his now cold tea.

Salmon coughed, waiting until Joshua met his eye. "Twenty kings have combined forced against us."

Joshua nodded. He hoped their cities were small.

Ethan continued to draw in the mud. "That's not all." He seemed to take his time explaining.

Joshua struggled to wait.

"They have horses."

"How many?"

Ethan tossed his stick into the fire. "Enough horses to be a city all by themselves. They corral them behind their camp to the north."

Joshua poured himself another cup of hot water. He didn't want another cup, but he could hold it while he thought. He flexed his fingers around the vessels, savoring the warmth.

"That is not all." Ethan poured another vessel of tea and waited until it had steeped.

Salmon interjected, "They have chariots."

Joshua's voice rose, "Like Egypt?"

Salmon lowered his voice, "They're made of wood, covered with leather. One king arrived while we watched. They excel at a frontal attack, but they cannot maneuver turns."

Ethan shrugged. "That's why they congregate in the plains. They'd be useless in the hills."

Joshua considered. "But their frontal attack?"

Ethan nodded. "Would be deadly. No man would stand against it."

Joshua sipped from the scalding drink, without feeling it. "If we sent our archers behind their camp, up on the hills, and shot their horses in the corrals before they were ready?"

Salmon shook his head. "After one arrow, there'd be pandemonium. We must break down their forces without their knowledge."

Joshua sipped again of his tea. He picked at a piece of fish on the coals before him. It had cooled with the rain. He didn't taste it.

Salmon motioned to the fish. "Are you going to eat that or just play with it?"

Joshua pushed it toward him. "Go ahead."

Salmon nodded to Ethan.

Ethan took a fish. "I'd better get mine, before you eat it all." He took a hardened flatbread to scoop up the fish.

Salmon's eyebrows raised. "All finished?" With Ethan's nod, he grabbed the rest. He ate with his eyes closed. "This is good." He licked his fingers and smiled. Then he seemed to remember what they were doing. He wiped his hands down his cloak. "We could position the archers on the hillsides around the plains. They could focus on the chariots, preventing their advance. We might not be mowed down like grass."

Hezron's special division of men, skilled with bows, slings, and rods, excelled in long distance fighting. Looking at the enemies' chariots and cavalry, this might save his men.

Joshua shook his head. "But we would still lose too many men. Our problem is the horses. How do we immobilize their forces and make them fight us on foot?" The tea sloshed inside him now. He put his vessel down and stood. He adjusted his sheath, letting his hand rest on his sword's hilt.

Salmon repeated Moses's words, "'A thousand may fall at your side and ten thousand at your right hand, but it shall not approach you.' How can we keep the horses from approaching us?"

Joshua looked at his men around him.

His footmen clustered in groups around small fires. They were seasoned fighters, knowing the taste of victory. They had learned to work together, as a unified front.

But not against horses.

And not against chariots.

He removed his hood and raised his head to the rain.

The rain continued to fall. Its cold, icy fingers touched his up-turned face. He closed his eyes, silently asking the Lord what he should do. Then he waited.

He didn't like to wait for news of the battle. He didn't like to wait for the Lord to answer. But most of his life, learning at Moses's side, was spent waiting. Waiting at Mount Sinai when Moses received the Law. Waiting for water in the desert. Waiting for manna to be sent. Waiting before each battle for confirmation of God's presence.

Joshua hated waiting. But when he didn't wait, like at Ai and Gibeon, his men suffered. He would wait now. He would wait until he knew what to do.

The rain paused. The sun broke through a cloud for a brief moment.

Then the Lord spoke. "Don't be afraid. I will deliver all of them into your hands. Hamstring their horses. Burn their chariots."

Joshua nodded. He put on his hood again.

Salmon studied Joshua. His eyes twinkled. "The Lord has spoken?"

Joshua nodded. "If we hamstring their horses ..."

Salmon nodded. "I once saw a horse's hamstrings damaged by a cart accident. It could no longer pull a heavy load across the desert, but it was still useful for light work."

Ethan stood beside them. "If we went at night, they would harness their horses to their chariots in the morning and have chaos."

Joshua smiled for the first time since hearing the news.

Ethan and Salmon grinned at each other.

Ethan nodded. "How many men should we take with us tonight?"

They made plans.

The rains continued to fall.

In the morning's early grey light, the rains still poured. Joshua stood before his men armed for battle. They had positioned Hezron's archers, along with the sling and rod throwers, on the hills above the enemy.

On the other side of the enemies' camp, Joshua's strong desert footmen would strike first, before their enemy assembled. He raised his sword over his head. "Fear not, men. The battle is the Lord's."

His men raised their swords and responded in unison. "The battle is the Lord's."

They rounded the hillside, stormed into the enemies' campsite and attacked.

A cry sounded. Pandemonium erupted as men tried to grab their swords and prepare for battle.

The enemy barely had time to see their killers, before being felled by their swords.

Behind the campsite, men hurried to harness horses to chariots. The horses strained against their leather strappings, churning the mud where they stood, but they could not move the chariots. Men angrily whipped their horses, trying to make them move. But they could not. They unleashed the heavy chariots and mounted the horses bareback, charging toward the fight.

Arrows strung on bows flew from surrounding hillsides, striking down horses and riders before they could reach the footmen. Those still able, slid from their horses, and pulled out their swords.

In the meantime, the desert footmen had already pushed the men beyond their campsite and up into the forests to the north.

Swords clanked.

Men groaned.

Sounds were muted by the falling rain.

Joshua's sword grew so heavy, it required two hands to wield it.

He rubbed his hands to ease the numbness.

Someone lunged at him with drawn sword.

He must focus.

Mistakes cost blood.

He shifted his sword with both hands. By deflecting the enemy's sword, he exposed the man's neck.

The man fell.

Joshua turned in time to avoid the thrust of another who flanked his left.

Ethan sliced through the man from behind and nodded at Joshua before turning back to face the front.

The sun melted the rain clouds. The day faded into evening.

Joshua's throat was dry. He pulled his water skin from his side and drank, his water trepid now from the warmth of his body. He wiped his mouth with the back of his hand, tasting his sweat. Digging in his pocket for a dried fig, he shook from weakness. He chewed, savoring the sweetness.

He surveyed how his men fared. The plains where the enemy had planned for victory had become a pool of water, flooded by the mountain streams and the rains.

His archers had kept the horses from mowing down his footmen. Those with slings had brought disorder among the horses. Many riders were thrown. Their horses ran off.

His footmen had pushed the armies into the enemies' back lines and surrounding hills.

The Lord had prevailed.

Joshua rubbed his arm. The sword's weight had grown heavier throughout the day. He wiped his sword clean in the grass before returning it to his scabbard.

The rain had stopped. The dry stream beds had filled with the water from the mountains as they rushed into the waters of Merom. The ground, thirsty for cleansing, would be washed by the blood of the slain.

And the Lord would be pleased.

Renewed by his brief rest, he looked at what must be done.

Chariots must be burned. The city of Hazor destroyed. The kings killed. The cattle and spoil collected.

The Lord had destroyed the power of these men who thought they could fight God and win.

No city had begged for pity.

They would not bow to a God Who would only accept their all.

They wanted their pleasure, gods, and comfort.

He took it all from them and showed no mercy.

The day began without the rain of the previous day. The desert people had conquered the people of the north and had removed the spoils from the city of Hezron. Now they must burn it.

Mikar wiped his face with his arm. He grew weary of serving these ungrateful, demanding people. But he would not serve long. He would continue spying under the guise of a submissive servant. By serving, he gained information and found people he could influence. He listened and watched and waited.

Yesterday's rains made the smoke blacker. It filled the air. The city would burn for several days.

How many cities had these people destroyed?

He had lost count.

When they entered the temple, destroying the gods, Mikar clenched his fists. No one destroyed the gods without paying. The gods had served him well. He, in turn, would continue to serve them. He knew where his power came from.

Nor did he forget his vow to make one pay who had turned from the gods. She had known the goodness of the gods but had forsaken them. Her beauty would serve the gods. And him.

Mikar thought he had taken care of her the first time, but just as they had prepared to fight in the south, he found out she was still alive.

The next time he would not leave until his task was complete.

Salmon looked over the battlefield, littered with bodies of men and horses. The sight sickened him, and he turned to watch the sunset. The reds in the sky only reminded him of the colors on the ground behind him.

The cool air swept down the mountainside, bringing the smell of the burning city, the charred chariots, and the smoldering horseflesh. He wiped his nose wishing he could wipe away the cause of the smoke as well.

Ethan came and stood beside him. "Another victory."

Salmon nodded. "Those horses were quality."

Ethan drank from his waterskin, savoring each swallow. Then he wiped his mouth with the back of his hand. "We'll still be able to use the horses that are still alive for light work and plowing."

"Those chariots were something, weren't they? We'd depend on the horses and chariots for future victories if we kept them. The Lord knows us, doesn't He?"

"And protects us from ourselves," Salmon laughed. "When we listen."

"You fight with more passion." Ethan took a sideways glance at Salmon.

Salmon adjusted his sword and shrugged.

"It wouldn't be because you have someone at home to fight for, would it?"

Salmon laughed. "It does make a difference. I don't want Rahab hurt."

Ethan nodded. "Marriage gives purpose."

Salmon nodded to the branches of a tall tree on the crevice of a cliff. "There's an eagle's nest." He studied it for a moment. "Ever see their mating dance?"

When Ethan shook his head, Salmon continued, "The male locks talons with the female. He carries her upside down, even though she's bigger than he. They spin in a downward spiral, almost crashing to the ground before he lets go and they fly apart.

"The dance tests the male. If he can carry the female, then he can hold up her babies when they learn to fly."

Salmon felt like that male eagle. Spiraling downward, holding onto Rahab, but without a hope of ever soaring. He sighed. He protected Rahab from outside dangers, but without her allowing intimacy, how could he ever really protect her heart?

He spent all his energy honoring his promise not to touch her. How could he have any energy left to guard her against others?

He didn't feel like soaring.

Ethan interrupted his thoughts. "Kamon has enjoyed getting to know Rahab."

Salmon shook his head to focus on Ethan's words. "I'm grateful you allow her to stay with Kamon while we fight."

"Any way to find out who attacked her?"

"Rahab told me maybe God wanted to show mercy to him."

Ethan laughed. "Over your dead body."

If the man was punished, would Rahab feel safe enough to be touched? Salmon had waited. He'd been patient. Sometimes, beyond what he could take. Was this what his marriage would be? Never consummated? Only able to see a beautiful woman and not touch her? Salmon shook his head. "It's unfinished business."

The sun disappeared behind the mountain. The smoke became more intense with the cooler temperatures.

Ethan pointed to the burning city. "How many people still hide in the hills? Sometimes I feel like I'm being watched."

Salmon nodded. "It's by God's justice we win the battles. It's by His mercy we are protected when we don't know it."

Ethan wiped his hands down his tunic. "It's been five years of fighting."

Salmon nodded. "Seems like the desert was a different lifetime. Were you in Egypt?"

Ethan nodded. "I was very small."

Salmon leaned against a tree. "It's been a long road to free-dom."

Ethan took an apple from his pocket and bit into it. "Want one?" He threw one to Salmon.

Salmon caught it and shined it on his tunic. "How did you find these?"

"You've been looking at the dead horses scattered all over the ground, while I've been looking in the trees. They're loaded with fruit."

Salmon shook his head. "And you stopped to pick an apple?"

Ethan shrugged. "Victory was sure." He crunched through his apple. "Are we finished?"

"With my apple? Do you have a meal in that pocket of yours?"

Ethan laughed. "No. Are we finished fighting?"

Salmon sobered. "Can we ever be finished fighting evil? Didn't it try to take over in the Garden with Adam? Haven't we had to fight it ever since?"

Ethan shook his head. "These people were consumed with pleasure."

"Did you see the pictures etched in stone in their temples?"

Ethan nodded. "Probably why God wanted the entire city burned. There was nothing good to save."

"I felt defiled by burning it. But in spite of the evil, I still knew God was there with me." Salmon crunched another bite. "No wonder He felt like vomiting. How does a people become so wicked?"

Ethan chewed his apple. "They look at themselves and can't see God. They become their own god."

"It'll be Passover when we reach the main camp. Rahab brings a fresh look at what we take for granted. She offers gratitude and worship to God that puts me to shame." Salmon tossed his apple core. She was healing. He must be patient.

They reached the stream. Ethan bent to drink. "Yes, the Pass-over will hold greater significance this year for all of us."

"Why?"

Ethan looked around the mountains and at the sky. "Because our God has brought us home."

CHAPTER 18

Their conquest was complete. The individual tribes would remove the remaining peoples. They marched home from conquering the northern lands.

Loaded carts with the spoils of battle lumbered into Shechem where the congregation camped. All the swords, armor, and knives, accumulated after each battle, had been redistributed to soldiers as needed. But the spoil they would disperse when the land was divided.

Joshua called the people together.

Eleazar stood beside him and raised his arms to silence the people. "When we went into Egypt, our people were few in number, only seventy. But we went by Joseph's invitation because the famine would be long. We have grown like the stars, just as God promised our father, Abraham.

Now we have left Egypt behind. And when we left, we brought Joseph's bones along with us as he requested. He wanted to be buried, not where he ruled and reigned, second only to Pharaoh in power, but here, in the Land promised by his God. Today we honor that request by burying him in the land Jacob purchased for one hundred pieces of silver. His bones may lie here, but he lives with our God for the obedience he showed."

They buried Joseph's bones.

The Land was theirs.

Eleazar dismissed them with a blessing.

Joshua watched the people return to their tents.

Caleb approached Joshua. He pushed aside the tent flap so they both could enter the Tent of Meeting. "May I show you a mountain that I want?"

Joshua laughed. "Just a mountain? You disappoint me."

Caleb walked to the map of the Land on a table in the middle of the room. "Remember when we spied out the land? We saw those fields rich with grain and the hillside rippling with grapes and orchards?"

Joshua nodded. "You wanted it then. Haven't changed your mind?"

Caleb laughed.

Joshua dipped his reed pen in the ink and circled the mountain and its surrounding area. "Your age hasn't slowed you down. We'll confirm it when we cast the lots with the others."

Caleb nodded. "I can wait."

Joshua finished marking the map. "Do you know what the Lord told me?" After Caleb shook his head, he continued, "That I was old and well stricken with age."

Caleb laughed. "He hasn't told me that."

"Well, I wasn't feeling so great before He told me that, but afterward, it was all I could do to get off my pallet in the morning."

Caleb looked down at the area circled on the map. He pointed to another area. "Include Kiriath-sepher in that circle."

Joshua extended the circle. "You will fight the city?"

Caleb shook his head. "Whoever claims the city, I'll give Achsah to wife." She was his last unmarried daughter. "I'll give the surrounding area to my son-in-law for his conquest."

Joshua shook his head. "Isn't claiming your daughter enough?"

Caleb laughed. "I may be strong, but I can't do it all. What I have been able to do, though, has always been done for the Lord."

The people had settled into a time of rest, waiting for home. Even though the land was now theirs, they weren't quite home until they could each claim their own section of land.

Joshua made his way through the crowd to the front of the assembly. He raised his hands. "Order, men. We're here to divide the land, to give each tribe their inheritance. Make room for the elders."

Those who held the stones to cast the lots moved to the front.

Joshua pointed to the map of the Land that was spread on the table.

Eleazar stood beside him, ready to record the results of the lots.

Joshua circled an area on the map. "We draw for who will have this land. Men throw your stones."

Phinehas stood back with his stone. He represented the tribe of Levi. He would not throw his stone for any land. The Lord had commanded the people to care for them. They would not be dependent upon the Land but upon its people, for their life.

Eleven men, one from each of the other tribes, threw their stones into the circle marked on the ground. Each stone was flat and held the tribe's emblem on one side and nothing on the back side. Everyone stepped forward to see the results.

Joshua nudged one stone toward Caleb, who stood beside him. "Judah gets it. The Lord has His Hand in the placement of these lots."

Caleb laughed, stepping away from the circle. He had been faithful forty-five years ago when the ten spies had reported against the Lord.

"Caleb has requested this mountain range. In honor of his faithful service, and in anticipation of clearing his mountains of the inhabitants, his wish is granted by the Lord. He has also made it known that the man who desires his daughter Achsah, may win her by claiming Kiriath-sepher."

Othniel, son of Kenaz, stepped forward. "I'll capture that city for your daughter, Caleb."

"Let it be done." Caleb nodded.

The meeting moved forward to subdivide the land by families.

Joshua circled another area of the land. "Men throw your stones."

Two emblems showed. "Ephraim and Manasseh will draw again to see which one receives the land." They dropped their stones again.

Joshua nudged Ephraim's stone to its owner. "Ephraim gets the land."

"The next land will be here." He gave the boundaries of another parcel. "That is Manasseh's, by the third lot."

Joshua looked around for the leaders within the tribe of Manasseh. "Could the families represented by Manasseh step forward and throw their stones?"

Zelophehad stepped forward. "Joshua. I represent Hepher my father, but I have no sons to carry on his name. My five daughters request an inheritance to carry on my name."

Joshua looked at Eleazar. "The law requires a son should inherit the land ..."

The daughters squeezed to the front of the assembly and bowed before Joshua and Eleazar. "Grant us an inheritance."

Eleazar smiled. "It's most unusual ... but I think warranted. Let them receive land."

"Thank you." They rose from their knees, smiling their thanks.

"Shall we continue dividing the land?" Joshua looked around at the gathered men.

One leader raised his voice over the group. "I'd like to walk the land. The only time I've seen it is marching through it in the night or in battle. If it pleases Joshua, Eleazar, and the leaders, grant us time to see what we will possess."

Joshua said, "A reasonable request."

Eleazar nodded. "Any objections?"

When none were given, Joshua instructed, "Take three men from each tribe to walk the land. Bring your descriptions to me. Then we will cast lots before the Lord. Any questions?"

Seeing none, Joshua ended the meeting. "We'll meet again in Shiloh and finish the division of the land."

When Salmon returned to his tent after the leaders' meeting, he settled on the cushions before the fire. He ate of the meal before them. "Three men from each tribe must describe the territories before they finish drawing the lots."

"You will go?" Rahab tried to hide her disappointment. She pushed another flatbread toward him.

"This is good." He chewed for a moment, then shrugged. "I'm a leader."

"You always leave..." Rahab stopped when she noticed his expression of determination. He left a lot. It seemed like he volunteered for extra duties so he wouldn't have to be at home. Did he regret his marriage already? She heated another flatbread.

"You will stay with Ethan and Kamon."

Ethan and Kamon convicted her of what she hadn't given to Salmon. She couldn't be a true helpmeet to Salmon and guard her heart. "Ethan isn't going with you?"

He shook his head.

She lowered her head and would not look at Salmon. "I won't stay with them."

Salmon's eyes widened. He opened his mouth to speak, then shut it. He dropped his eyes and finished his meal.

Rahab choked down the rest of her food. She felt like she was chewing on a stick. Why was she being so stubborn? Could she be safe and vulnerable at the same time?

The air felt heavy.

They finished their meal in silence.

She left the uneaten food by the fire and prepared for sleep. She heard Salmon preparing for the night.

Why had he suggested she go with Ethan?

She turned her back to him. She would not relent.

She felt him squat beside her.

She tensed.

Salmon coughed. "Rahab, look at me." His voice was intense, pleading, yet commanding.

She cringed. She would try to be strong and not relent. She turned to him.

He held a dagger in his hand.

She gasped. Would he use it on her? She could hardly listen to his words as she stared at the dagger.

He kept his voice level. "I'll leave my dagger under your pillow. When you need it, use it."

She stared at the dagger. She shook her head. "I couldn't use it."

Salmon placed it under her pillow and patted it. His voice became hard. "When you stab, stab low, twist, and pull up."

He moved to his pallet, laid down, and fell asleep.

Rahab could not. How could he fall asleep after telling her how to kill someone? Why did he say, "When," not "if"? She had blocked out her attack. But Salmon's warning awakened the threat. Did he think the attacker would return? She shifted from one position to another all night without sleep.

Early before the sun rose over the mountains, Rahab packed food for Salmon's trip. The silence of the night gained weight in the pre-morning light.

Salmon tied his waterskin to his belt and adjusted his food. Before leaving, Salmon stood in front of her. "You won't stay with Ethan and Kamon?"

"No."

Salmon's tone wasn't harsh or demanding. "I'd feel better if you did. Why won't you?"

She shook her head. She felt tears pooling. She lowered her head. How could she explain that they showed her how she should treat him? Why couldn't she overcome her fears to do what she should? She coughed then swallowed. "God will be with me."

Salmon nodded and stepped away from her. "It will be only a short time."

She felt cold air fill the space between them, like a chasm that she couldn't cross. She wanted to reach out and call him back, but he had already turned to leave.

Rahab sighed. A short time was forever when Salmon was gone. She wished he didn't have to go.

At the tent's opening, Salmon looked back at her for a long moment. He seemed to read her thoughts. "Ask Eleazar what Moses said about a thousand years." And he walked away.

Ever since they had returned from fighting, Mikar had watched for an opportunity to complete his task. When the harlot had lived alone, it had been easy. Now, living among the people and married, his opportunity was harder to find. The people would separate soon and spread across the entire country. His chance would be gone.

He must teach that harlot the consequences of forsaking the gods' pleasure and worshiping Another. He must also challenge this God.

Mikar had waited patiently.

But time for waiting was past.

After the sun rose, Rahab prepared her campsite for the day. She put away the food from their meal the night before. She still felt torn. How could she be Salmon's helpmeet when she wouldn't even obey his small request?

She tried to keep herself busy, so she wouldn't think of the long days and even longer nights she'd have to endure until he returned. How could one man's absence make time move so slowly?

The sun was creeping slowly, just ready to shed its light over the mountain range as she made her way to the Tent of Meeting. She would speak with Eleazar. As far as she was concerned, just this day could be a thousand years by the time it was over.

When Eleazar finally came to the Tent, Rahab asked what Moses meant about a thousand years.

He considered for a time before he smiled. "Ah. Moses spoke of dwelling in the Lord's presence. 'For a thousand years in His sight are like yesterday when it passes.'"

"What does it mean?"

Eleazar shrugged. "Time means nothing to God. We are confined by moments. He promises us something. It seems to us it takes forever for fulfilment. But for Him, if He says He will do it, He already has."

"So how can we understand His time?"

Eleazar laughed. His wrinkles raised around his eyes. "We won't."

Rahab shook her head. "Then why does He put us in time?"

"Time helps us to dwell in His presence."

"How?"

"God's presence is here now. But we lose His Presence when we worry about tomorrow, or remember yesterday's pains, or focus only on today's things." Eleazar shook his head. "But time is not un-important. Moses asked God, 'Teach us to number our days, that we may present to You a heart of wisdom ... Make us glad You have afflicted us, and for the years we've seen evil.'"

He paused allowing her to consider. "Does that help?"

She hesitated, then nodded. She walked back to her campsite. She must think about this.

How did she spend her days? Dwelling on her pain? Keeping safe because people had hurt her in the past?

She wasn't glad for her affliction. If she gave her pain to God, would she then know wisdom? If she spent her time in God's presence, would she feel pain?

Singing helped. The songs His people sang in worship focused on God.

In the days that followed, by thinking about the words of the songs, and remembering the Law, she thought less about her own pain and safety. Her joy became full.

She remembered Joshua's words when she had first come to camp, that "God would change her." She had foolishly thought it would hurt because she would have to do evil. Now she understood. The change would hurt because God would take away the evil from her own heart. He would make His desires to be hers. It would only hurt while she hung onto what she wanted to do. When she gave it up, the hurt would stop. And He would be pleased.

As she thought about God, she also remembered Salmon. She couldn't wait for his return. She wouldn't withhold what a wife should give because she feared rejection. She would submit to his affection. She went to sleep each night thinking of Salmon and God.

And Salmon's absence passed like a thousand years.

The nights were long and quiet. Rahab hadn't realized having Salmon sleep near her gave her a peace that allowed her to close her eyes without worry at night. With him gone, she found that she would shift and squirm on her cushions, trying to sleep. Often she would bump the dagger. The cold steel would startle her fully awake and she would have to tell God of her past pain and ask Him to heal those wounds and take the worry of any future attacker away.

She found, by concentrating on the words of the Lord, she could sleep.

One night after sleeping several hours, she awoke. She lay motionless, listening for what had awakened her. Nothing seemed different. Yet she felt she wasn't alone.

Dread crept over her. Had her attacker returned? Is that why Salmon had been so adamant about her staying with Ethan and Kamon? Why had she been so stubborn?

Panic shook her.

A foreboding filled her.

She sensed the other's presence closing the gap between them. The air felt black, thick, suffocating.

Her heart beat faster. She heard its pounding. Whoever was there must hear it, too.

She felt herself holding her breath. She had to will herself to breathe. Slowly. Deeply.

There was no moon.

Someone stumbled over wood she had left for the morning's fire. "Salmon?" She whispered. But knew it wasn't him.

When no one responded, she slid her hand beneath her pillow to hold the dagger. Could she use it?

She rolled, without a sound, away from her pallet and sat against the tent's canvas.

As soon as she moved, she felt a brush of air as something slashed through the pallet where she had just been.

She swallowed a scream, not wanting to give away her location. She couldn't squeeze any closer to the tent wall. She held her breath.

"Where are you, harlot?"

She felt air move around her knees as he shoved her bedding, feeling for her. It would only be a matter of time before he found her. She sat still, not breathing.

"The gods have come to take back their own."

Time stopped.

She had told Salmon she couldn't hurt someone. But this man was the one who had come before. She recognized his voice. She knew what he would do.

"Where are you, harlot?" His voice louder.

In the dark, she felt cool air as if the tent flap had opened. Was that Salmon? Could she alert Salmon, without giving away her location?

"Harlot, where are you? You were given to the gods. Yet you betrayed them. I will make you pay your dues."

As he spoke, he touched her knee and laughed. "Thought you could hide from me?" His hand moved up her leg.

She couldn't move.

He followed her leg up her tunic.

She smelled his rank breath. She swallowed the bile that rose in her throat as he breathed in her face. She shuddered, but couldn't scream.

She adjusted her grip on the dagger, relaxing her fingers, then tightening for a better grip. She held her arm back ready to strike.

Hit low. Bring it up and twist.

She was ready.

He grabbed and ripped her tunic. The sound seemed loud in the silence. "We will do again what we've done before, only this time, I'll make sure you don't live to make the gods unhappy."

He pulled her toward him.

His jerk gave momentum to her lunge with the dagger.

Holding the dagger with two hands, she thrust the dagger forward low with as much force as she could. She twisted it. She felt his warm blood pour down her hand. Cringing, she lifted the knife upward.

He grunted and fell on her. "Curse you, harlot. For believing their lies about this God."

She did not let go of the dagger, but kept twisting and turning it. She could smell the blood. She tried not to think of what she was doing.

"Rahab?" It sounded like Salmon, his voice very close.

Her voice trembled, "I'm here."

He grabbed the man and threw him to the ground.

Salmon reached for Rahab. "Are you all right?"

Rahab fell into his arms. "Salmon, I'm sorry. I should have listened."

Salmon squeezed her tightly. "Shh. It's over."

Rahab held onto him. Her entire body shook as she sobbed.

He rested his chin on her head. "He won't bother you again."

Rahab clung to him. Her fear found comfort in Salmon's arms. She trusted Salmon. That night she gave herself to him.

As she gave to her husband, she knew a deeper love for God. Was that what happened as man and wife became one flesh?

When the darkness of the night was replaced by the new day, Salmon turned from holding Rahab to deal with the body on their tent floor.

Salmon took his dagger from the man's back and wiped it on a cloth by the fire. He replaced it in his sheath. He searched the man's pockets and removed the gold piece taken from Rahab during the first attack. He examined it in his hand. He had been the first attacker.

By the awl in his ear, the man was one of the Gibeonite servants. Was this a sign of what would come if they left any in the land?

Salmon rolled him over with his foot. The man was stabbed in the front. Salmon raised his eyebrows at Rahab. "You stabbed him?"

She could only nod. "I forgot about God's mercy."

Laughing, he hugged Rahab. "No, you remembered God's justice." Salmon stopped laughing. "He wouldn't leave our tent alive. But I hadn't counted on your help." He shook his head and laughed again. "The Lord is gracious."

"Why do you say that?"

Salmon squeezed her. "Now I can sleep in peace."

"You couldn't before, after you told me that God was with you?"

Salmon smiled. "I needed to protect you." He gave her the gold piece.

She gave it back. "I once needed the gold to remind me of my worth."

Salmon's eyebrows raised in question. "Not anymore?"

"You've shown me my value.

"Eleazar told me once, 'When I knew of my unworthiness, and accepted God's mercy, I would know God better.' I now understand what he meant."

Salmon hugged her. "You are my treasure, more precious than gold."

Rahab rested her head on his chest. Her fear of his rejection seemed so small. "I'm sorry it took so long to submit to you. I thought you would grow tired of me and cast me out."

Salmon squeezed her. "Gold doesn't lose its value. Nor do you. You just grow more precious." Salmon laughed. "But the time was like a thousand years to me as I waited for you to trust me."

"A thousand years for me was a moment away from you."

Salmon laughed. "Those moments couldn't get any longer."

"Eleazar told me to be glad God has afflicted us, and for the years we've seen evil. That helped me to look past the pain and thank Him."

Salmon studied her, tucking her hair away from her face to see it better. "So, did you?"

"That's what made me give myself to you."

Salmon hugged her again. "Then I can thank God for the evil, too."

The sun had almost reached its zenith when Joshua reached the cave away from their campsite. "Shalom."

Salmon turned from placing the last boulder over the grave of Rahab's attacker. He wiped his hands down his tunic and smiled. "Be at peace."

Joshua gestured to the grave. "Resolution has been made."

Salmon smiled. "Justice is good. In all the battles we've fought, but I've never had this much satisfaction of its finality as this one."

Joshua fingered his dagger's hilt. "You experienced the evil personally. It effected your family."

Salmon shrugged. "There have been many graves. Death's finality never got easier. In a way, their evil sealed their death. But with this death," He paused searching for the right words. "Evil cost us. Its removal gave freedom and peace in a tangible way."

"It's good to be on God's side." Joshua studied Salmon. "Not always easy, but always best." He paused not knowing how to say what he had come to say. He licked his lips and tried to speak again. "I was wrong."

Salmon's eyebrows raised but he didn't speak.

"I was wrong about Rahab." Now that he had started, the words rushed out quickly. "Remember when we first visited her campsite, I told her God would show Himself to her, and she would know Him."

Salmon nodded, a quizzical look on his face.

"I thought God would change her to be more like our people, to live like us and be like us. That's what I thought God would do."

Salmon smiled and nodded. "It's not the Law that saves us. Sometimes our people think by living the Law God will be pleased. And in a way, He is. But the Law orders our lives so that me must look to God. So we don't forget Him in our daily lives. The Law sets us apart as a unique people, not so that we can glory in the Law but so we can glory in the God Who gave us the Law."

Joshua nodded. "She found God, and so changed, maybe in spite of our people who should have showed her God. But as God changed her, He showed me my pride in thinking only our people were worthy of His mercy. He convicted me of my arrogance that only those whom I thought were worthy could please Him."

Salmon nodded. "He wants all to know Him. God's mercy reaches anyone."

Joshua added, "God reached someone like her, who knew she was wrong, rather than someone like me who didn't think I had anything to change. She continues to show me our God."

"Rahab shows me how to search for God, too." Salmon laughed. "She makes me know God so I can answer the questions she asks me."

Joshua smiled for the first time. "God's mercy works on all of us."

"He does, indeed."

CHAPTER 19

The leaders had returned from mapping out the Land. The entire congregation assembled at Shiloh where the Tent of Meeting would stay. Joshua raised his arms. "Men of Israel. Assemble yourselves. Let us divide and settle."

Lots were thrown, boundary lines were drawn, the land was divided.

The Lord portioned out the land for the people.

Joshua admonished them. "The Lord has given us the Land. We have fought these five years to claim it. Remember His command to remove all the people who did evil. Otherwise, they will turn your hearts from God. The Lord will strengthen you. We're not finished yet."

Joshua looked at Eleazar and Phinehas. "The land is rich, flowing with milk and honey, promising wealth to those who obey God. We must take care of the Levites who receive their inheritance from the Lord by way of our offerings. The Lord promised the Levites would have cities with pastures for their use."

Eleazar nodded. "Another reason why all of you should not forsake the Lord's Words. My family would starve."

They laughed.

Joshua raised his arm toward the families of the Kohathites, of the Levite tribe. "We will cast lots for which cities will host the families of the Kohathites."

They cast lots. The family of Kohathites received twenty-three cities, scattered throughout the land.

They cast lots for the families of Gershon and Merari. All of them were provided places to live, raise their cattle, and grow their food.

Joshua looked at the map. "We have one more item for business. Moses described the cities of refuge."

Caleb interrupted, "Where do you want to settle, Joshua?"

Others took up the question, "Yes, Joshua. Where will you be?"

Joshua looked over the crowd of faces and tears welled in his eyes. He had come from following Moses's footsteps to leading this people by listening to God's words. He had watched as God delivered them from Egypt, provided for them in the desert, and now given them their land. He had been there in their hardships, their struggles, their growth. The battles had brought them closer, making them depend upon on one another. He couldn't think of anywhere he would rather be than with this people. He had even come to learn that the harlot, though a foreigner, could find and know God. He swallowed and wiped his eyes with the sleeve of his cloak. "When I spied out the Land forty years ago, I saw a land ripe for our taking. I saw our God wanting to bless. Now, I see how God has provided. It is more than enough.

"It's my desire to be in the center, where any of you can reach me at a moments' notice. If I could be granted the city of Timnath-serah, in the hill country of Ephraim, I would be pleased."

Caleb nodded. "Let it be granted."

The leaders shouted, "Amen."

Joshua swallowed. "Thank you." He nodded to Eleazar. "Now for the cities of refuge ..."

Eleazar looked over the crowd of men. "These cities of refuge are established for accidental killings. A person can run to the nearest of these cities, present his cause and, if pardoned, dwell in the city until the death of the high priest. Then he can return to his land, without threat of punishment."

They designated six, scattered throughout the land.

Joshua looked over the men. "Any other items of business?"

His eyes fell on the leaders of the two and a half tribes that had requested their land across the Jordan. He smiled. "The warriors, always ready to march into battle first, are anxious to return to their wives and families."

Everyone looked to the tribal leaders of Manasseh, Reuben, and Gad.

"You have fulfilled your promise to Moses before God to help us conquer the land. Without your obedience, we would have struggled to march at a moments' notice all night long to reach Gibeon, where we fought the five cities. Countless other times, your presence protected our families." Joshua swallowed before he could continue. "We will miss the camaraderie found in your presence. But it's now time for the Lord to give you rest with your families. Love God. Walk in all His Ways. Hold fast to Him. Serve Him with your entire heart.

"As you return to your own families, take your portion of the spoils of the land. Share with those who took care of your families while you fought."

As the leaders crowded around Hezron, he wept. They had become one people before their God, not only by traveling through the desert, but by fighting for Him and with Him in the Land He had given. They had become God's people.

Not one of their enemies had prevailed. Not one of the promises of the Lord had failed. Everything had come to pass.

CHAPTER 20

The sons of Gad, Manasseh, and Reuben journeyed home. After they crossed the Jordan River, Hezron looked back. He felt like he had left part of his life back there with the men he had fought, slept, ate, and marched with for five years. It was hard to leave. Yet he was ready to go home. "Men, our territory is far from the city of Shiloh where the Tabernacle is. Let's build a monument here on this side of the River for our children, so when they question how we could be part of the Land, while being so far away from it, we can point to the monument, representing our devotion to the Lord."

The others agreed. They began at once, anxious to return to their homes, but hesitant to break the bonds that had been established through battle.

The monument on the other side of the Jordan stretched toward the sky. When Phinehas saw the monument, he told Joshua and Eleazar, "Look! They crossed the River and have already forgotten God. We must discipline them for their wrong!"

Joshua sighed. "Choose ten leaders, one from each of the tribes. Go and ask them why they've done this."

When Phinehas and his group crossed the other side of the Jordan, Hezron bowed to them. He raised his arms to embrace them. When he saw Phinehas's face, he dropped his arms. "What's wrong?"

Phinehas fingered his sword. "How, after the Lord has given you the victory over this entire Land, could you turn your back on Him and build an altar to the other gods?"

Hezron shook his head, his expression one of confusion. "Turn our backs on Him? We built this to remember what God has done.

"We made the monument, not as an altar to sacrifice offerings, but as a witness between your descendants and ours that we are part of the Lord's inheritance." By the time Hezron had finished, he had tears in his eyes. "We wish not to forsake the Lord, only remember Him."

Phinehas nodded. "Today, God is in our midst. You are not unfaithful. We'll call the altar 'Witness' for it is a sign between us that the Lord is our God."

EPILOGUE

Eleazar came out of the Tabernacle after sacrificing for the people one Sabbath. He had removed his priest's robe and breastplate.

Joshua glanced at Eleazar. "You don't look well."

Eleazar nodded. He walked to his tent. "Our God has been faithful. My life is complete."

Joshua followed him. After helping him sit, he offered him a dipperful of water.

Eleazar sipped. "I remember asking my father what wisdom he would give me." He laid his hand on Joshua's arm. "Do you know what he said?"

Joshua leaned forward as Eleazar's voice grew softer.

"Obey God."

Eleazar, the son of Aaron, died.

Phinehas buried him at Gibeah in the hill country of Ephraim.

Joshua and the people mourned.

Rahab found she could not out-give her God. When she obeyed His commands, He rewarded. Not always in tangible ways she could see, but in deeper ways, where her heart was at peace, without fear. She had been afraid to give, wanting to hold control, but when she gave of herself, she received more. By being vulnerable and willing to accept pain, she was loved more. By releasing control, she knew oneness.

She learned her love and service to Salmon reflected what God wanted for Himself. Her love deepened for Salmon and her God.

Submitting was not easy. She still struggled to meet Salmon's needs. Those times tested her obedience to God.

But God gave mercy as she strove to do right.

God blessed her union with Salmon. He gave them a son. They called him Boaz.

God took an unworthy and unwanted woman and made her pleasing to Himself. Isn't that what God wants of all His people?

Out of her lineage, God would bring His Coming One who would save from destruction all people, not from just one city, but from the world.

The Lord gave rest to Israel from all their enemies on every side.

The years passed, Joshua called all Israel to the Tent of Meeting in Shiloh. "I am old. God has been faithful. You have seen the Lord fulfill all His Promises. Look what He did for you in battle: one of you put to flight a thousand. The Lord fought for you. He has done all that He promised.

"Drive out all the rest of the inhabitants. Let none remain. Otherwise, they will ensnare, trap, and whip you, like thorns in your eyes, until you perish from off this good Land given by God.

"Keep the law. Don't turn from it to the right or the left. Cling to the Lord. Love Him.

"I tell you of your history, not so you grow weary but so you remember God's faithfulness.

"God gave you land you didn't work, cities you didn't build, vineyards and olive groves you didn't plant.

"Now, fear the Lord. Serve Him. Make a solemn choice today Whom you will serve.

"As for me and my house, we will serve the Lord."

The people answered Joshua, "How can we forsake the Lord Who has done so much for us?"

Joshua looked over the people and shook his head, remembering how quickly they forgot in the desert. Had they really learned? "God is a jealous God. Don't think you can serve anything else and Him too. If you forget, He will turn His Face away from you."

The people answered him, "We will serve the Lord."

Joshua wrote these words in the book of the Law of God. He placed a boulder under an oak tree as a sanctuary of the Lord witnessing the people's promise.

He had learned the truth of the Lord's words, "I am with you." Even to those, like the harlot, who were not one of His chosen ones. Or maybe, because she was one of His chosen ones.

Joshua, the son of Nun, the servant of the Lord, died, being one hundred and ten years old. He was buried in the hill country of Ephraim, his inheritance.

The people mourned Joshua.

They served the Lord all the days of Joshua and the elders who survived Joshua.

The people saw God when He made His Name known in Egypt.

The people knew God when He brought them through the desert.

The people remembered God when He gave them their Land.

And the Lord was with His people and gave them peace.

THANK YOU

If you have enjoyed *I Am with You*, help spread the word. Post a review (how you liked it and why).

What is a reviewer?

Someone who reads my book and tells others what they thought of it.

What do you do?

1. Read the book.
2. Write three sentences about the book.

a. The What sentence: summarizes the book.

b. The Why sentence: tells what the book did for you, why others should read it, why you chose to read it. Example: you wanted to visualize the journey of the Israelites.

c. The How sentence: tells how well you liked the book.

3. Post your review here:
www.amazon.com
www.goodreads.com
www.sonyacontreras.com

Please allow me to use your review for marketing. Include a note in your message giving me permission.

Thank you.

SUMMARY REMARKS

Chapter 1: the story between Satan and Michael is based on Jude 1:9.

Chapter 5: The archeology of Jericho records a wall crumbling. The north side of the wall did not fall with the others, but remained standing. That's where I put Rahab's house.

A special store-room is found in the archeological digs that suggest the king made his last stand there before his great city fell.

In Chapter 4, Moses's song is recorded in Psalm 90–91.

In Chapter 5, the references of Moses's words were Psalm 90:12 and Psalm 91:5-10.

In accepting Rahab's family into the Jewish community, I relied on these qualifications: renunciation of idolatry, acceptance of Torah and dietary laws. Additional requirements for strangers and aliens include: be loyal to God (Lev. 20:2), participate in festivals (Deut. 16:11, 14) could offer burnt offerings (Lev. 17:8, 22:18), if circumcised, could sacrifice lamb (Ex. 12:48–49). Edomites and Egyptians were admitted (Deut. 23:8–9,), but up to the tenth generation, Ammonites and Moabites were not (Deut. 23:4). Jews were allowed to have alien slaves (Deut. 25:45–46).

Chapter 6: the city of Ai, stood on a high, well-guarded hill. Only by drawing the men out of the city could Israel have fought them.

In Chapter 11, the reference to eagles' wings comes from Exodus 19:4-6.

In Chapter 12, the story about the cruelty of Sodom documented by Emil G. Hirsch and I.M. Casanowicz from Vol. 6, p. 605 of the Jewish Encyclopedia.

Chapter 12: "Be sure your sin will find you out" is from Numbers 32:23.

Chapter 14: "Bone of my bones, flesh of my flesh" comes from Genesis 2:23.

Chapter 15: the story of hornets driving out the kings is found in Joshua 24:12.

Chapter 16: Moses's words are found in Psalm 91.

In Chapter 17, the Psalm of Moses was Psalm 91.

In Chapter 18, the Coming One is the Messiah for the Jews. Rahab is in the lineage of Christ, as mentioned in Matthew 1:5. She is also mentioned with those who had faith in Hebrews 11:30–31.

Yam Suph, from the Hebrew Bible/Old Testament, has been translated Red Sea. More recently, a better translation of Sea of Reeds or Sea of Seaweed has been suggested. The location for Israel's crossing substantiated by archaeological records lies not in the modern day Red Sea area but at Lake Bardawil, close to the Mediterranean Sea. This Lake Bardawil, walled in by mountains, trapped the Israelites, with no way of escape. Aardsma gives depth calculations, substantiating the number of people crossing in the given amount of time.

According to the current standard of capitalization, pronouns referring to God (i.e. Who, His, He) and nouns speaking of His body parts (i.e. hand, finger) should not be capitalized. When those words have referred to little gods, I honor that standard. But for the sake of respect for God, as well as clarity in the text, I have chosen to capitalize them, regardless of the standard. I trust the reader was not overwhelmed by the grammatical "mistake" of this choice.

The Bible tells the story in Joshua. Read it for yourself and rest in Him.

I pray that you not only enjoyed the book, but saw God better through it. Let me know at www.sonyacontreras.com.

ACKNOWLEDGEMENTS

The New American Standard Bible by Zondervan Publishers was used when the Bible was directly quoted. The plot follows Joshua.

To interpret the archeological data, especially some that were written in French, I relied on Dr. Gerald E. Aardsma's conclusions. He researches from a conservative Christian perspective, assumes historical integrity of the Bible, and shows that the sacred and secular dates harmonize without difficulty when the date of the Exodus is right.

No book comes together without others. My husband's prayer group faithfully upheld me through the book's many revisions. Thank you, men.

My younger boys waited quietly, as I finished a thought before I could read to them. I thank you, James, Joshua, and Jeremiah.

My boys listened as I developed plot ideas, considered character flaws, and wondered about life during ancient times. Thank you, Josiah, Jonathan, Jonas, Jacob, James, Joshua, and Jeremiah.

Technology overwhelms me. If it were not for my son Joey John fixing formatting problems, this book would never look presentable. Thank you, Joey John.

The Holy Spirit is the Comforter, but if there was anyone who could be personified as the comforter, it would be my best friend and husband, Joey. He came beside me and read the book in its roughest form and said, "It is good." He supplied the funds for all the steps. He celebrated its completion, assuring me that the sales would come. He reminded me of my purpose—for God and God alone. The words "thank you" are not enough.

MAP

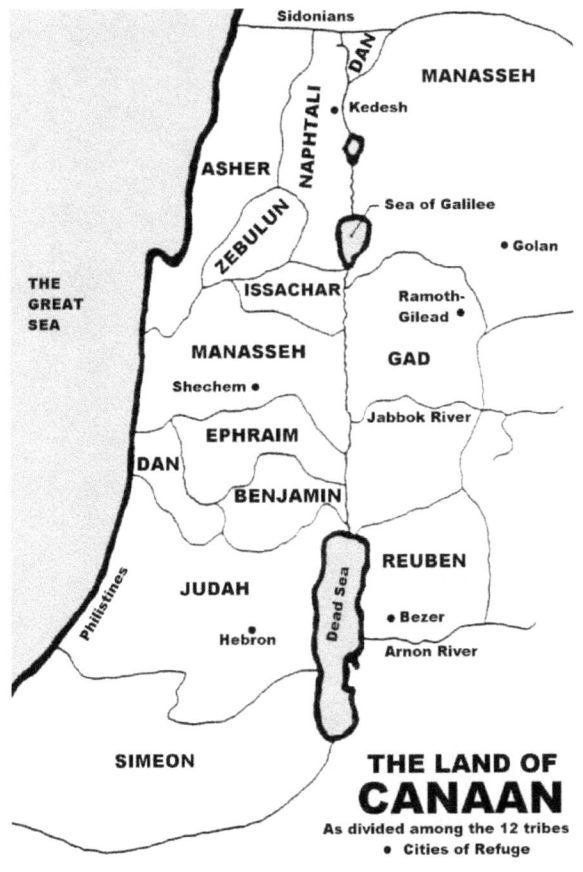

Sidonians

DAN

MANASSEH

NAPHTALI

• Kedesh

ASHER

ZEBULUN

Sea of Galilee

• Golan

ISSACHAR

Ramoth-
Gilead •

THE
GREAT
SEA

MANASSEH

GAD

Shechem •

Jabbok River

EPHRAIM

DAN

BENJAMIN

REUBEN

Dead Sea

JUDAH

• Bezer

Philistines

Hebron •

Arnon River

SIMEON

THE LAND OF
CANAAN
As divided among the 12 tribes
• Cities of Refuge

GLOSSARY

Abba   Hebrew, endearing form of father

Ark of the Covenant where the presence of God rested (described in Exodus 37:1–9)

Coming One the promised Messiah for the Jews

Cubit   form of ancient measurement, length from middle finger tip to elbow bottom

Elizur   stoned for picking up sticks on the Sabbath in Book 2, *I Have Called You...*

Finger   smallest subdivision of cubit, equal to ¼ hand-breadth

Handbreadth width of hand at base of four fingers (1/6 of cubit)

Korah   swallowed up by the ground when he usurped Moses's authority (see Number 16)

Reed Sea commonly called Red Sea, see summary remarks for further explanation

Salmon   also called Salma in I Chronicles 2:11

Sea of Chinnereth   now called Sea of Galilee

Shekel   weight of barley, 180 grains or 11 grams

Sodom   destroyed by Angel of God for wickedness in Genesis 19

Women of Moab   sent by the king of Moab to entice Israelite men when Balaam, the prophet, wouldn't curse them (Number 25)

Zerahite Judah was the father, Tamar (his daughter-in-law) was the mother, she played the harlot to catch Judah for his deceiving her (see Genesis 38).

BIBLIOGRAPHY

Alphin, Mark. 2011. *Hamstrung?* Mar 11.
https://reachingfinland.wordpress.com/2011/11/30/hamstru
ng/.

n.d. "Bald Eagle Mating Ritual--Sky Dancing." *Bird Note.* Accessed
June 2016. http://birdnote.org/video/2012/07/bald-eagle-
mating-ritual-sky-dancing.

Bradshaw, Den. 2014. "How To Not Get Knocked Out." *Guys Survival
Guide.* January 22. Accessed March 2016.
http://guysurvivalguide.com/survive/survival/how-to-not-
get-knocked-out/.

Britam. n.d. "Esau and the Edomites: The Family of Esau." Accessed
February 20, 2015.
http://www.britam.org/Edom/2EsauFamily.html.

Craig, William Lane. 2007. "Slaughter of the Canaanites." *Reasonable
Faith.* August 7. Accessed February 20, 2015.
http://www.reasonablefaith.org/slaughter-of-the-
canaanites.

Danaher, John. 2010. "DId God Command Genocide? (Part 1) The
Problem." *Philosophical Disquisitions.* March 12. Accessed
February 2, 2015.
http://www.philosophicaldisquisitiosn.blogspot.com/2010/0
3/did-god-command-genocide-part-1.html.

—. 2010. "Did God Command Genocide? (Part 2) Copan's Casuistry."
  Philosophical Disquisitions. March 12. Accessed February 20,
  2015.
  http://www.philosophicaldisquisitions.blogspot.com/did-
  god-command-genocide-part-2.html.

—. 2010. "Did God Command Genocide? (Part 3) Canaanite
  Wickedness." *Philosophical Disquisitions.* March 12. Accessed
  February 20, 2015.
  http://philosophicaldisquisitions.blogspot.com/2010/03/did-
  god-command-genocide-part-3.html.

Deffinbaugh, Bob. 2014. "The Sin Offering (Leviticus 4:1-5:13; 6:24-
  30)." *Bible.org.* May 18. https://bible.org/seriespage/5-sin-
  offering-leviticus-41-513-624-30.

Duigon, Lee. 2010-2016. *"Gay Activists Threaton VIolence"*
  Chalcedon-Equipping to Advance the Kingdom. Accessed
  November 2015.
  http://chalcedon.edu/research/articles/gay-activists-
  threaten-violence/.

Ephraim Stern, Editor, Ayelet Lewinson-Gilboa, Asst Editor, Joseph
  Aviram, Editorial Director. 1993. *Israel Exploration Society,*
  Vol 4 and Carta Jerusalem. The Israel Map and Publishing Co.,
  Ltd: Simon and Schuster (A Paramount Communication Co. .

Hall, Rayne. 2012. "Guest Post: Writing Sword FIght Scenes 101."
  Tara Maya: Science Fiction and Fantasy. December 2.
  Accessed January 4, 2015.
  http://taramayastales.blogspot.com/2012/12/guest-post-
  writing-sword-fight-scenes.html.

2011. *Hamstringing Animals.* June 11. http://eco-
  bible.org/wiki/Hamstringing_Animals.

n.d. "Has the "Missing Day" in Joshua Been Proven Scientifically?"
  Bible.org. Accessed February 20, 2015.

http://www.bible.org/question/has-%E2%80%9Cmissing-day%E2%80%9D-joshua-been-proven-scientifically.

Hirsch, Emil G., and I.M. Casanowicz. 2002-2011. "Insects." *Jewish Encyclopedia Vol. 6 P. 605.* Accessed March 2016. http://www.jewishencyclopedia.com/articles/8125-insects.

n.d. "Hivite Meaning/Hivite Etymology: Discover the meanings of thousands of BIblical Names in Abarim Publicaions Biblical Name Vault." *Abarim Publications.* Accessed February 20, 2015. http://www.abarim-publications.com/Meaning/Hivite.html#.VOdJZfnFF9ik.

Institute for Creation Research. n.d. "The Wickedness of These Nations." *Institute for Creation Research.* Accessed February 20, 2015. http://www.icr.org/books/defenders/1118.

Leahy, Dana. n.d. "Knocked out: Myths and Facts about Concussions." *Startswithyou.com.* Accessed 2016 March. http://www.startswithyou.com/organize/1560_Knocked_Out_Myths_and_Facts_About_Concussions/.

Lieber, David L. 2008. "Strangers and Gentiles." *Jewish Virtual Library: A Division of the American-Israeli Cooperative Enterprise.*

Marquet-Krause, Judith. 1933-1935. *Les Fuilles De 'Ay (Et-Tell) [The Escavation of Ai at the Ruins].* Entreprises Par Le Baron Edmond de Rothschild, Funded by Rothschild.

Meggitt, Jane. n.d. "The Mating Behaviors of the Golden Eagle." *Pets on Mom.Me.* Accessed May 2016. http://animals.mom.me/mating-behaviors-golden-eagle-11151.html.

n.d. *Merom.* http://biblehub.com/topical/m/merom.htm.

National Eagle Center. 2015. "Eagle Nesting and Young." *National Eagle Center.* Accessed May 2016. https://www.nationaleaglecenter.org/eagle-nesting-young/.

Padfield, David. n.d. "The Adominations of the Canaanites." Accessed February 20, 2015. http://www.padfield.com/acrobat/history/canaanite-abominiatons.html.

Ramsland, Dr. Katherine. 2010. "Stab Wounds Don't Always Kill." *The Writer's Forensics Blog.* Accessed July 2, 2016. https://writersforensicsblog.wordpress.com/2010/02/20/stab-wounds-don%E2%80%99t-always-kill/.

Rich, Tracey R. 1998-2011. "Quorbanot: Sacrifices and Offerings." *Judaism 101.* Accessed May 2016. http://www.jewfaq.org/qorbanot.htm.

Slick, Matt. n.d. *Christian Aplogetics and Research Ministry: Moloch, the Ancient Pagan God of Child Sacrifice.* Accessed November 2015. https://carm.org/christianity/miscellaneous-topics/moloch-ancient-pagan-god-child-sacrifice.

—. n.d. "What is Casting Lots." *Christian Apologetics and Research Ministry.* Accessed March 2016. https://carm.org/what-casting-lots-in-the-bible.

Southern, Paul. 2005-2016. *SBG Exclusive Black Dragon Force: How to Sharpen Swords 101: A Beginner's Guide.* Accessed March 2016. http://www.sword-buyers-guide.com/sharpen-swords.html.

State of Israel. 2013. *The Land: Geography and Climate.* http://www.mfa.gov.il/mfa/aboutisrael/land/pages/the%20land-%20geography%20and%20climate.aspx.

Stiles, Wayne. n.d. "Sorting Out Those Odd Canaanite Names and Places." *Wayne Stiles: Connecting the Bible and Its Lands To*

Life. Accessed November 2015.
https://www.waynestiles.com/sorting-out-those-odd-
canaanite-names-and-places/.

—. n.d. "Sorting OUt THose Odd Canaanite Names and Places."
Wayne Stiles: Connecting the Bible and its Lands To Life.
Accessed Nov 2015.

Struthers, William M. 2009. *Wired for Intimacy.* Madison, WI:
InterVarsity Press.

2016. "Tawny Eagle." *Wikipedia.org.* April 11. Accessed May 2016.
https://en.wikipedia.org/wiki/Tawny_eagle.

The Church of Jesus Christ of Latter Day Saints. 1980. "Joshua 1-24
The Entry into the Promised Land." In *Old Testament Student
Manual Genesis-2 Samuel*, 234-243. The Church of Jesus
Christ of Latter Day Saints.

The Israel Ministry of Tourism, Government of Israel. 2011.
Geography and Nature of Israel.
http://www.goisrael.com/Tourism_Eng/Tourist%20Informati
on/Discover%20Israel/Pages/Geography%20and%20Nature.a
spx.

2014. "The Lost Day." *Snopes.com.* June 25. Accessed February 20,
2015. http://www.snopes.com/religion/lostday.asp.

The Quartz Hill School of Theology. n.d. "The Religion of the
Canaanites." *Quartz Hill School of Theology.* Accessed
February 20, 2015. http://www.theology.edu/caanaan.html.

2011. *The Victory at Merom Waters.* September 21.
https://mysteriesofthebible.wordpress.com/2011/09/21/the
-victory-at-merom-waters/.

Townsend, Lee, Extension Entomologist. October, 1995. "Sheep
Pests." *Entomology at the University of Kentucky, College of
Agriculture.*

Wade, RIck. 2001. "The Charge of Genocide." *Probe Ministries.* Accessed February 20, 2015. https://www.probe.org/god-and-the-canaanites/.

n.d. *Waters of Merom.* https://www.biblicaltraining.org/library/waters-merom.

n.d. "Who Were the Philistines?" *Got Question.org.* Accessed February 20, 2015. http://www.gotquestions.org/Philistines.html.

Wikipedia. 2016. "Golden Eagle." *Wikipedia.org.* May 31. Accessed June 2016. https://en.wikipedia.org/wiki/Golden_eagle.

2012. "Yahoo Answers." *What Part of the Stomach Do You Stab Someone To Kill Them?* Accessed July 2, 2016. https://answers.yahoo.com/question/index?qid=201209211 31325AAgVaPI.

KNOW HIM

God has paid the way for man to enter His presence. Not through our works, but only through what God has done for us.

We could never satisfy a holy God's requirements. We fall short of what God wants. So His Son died, a substitute for us. His holiness can now be satisfied. Our judgment can be removed.

Please do not hesitate to accept His Work on the cross in your life. Tell Him you fall short of His holiness. Recognize He paid for your sin. Ask Him to remove your sin. His requirements are satisfied. Thank Him. Serve Him.

Knowing about Jesus is not knowing Him.

Know Him and be His.

ABOUT THE AUTHOR

Growing up with five sisters, Sonya Contreras asked God many questions, even when she did not like His answers. Graduating from Cedarville University and Institute for Creation Research with a Master's Degree in Science Education did not stop her questions. Marrying her best friend and homeschooling their eight sons, she found that dreams do come true, in spite of unanswered questions. Trusting God, Who knows all answers, she shares questions that matter weekly at www.sonyacontreras.com.